GHOSTTOWN

A WHITNEY LOGAN MYSTERY

GHOSTTOWN

MERCEDES LAMBERT

*With a foreword by Michael Connelly and an
afterword by Lucas Crown*

FIVE STAR
An imprint of Thomson Gale, a part of The Thomson Corporation

MYSTERY

Detroit • New York • San Francisco • New Haven, Conn. • Waterville, Maine • London

THOMSON

GALE

LIBRARY OF CONGRESS CATALOGING-IN-PUBLICATION DATA

Lambert, Mercedes.
  Ghosttown : a Whitney Logan mystery / Mercedes Lambert ; with a
  foreword by Michael Connelly and an afterword by Lucas Crown. — 1st ed.
    p. cm.
  ISBN-13: 978-1-59414-588-9 (alk. paper)
  ISBN-10: 1-59414-588-1 (alk. paper)
  1. Indians of North America—California—Fiction. I. Title.
PS3562.A454G48 2007
813'.54—dc22   2007011878

First Edition. First Printing: August 2007.
Published in 2007 in conjunction with Tekno Books and Ed Gorman.
Printed in the United States of America on permanent paper
10 9 8 7 6 5 4 3 2 1

"Go on—beat it," he said. "Stay off our reservation and you won't make any enemies."
—Lt. Dergamo, Bay City Police, to Philip Marlowe
RAYMOND CHANDLER, "THE LADY IN THE LAKE"

DOUGLAS ANNE MUNSON:
AN APPRECIATION

If writers are immortal, if their work continues to live on the page and shelf long after they are gone, then what about the work that is never published and never put on a shelf? Are these works the ghosts of what could have been? Or what should have been? Do books never read deny the author immortality?

The book you are about to read may answer those questions, or at least chase away a ghost. Appropriately titled, *Ghosttown* is in many ways Douglas Anne Munson's last will and testament. Written under the name Mercedes Lambert, it is the last novel she completed before her death in late 2003. Thankfully published for the first time here, the story completes the cycle of Mercedes Lambert novels, following *Dogtown* and *Soultown* and featuring attorney Whitney Logan and her translator/secretary Lupe Ramos. Once again Munson/Lambert uses the novel to explore the dark edges and cultural friction of the city of Los Angeles. Once again her characters are equally tough and vulnerable. Once again she has given us a story we won't soon forget.

But this time there is something new to go along with the usual fare. *Ghosttown* seems to me to have been written with a palpable sense of the author's knowledge of the creeping cancer and the coming end. The novel is a mystery for sure, but it radiates with spiritual exploration as well. It is full of the possibilities of otherworldly things, of what might lie waiting for us on the other side. The book, written sparely and under the

7

philosophy of less always telling more, shows the skilled hand of a veteran. The story revolves around Tony Red Wolf, the mysterious client who attracts yet repulses Whitney Logan. He's on some sort of a journey and Whitney wants to be along for the ride.

Munson's own journey to the Los Angeles of her fiction began in Tennessee. Named after an uncle who was killed in World War II, she was the daughter of a transient newspaperman who moved from town to town chasing jobs. Life wasn't happy; she once said she never had a childhood friend. It was law school at UCLA that finally brought her out west. Upon graduation she worked in corporate law for a few years but wasn't fulfilled. She decided to go out on her own and that brought her down into the trenches of the justice system—the children's dependency court in downtown LA.

It was in those trenches that the writer was born.

I never knew Douglas Anne Munson but I knew her books. I read them all and loved them all. I loved them most because in the crowded field of authors who chose Los Angeles as the place of their fiction, she was unique. She was brave. She kept her head down and wrote what she wanted to write, explored what she wanted to explore. It didn't matter who would publish it or who would read it. These were the stories she had to tell—if only to herself. In doing so she gave us characters we hadn't seen before and took us to places we had never known.

El Niño, published in 1990, is perhaps her masterpiece. In it she simply wrote what she knew. The book is an exorcism of the frustration and pain accumulated during a decade as an attorney representing parents in the dependency courts. Munson was a court-appointed lawyer and her clients were most often people who abused and neglected their own children. The novel (later published in paperback under the title *Hostile Witness*) is a searing yet wholly accurate account of that world and of an attorney who sees too much of it, thinks too much about it, and drinks too much to forget it. One reviewer called the book "an anguished tour of several kinds of hell." But another said the book was important to anyone "who seriously cares about what happening to our society on the edge of the 21st century."

For Munson the book was no tour. It was her life. She had lived it, seen the depravity and poverty she put in the book in her own client's lives. Luckily for us, she had her typewriter to go to when the burden became too heavy. *El Niño* is what came of that experience and because it was published we are all the better. We know something about the world that we didn't know before. We feel something we didn't feel before. I think there is nothing better that can be said about the work of a writer.

After *El Niño* came the Mercedes Lambert books, first *Dogtown* and then *Soultown* and now *Ghosttown*. In these books the author once again wrote about a young woman with a law degree standing before the gaping maw of the justice system. Whereas Sandy Walker of *El Niño* was tough and cynical and damaged, Whitney Logan is young and naïve and vulnerable. Munson/Lambert teams her with Lupe Ramos, the Chicana prostitute who eventually graduates to legal secretary. I dare say a more unique pair of detectives has yet to be written. The books are lively, meaningful, and, most of all, they ring true.

Carolyn See wrote in the *Los Angeles Times*, "Who says an entertaining, charming, unpretentious detective story can't be . . . an authentic agent of social change? Without ever making a big deal of it, the author takes on dozens of issues that define our weird metropolis." She was reviewing *Dogtown* but the sentiment and appreciation certainly would apply to every book Douglas Anne Munson wrote.

See ended her glowing review by saying she hoped to learn more about the characters of Whitney Logan and Lupe Ramos in books to come.

She was right in hoping for that. For these characters, one book was not enough. Now we have three and I still feel shorted. After this I will miss Whitney and Lupe and the strange, wonderful people they encounter. I will miss them for a long, long time.

To me it always comes down to character. All novels, no matter what the genre or subject, live or die with their characters. It is the characters that hold the keys to the gates of a writer's immortality.

I think in this case it is the characters who will stand well as the author's epitaph and who will open up those gates. Douglas Anne Munson may be gone too soon, but she wrote characters that will never die.

—Michael Connelly

CHAPTER 1

A low groan echoed down the hall. Was someone hurt? Another groan. Had some of the Vietnamese gangbangers from down the street snuck in to get loaded again? I was sick and tired of working in a shooting gallery. I edged quietly towards where the groans had come from.

"Let me suck that big dick of yours. That's right, baby, big and hard."

I ground to a halt outside the oak door and listened to the voice coming from inside my office, the Law Office of Whitney Logan. It was only ten in the morning.

"It's so big. I want to suck it 'til you come in my mouth."

It was the voice of Lupe Ramos, my secretary. Goddamn it to hell. She must have pulled some *mojado* up off the street for a quickie. When she started to work for me in August she'd sworn she'd stopped prostituting. It was barely mid November now. She'd done six months with the county earlier in the year and was on probation. Her second conviction. She'd be going to the state if there was a third. I'd tried to help her get her life straightened out. I'd given her a job although I couldn't afford it. Just last week I'd told her probation officer, a stressed-out-looking black guy named George Carver, that everything was fine.

"I want you to put that big cock inside me. I'm getting so wet . . ."

I shoved the door open. "That's it! Get your stuff and get

11

out!" Lupe was in the chair behind my desk with her back to me. She waved one hand over her head in my direction either in greeting or telling me to shut up. Her feet were propped on the sill of my window that looked out over Hollywood Boulevard. She glanced up in annoyance from the phone cradled against her shoulder. A thin stack of index cards used to update my records was in her hand and a pile of my legal files in her lap.

"Yeah, do it to me, baby . . ." Lupe put her hand over the mouthpiece. "I thought you were going out to West LA traffic court," she hissed.

"What the hell are you doing?"

"Harder . . ."

I tossed my purse on the desk where I noticed a printed form divided into columns and squares like a page from an accounting book. The top of the form screamed, in bright pink letters, HOT BOX TALK. "You set up a nine hundred sex-talk line on my phone."

"Harder . . ."

I grabbed it from her. "Take a cold shower, you jerk!" I slammed the phone down.

"You sure know how to talk the talk, girl." Lupe shoved her feet into her black patent leather high heels that lay on the floor beside my chair, dumped the files and cards on the desk, and stood up. "Explains why you're such a big success with men."

I picked up the HOT BOX TALK accounting sheet. "How long's this been going on?" Her tiny numbers were indecipherable.

"I can still get all my regular work done," she said, indicating the pile of completed files on the desk.

"How long?"

"Less than a week," she shrugged.

I knew she was lying. "I can't believe you'd do this to me—"

" '. . . after all I've done for you.' Look, Whitney, I didn't put on a nine hundred. You know how much it costs to set one up? The service forwards calls to me. I'm an employee, a part-time employee. Like you must think I am, since you didn't pay me the full three fifty you owe me. Besides, I've always wanted to be an actress."

"You're not an actress, you're a sex industry worker."

"Entertainer!"

"You think when Bette Davis was making movies she expected guys to be fiddling themselves?" The phone rang again and I grabbed it before she could. "Wrong number, jack-off. Don't ever call here again!"

"Ms. Logan, Whitney Logan?" a woman's voice asked. "This is the clerk of Division Forty."

Then I recognized her voice. I talked with her every time I went into court to try to hustle up some work or to do an arraignment. Being friendly with the clerks is supposed to be a good way to get court appointments. I depend on court appointments for clients. The fifty dollars an hour it pays has been the only thing that's made it possible for me to keep my office.

"Sorry, I've been having a prank caller." I glared at Lupe, who couldn't conceal a smirk.

"Of course," she said. I could tell she was pissed. "Can you come pick up a case? We got guys oozing out of the tank today."

I told her I'd be right there, made my apologies again, and thanked her for calling me. I tossed a fresh legal pad into my briefcase and checked my wallet to make sure I had a supply of business cards.

"Sorta like being invited to a party that's already started, isn't it?" Lupe opened the office door for me.

The phone was ringing again before I got to the stairs.

It had been more than a year since I'd met Lupe outside my office building one sweltering August afternoon. Then she'd been a skinny little hooker with hot pants and halter tops prowling the street in stilettos. I'd needed her to act as a Spanish interpreter when I was paid to find a missing housemaid. Instead Lupe and I had found a dead girl, a girl our own age, in a deserted loft on the edge of Dogtown. Things went all to hell then. I thought I knew everything about everything in those days, but Lupe ended up with a gun in her hand. A man ended up dead.

It had taken me a long time to expiate the guilt and shame that I had brought down on myself in Dogtown. I still couldn't say I'd gotten rid of it all. Lupe disappeared after that bloody August day. I found her months later in jail for hooking. After she got out I tried to help her get her son, Joey, back from her brother, but the little boy had been hidden in Koreatown. Koreatown can be a bad place for people who don't know their way around, and I was a stranger there. We found more dead people. All Lupe had wanted was a job in an office so she could get off the streets, but I'd taken her on another death trip.

Me, all I'd wanted was to pay her back for having shown me who I really was. I wasn't a big-deal lawyer just because I had a degree from one of the best law schools in the country. I wasn't the deified crusader for justice I'd hoped to be when I opened my own law office. I was just another woman trying to make it on her own in a big city that would one day disappear into the Pacific. In the meantime, everyone else was trying to make it, too. And some of them weren't very nice people.

A couple of days ago Lupe told me that if work didn't pick up and I didn't pay her when I was supposed to, that she'd leave. We'd been through so much together I thought we were, in some mismatched way, friends. Did she still have it in her to go back on the streets? Her brother Hector was on her mom to toss her out because she wasn't bringing home enough dough to support them. I thought Hector should get off his fat ass and get a job himself, but after his part in the messy affair in Koreatown, he seemed a broken man. Hector promised that if they kept Joey and got rid of her, he could bring in a couple of real cash tenants.

I made myself put Lupe out of my mind as I parked in the usual lot across the street from the Criminal Courts Building at Broadway and Temple. The same guy wrapped in a sheet who believes himself to be the Messiah of the Harbor Freeway panhandled me. The lobby of the CCB was full of the usual gangbangers, dope dealers, and guys who looked like they'd gotten lost on the way to the track at Santa Anita. Division 40 was packed with the usual angry black men in Lakers t-shirts and gold necklaces, the usual perfumed Latinos in cheap patterned rayon shirts. The DAs, male and female, had short hair and Brooks Brothers suits. The public defenders wore their hair longer and believed in sports coats and separates. The private lawyers looking for work, like me, paid more than they could afford for their clothes and shook hands enthusiastically with anyone who crossed their path.

I checked in with the clerk who gave me an icy stare.

"Sorry about that on the phone," I offered again hopefully. "Lot of weirdoes out there . . ." She had already dismissed me and gone back to her work. I'd given her a five-pound box of See's candy each year for Christmas. Did she want ten pounds? Maybe she wanted scotch. I never seemed to be able to figure it out with her. It was the usual cold shoulder.

Everything was the usual. Although Burt Schaefer who threw me some of his overflow had given me my first manslaughter case and it should have been worth at least five grand to try, I was barely making enough money to pay my rent, pay Lupe, and take care of myself. I'd done a lot of work preparing for the manslaughter trial and started to pick a jury when the Armenian who was alleged to have stabbed his wife, in a drunken domestic dispute, got cold feet and begged for the previously offered deal of eight years rather than go to trial with me. Goodbye five grand, goodbye career advancement. I ended up with less than seventeen hundred dollars for prep expenses. It was like being ready to jump out a plane for the first time, engines revving, the chute on your back, and the airfield shuts down because of fog. I knew I was getting better all the time as an attorney, but I still had no way to show it and nothing to show for it.

My landlord, Harvey Kaplan, in his usual stoned way gave me as much latitude as he could and still make his mortgage payments. I lived in the same ratty apartment in Sherman Oaks I'd lived in during law school. I had my usual workouts— weights, running, and tae kwon do. The usual downbeat drunken three a.m. phone calls from my father. Besides the missed opportunity to do my first felony trial, the only thing different lately in my life was that I'd gotten rid of my old Datsun and bought a red '64 Chevy Malibu with the idea of restoring it and having a V8 dropped into it. Strange hobby for a girl with no interest in things mechanical, but I figured as long as I lived in LA I wanted to participate in car culture. Now I was too broke to have the work done on it. I thought I'd thought be able to have the engine put in, cherry it out with a fresh paint job, original upholstery, and tinted windows, but there had been something wrong with it nearly every week since I bought it.

The clerk's voice interrupted my slide into self-pity. "The file on top's yours."

I picked it up. A drunk in public and disorderly conduct. The usual crummy case dished out to me in Division 40. I'd already had dozens of GTAs, possession for sale, assault and battery. Scores of hookers and small grifters. I wanted manslaughter trials, big drug cases. I was getting tired of paying my dues.

I skimmed the report. Three men and a woman seen drinking and fighting in public. Two men and the woman fled. Suspect belligerent and intoxicated, picked up in Winston Alley around eleven the night before last. My new client's name was Tony Red Wolf.

I found Tony Red Wolf crouched on the floor of the lockup with his back to the wall staring impassively ahead as though he didn't see any of his surroundings. Around him were eight or nine black guys who talked loudly, engaged in mock shoving matches, and took turns pissing in the toilet in front of me.

"Yo, baby," called someone from the back of the cell. I was aware of the click of my black Charles Jourdan heels across the concrete floor.

"Mr. Red Wolf?"

"Hey, Chief, she's here to see you. Why don't you do a rain dance for her?"

Tony Red Wolf got slowly to his feet. He was over six feet tall. His long black hair hung to the middle of his back and was tied off in a single braid. His face was chiseled, nearly gaunt, hard. Eyes—indigo. He looked about forty. He didn't acknowledge the guy who'd spoken, although I saw his eyes shift almost imperceptibly towards the man and memorize him. I've learned to watch peoples' eyes in tae kwon do. I wondered why the sheriffs had put him in with the black guys instead of the Latinos. He could have been mistaken for Latino, but for the reddish yellow tinge of his skin.

"Mr. Red Wolf?" I saw the edge of a red tattoo peeking out from beneath the short-sleeved blue county overalls he wore. He was slender, but muscular, as though he'd been buff before he started drinking and stopped eating. Like me, he had a scar along the edge of his chin, but his was jagged as if a knife had made it. I took a quick glance at the police report. According to it, he was thirty-five.

I handed him my business card, which he stuffed, without looking at it, into the pocket of his overalls. I started to read him the report. "Suspect armed with a broken bottle—" He made a dismissive gesture with his hand like he didn't care what was in it.

"Says you were drunk and told the cops you'd been fighting over a woman," I summarized.

"I didn't say shit to the cops."

"Was there a woman? Perhaps your girlfriend?" I asked, still referring to the report. "Says here the cops recognized the woman as one Shirley Yellowbird, but she got away."

He didn't say anything. I was trying to keep my voice low so we'd have some semblance of privacy. I've always thought one of the worst things about jail would be having to listen to the inane and repetitive conversations of others. The black guys were getting louder and shoving each other around with increasing hilarity. "Fool!" "No, you the fool." "Yo momma!"

"Look, Mr. Red Wolf, you want to get out of here, right?"

He glanced back at the black guys and nodded. "Indian can't stand being locked up. Kills his soul, makes him want to die."

I was a bit startled to hear him referring to himself in the third person, but at least he was starting to speak. "Okay, so tell me something I can use when I talk to the DA. This sounds like a case they'll probably give you six months on since you were brandishing a weapon. That's three months actual time—"

"I'm not doing any time in any *wasichu* jail." He started to turn away from me.

"Excuse me, what's *wasichu?*"

"White man."

I fell silent for a few respectful seconds. "Okay, so who's Shirley Yellowbird?" I was feeling silly with these names from Central Casting. I'd never thought about Indians in Los Angeles. I'd never seen any. According to the report, Shirley was a twenty-two-year-old woman about my height, five-five. About thirty-five pounds heavier than my one-fifteen. "I'm here to help you."

Tony Red Wolf looked me up and down, at my Charles Jourdan heels, the black suit I hadn't finished paying Saks for yet.

"You look *wasichu* to me."

I felt lousy as I looked at Tony Red Wolf in his emaciated and hungover state. A man with his own personal history of demon-wrestling. I wanted to imagine him as a kid or a teenager when he must have been tall and proud. I wanted to imagine him running, laughing, his hair flying behind him. I felt like I was seeing the last of a nearly extinct species in a zoo. A collage of familiar textbook pictures of old black-and-white photos taken in the last century of Indians on reservations, signing peace treaties, doing the last corn dance or bear dance or whatever animal dances there were rumbled through me and I felt ashamed and sick of being white.

"I'm on your side."

Tony Red Wolf spit on the floor near my foot.

It was the same everywhere for a white girl, even one who belonged to the National Lawyers Guild and wanted to work for peace and justice. Lupe did it, too, bagged on me all the time for being white. So much for the new multicultural Los Angeles. I felt like spitting back at him. "Okay, fine, I'm a pig. Everything that's wrong with the world is my fault. You want to get out of here or not? If you do, tell me right now because I'm here to make a living. Your pissant little case is worth about three hundred bucks to me. I'm behind on my rent, I've got a car that's barely running, and I don't like being in jail, either." I stopped, breathless, my hands on my hips.

The cell was silent. Tony Red Wolf stared at me. All the black guys were watching. I turned to go.

"What kind of car you have?'

"Sixty-four Chevy Malibu."

He laughed. "I can fix any kind of car."

"Great," I whispered. "And I know how to get guys like you

out of jail. Want to try this again or you want to go someplace where they'll let you make a nice shiny new plate for my car?"

We glared at each other through the bars. The black guys hooted and started pushing each other around again.

"Tell me who Shirley Yellowbird is."

"Don't matter who Shirley is—"

I was totally fed up with being the scapegoat for the world. When the big earthquake tore through Los Angeles two years ago it was all I could do to keep from running outside my apartment screaming, "I didn't do it." I put my pen away. I'll buy all the goddamn Charles Jourdan shoes in the world I want. "I'll go tell the judge you want to start your six months now."

He stepped closer and lowered his voice so I had to lean against the bars to hear him. "That night, a guy shoved Shirley. Guy named Ernie Little Horse."

"Why?"

"Didn't want to go with him."

Was that how the cops recognized her? "She's a prostitute?"

Tony Red Wolf gave me a dangerous look.

"Sorry, I don't know who she is. I'm just trying to figure out who all the players are."

"Shirley's no prostitute. She likes to have a good time, drink some, smoke some . . ."

"Crack?"

He laughed like I was some idiot social worker.

"Look, Mr. Red Wolf, I don't want to be culturally insensitive, but I don't know what the hell you're doing in a place called"—I checked the report again—"Winston Alley at eleven at night, with two guys and a drunk woman. You could be playing bridge, or dealing drugs. You could be inventing a new form of rapid transit for all I know."

He shook his head impatiently. "Me and Shirley and Ernie Little Horse were drinking in the alley. Dwayne Yazzi came along. He said he had some crack with him. Ernie wanted some. He told Shirley he'd give her a taste of his. Dwayne said he'd give Shirley some if she went with him. Shirley was playing like she was deciding what to do. Ernie and Dwayne started arguing about who she'd go with. Dwayne grabbed Shirley by the arm and tried to pull her out into the street."

"That's when Ernie hit him?" I guessed.

"Yeah, smashed the bottle we were drinking and tried to cut Dwayne."

My eyes wandered to the scar on Tony Red Wolf's chin. My scar's nearly invisible. My mom says I got it as a baby when my high chair collapsed.

He caught my gaze. He ran his finger along the scar like a person tracing a street on a map. "That's an old one. Got it when I was a boy in boarding school." He crossed his arms across his chest as though signaling an end to the reminiscence. "I tried to break up the fight and the rest is history."

I had a hard time imagining Tony Red Wolf in a fancy boarding school, wearing a uniform with an Eaton tie and a pair of little oxfords. Probably a reform school. He seemed full of shit to me. A moment of silence must have hung like a canopy over us because suddenly the black guys sounded real loud again and the claustrophobia of the cell felt overwhelming to me. "Well, I'll do my best with it. Got any priors?"

He shook his head, but Tony Red Wolf had seen that I wasn't very impressed with his story. He started to walk away from me.

"Mr. Red Wolf?"

He turned back reluctantly.

"I think the carburetor needs to be rebuilt."

He smiled for the first time and went back to his place against the wall. One of the black guys, the same one who'd hassled him when I came in, lounged against that space. Red Wolf went right up to him in an unhurried but deliberate way. The black guy pushed himself away from the wall, his easy slouch turning into an aggressive ready stance. "Yo, Chief, there's lots more wall."

"This is my part of the wall. Indians were here first." Red Wolf seemed to grow larger as the two men stood close to one another, face to face. The black guy cracked his knuckles and inched forward. All the men in the cell stopped talking. The drone of the central air-conditioning became very loud. I noticed a fly on the bars of the cell. Neither Red Wolf nor the black man moved. I wondered if I should go call for the sheriff.

Red Wolf raised his scarred chin, challenging the black man. The brothers, excited that some shit was going to go down, edged closer to the two men. It seemed to grow much hotter in the lockup. Time seemed to slow down. The black man started to raise his fist. Like a rattlesnake striking, Tony Red Wolf's hand shot out and grabbed his opponent's wrist. He didn't push with any force, but his grip was immovable. The black man shifted slightly, his weight moving backwards, his shoulders dropping almost imperceptibly. If Tony snapped the wrist back and twisted suddenly, he could break it. There was another second of unbearable silence before the black guy said, "Yo, Chief, just keeping it warm for you!"

Tony dropped the man's hand.

The black guy laughed and turned back to his colleagues. They hooted and gave each other high fives. Settling into his crouch against the wall, Red Wolf's eyes retained the unblinking discipline I'd seen on the faces of the best black belts in tae kwon do competitions, but colder. A look that said today's as good a day as any to die. Then he seemed to sigh inaudibly, closed his eyes, and looked like a tired middle-aged man who drank too much.

I went back into the courtroom feeling a bit disoriented for an instant. I wondered if the black guys would stomp on Red

Wolf while I was gone or if the electricity I'd felt in the air was real. I glanced at my watch and noticed that it had stopped at eleven-fifteen when I'd gone into the lockup.

"Logan, you get the Indian in back?" the DA asked me.

"Yeah, it doesn't sound like much of a big deal. Drunk in public, present at a location where a fight was occurring."

"With a broken bottle in his hand, waving it at a screaming woman."

"Get out, that was one of the other Indians. They were arrested, too, weren't they?" I bluffed.

The DA shook her head as she read the report. "There weren't any other Indians. Just your guy and the woman who ran away."

What about Ernie Little Horse and Dwayne Yazzi? I didn't say their names because what Red Wolf had told me was technically a privileged communication. But it wouldn't be the first time a client lied to me. "In the police report it says there were four people when the police vehicle approached the location and they saw a man with what appeared to be a bottle in his hand. It was dark and they were far away. They can't positively ID anyone. No indication they picked up a bottle and fingerprinted it. Sounds like the others got away, the cops were pissed and got it in for my client. Not exactly a career maker for either of us, although it would give us the opportunity to shop for new suits to wear in front of the jury."

The DA laughed. "I got bigger fish to fry today—we'll make it a straight drunk in public." She consulted a printout from the criminal index unit. "No priors. Ninety days with credit for time served."

I shook my head. I'd do my best even if it was for three hundred dollars and a guy who treated me like an asshole. "If he's a drunk, why not put him on a diversion program? Isn't it better to rehabilitate someone rather than just dry him out?"

"Right, and some day pigs will fly."

I wondered about it myself. If something worked, wouldn't my father stop drinking? "He screws up, then you put him in jail. Throw away the key."

"Fine, go over all the conditions with him. You know Harper hates it when all he gets are blank looks while he's making his orders."

Judge Harper was new. He'd been sent over from law and motion. He wasn't used to the boredom and contempt on the faces of the underclass yet.

Tony Red Wolf rose to his feet as soon as I came into the lockup.

"Here's the deal, Mr. Red Wolf." You might not like it, but it'll get you out of here. "You're going to have to say you're an alcoholic—"

He looked past me as I recited the conditions. I wasn't sure if he was listening.

"Okay," he interrupted.

"I'm sorry if it seems undignified. I don't have any idea if you're an alcoholic or not. That's your business—"

"I said it's okay. You did the best you could, pale girl. Got something for me to sign?"

I slipped the paper and my pen under the cell door. He read the form quickly, signed it, and pushed the things back under the door. He didn't look at me again or say anything as we stood in front of the judge. When it was over he was led back into the holding area to be processed out for discharge later in the day.

I'd probably get cut down to two hundred bucks because I managed to finish by noon. I retraced my steps back to my car. The smog was yellow and poisonous although an unexpected Santa Ana wind had blown through town. It was hot again. I rolled down all the windows. Lupe calls this Mexican air conditioning. I pulled out my Thomas map guide to the city and studied it. I started the Chevy and coaxed it out of the parking structure.

The sprinklers were on in the patch of grass in front of City Hall. To the east was JTown and beyond that the bridge to East Los where Lupe still lived with her mother, her son Joey, and her creep brother, Hector. To the west was Hollywood and then the ocean. Sometimes a cool breeze blew off the ocean, but not today. The sky was cloudless. It hadn't rained in months. I headed the car south down Spring Street. Winston Alley was a filthy path of broken bottles, empty discarded chip bags, and used rubbers. It smelled of urine and vomit. Less than three hundred feet away was skid row, the Nickel, where men sleep outdoors under cardboard boxes because the missions are full. As I drove away I noticed a hawk soaring overhead, a strange black form against the yellow sky.

CHAPTER 2

Kicking back on my couch that night after tae kwon do, I found myself with nothing to do and staring blankly at the amber glow from a bottle of Southern Comfort on the coffee table. I'm not interested in television. Never watch it unless the Lakers make the playoffs. Or there's big news. Like the riots three years ago.

I don't think it's so bad to have one or two drinks before bed. Helps me sleep. Some nights I toss and turn before falling into fitful slumber punctuated by disturbing dreams that center around my father. Other nights that seem to never end I worry about whether I'm going to have enough work to survive. I get out of bed and plan elaborate budgets involving money I may or may not make during the month.

I never expected things would go the way they have. My own office on a rapidly deteriorating stretch of Hollywood Boulevard instead of the Public Defender's Office. Lupe Ramos, an ex-prostitute, for a secretary. Harvey Kaplan, formerly one of the best criminal attorneys Los Angeles ever saw, now a burnt-out pothead involved in a dubious sect of religious geeks, as my office landlord. The only thing I want is to be a good criminal lawyer. Serve the people. I've done everything I could think of to find clients. Court appointments, overflow from other lawyers, fliers in English and Spanish in the area surrounding my office. Everything but stand on corners myself.

It's true my folks are loaded. They'd give me money if I asked for it, but the whole point of being in Los Angeles is to be away

26

from them and reinvent myself.

Why was I having such a hard time of it? The economy? Was it astrological? I drank the Southern Comfort. Should I put an ad with my picture in the phone book? Abandon the office and try to work for someone? I didn't want to do that. The truth is I can't network. Despite the East Coast private schools when I was a kid, the summer camps where I learned to ride and play tennis, and the sorority in college, I'm a hopeless clod. Everything I know about how other people do things I read in books. Put me in a room full of people and I either put on a mask and become so outgoing I'm nearly giddy or I plant myself in a corner and watch.

I don't believe in psychotherapy. I believe in running, working out with weights, tae kwon do. I believe God is an accountant. I believe that with a good pair of designer sunglasses and an expensive pair of black high heels you can go anywhere in the world.

I poured another shot of Southern Comfort. I'm a loner. Always have been, guess I always will be. Lupe's the closest I've ever had to a best friend. I've been to her son Joey's birthday party at her mother's house on Floral in East LA. We've eaten lunch together, sometimes dinner after work, but we never really do anything together. It would probably be nice to see a movie with Lupe, go bowling, whatever the hell it is that friends do when they get together, but we have our own lives in different parts of town.

Lupe was probably at that very moment watching TV with her mom. Hector was standing in the front yard with some of his fat *cholo* homeboys drinking beer. Joey, who was four or five by now, had been put to bed. I bet Lupe and her mom made popcorn and watched the old black-and-white movies with Joan Crawford, Lana Turner, or Rita Hayworth that Lupe loved. Or maybe her life was no bed of roses, either, and she was simply trapped in a small rundown house with her old lady who insisted on watching all the game shows, a kid she couldn't afford to raise, and no future.

I felt glummer by the second. I poured another shot. I fooled with the twist-on cap of the bottle. I thought about putting the bottle back in the kitchen. I drizzled a quarter inch of Comfort into the glass. I don't have anyone. I haven't been with a man for over two years. The last one—I could barely remember his name—had wanted to spend the night in my apartment. The idea of someone dropping his pants on my floor and hanging his coat in my closet was too much. I've fought hard for my freedom. I wouldn't mind a fuck in a motel or a good ram at some guy's pad, but it wasn't happening. I get enough exercise so I don't think about sex too often and when I do, I take care of business myself.

The drink I'd had in hand seemed to have disappeared while I was thinking about my nonexistent sex life, so I poured another. I was starting to get pretty buzzed. I'm sure it's damn weird to go two years without a man.

The point is, I am good-looking. No beauty queen, but good enough. Good body, good skin, good hair that is nearly platinum from being outdoors so much, gray eyes. My features are conventionally WASP. I don't have the big, bee-stung lips popular now. My little rosebud mouth is tiny. I bite my nails. My tits are too small and I should probably get some of those dangerous implants. I reached for the Southern Comfort again and studied the label a bit before pouring another drink.

Men don't notice me. That's not true. Some of the muscle-heads at Gold's Gym look at me and talk to me while I'm work-ing out. Not interested in bodybuilders. Some of the sheriffs at the courthouse look at me and want to tell me about their guns or RVs. Not interested in cops. Mexican busboys will bring me extra baskets of chips without being asked and I've had guys at the grocery store try to pick me up by asking me questions about fruits and vegetables.

Yet, once in a while, there was a night I didn't want to be alone. When I wanted a man next to me. It was probably the unexpected Santa Ana wind. I felt restless and discontent. I'd probably be better off if I called one of the 900 talk lines like the one Lupe worked for and let some hot stud get me all worked up. That would add some spice to my solitary sexual adventures. I brought the phone and the *LA Weekly* over to the couch and began going through the ads. There were gorgeous brunettes, big black men. Hunky guys with long blonde hair. I slammed down the shot and put my hand on the phone. What would I say? "Touch me, spread my creamy white thighs. . . ."

The guys were probably gay or overweight senior citizens.

I threw the paper on the floor. I should call my office to check for messages. I stared at the phone. The phone and the room were getting fuzzy. Maybe I'd have some work for tomorrow. It was too difficult to get up for paper to write down messages. It was way too much effort to dial the number. I passed out on the couch.

It was four in the morning when I woke up with a hangover and cottonmouth. I drank a couple of Cokes, swallowed a fistful of aspirin, and sat down on the floor of the shower with the cold water on. I hate myself when I get drunk like that. It doesn't happen too often, but when it does I feel guilty as hell. I forced myself to eat two pieces of dry toast, a fried egg that almost made me heave, and another Coke. Finally, I was able to return to the telephone.

The line buzzed and beeped while I punched in my code numbers for the voicemail service. If I was lucky there'd be a call from someone who got popped for drunk driving.

"Three forty-nine a.m.," intoned the computerized voicemail. "Mzz Logan . . . izz Red Wolf . . . 'member me . . . needa

lawyer . . ." He sounded breathless, agitated, probably drunk.
". . . girl . . . badgottacomeSan Gabriel . . ." The phone made a
clattering sound as though he'd dropped the receiver.

" 'Four twenty a.m.' . . . Red Wolf. Kilnmission . . .
comeon . . ." He still sounded messed up. A fight? Car accident?
Did a man who frequented Winston Alley even have a car?

I could probably get the court to appoint me on his case, if
there was one, and any case is better than no case. I put on a
dark brown linen suit in the event I did end up in court. He
could be screwing with me, I thought as I tucked in my ivory
silk blouse. Maybe he was just a drunk. Maybe this was the
equivalent of my father's bonkers besotted middle of the night
calls.

It was too nutty. I'd seen Winston Alley. I started to take my
suit off, but I felt too wrecked to push myself through the grind
of another day. At first I thought Tony Red Wolf had been talking about a homeless shelter or soup kitchen like the ones on
Main where apparently he hung out; but, after replaying his
messages and studying my map book, I decided he was talking
about the San Gabriel Mission. I put on brown and white
spectator pumps, my pearls, a slick of Beige de Chanel lipstick,
and felt strong enough to face a new day. I was going with the
chance some work might develop out of the call.

After leaving a quick message for Lupe that I'd be in later
and a stop at an all-night donut stand for joe to go, I headed
east. It was still dark, just a few minutes after five. Traffic was
easy on the Hollywood freeway. Most mornings I'd be on my
way to Gold's Gym in the opposite direction. I sipped the black
coffee, loaded an Etta James tape into the cassette player, and
noted the eroded moon. Silhouettes of palm trees clustered in
Silverlake, Echo Park, and Varrio Loco Nuevo loomed above
the freeway. On the hillside to the north the observatory was illuminated like a spaceship hovering above the city. Arching to

the south was downtown, a string of skyscrapers edged in purple neon.

I followed the curve of the freeway farther east over the concrete riverbed, over the railroad tracks, past the jails and past Dogtown.

The San Gabriel Valley was once the world's greatest citrus belt. Small towns with Victorian architecture sprang up along the Pacific and Santa Fe railroads. Today there are few trees and the ugliest smog in the county. Nothing but miles and miles of gray box-shaped houses and neon-lit Chinese restaurants strung along the freeway and hyphenated by miniature golf courses with castles and windmills. Like the rest of Los Angeles, the valley was predominantly Anglo until about fifteen or twenty years ago, when it became a major destination for upwardly mobile Chicanos. Thousands of Mandarin- and Cantonese-speaking Chinese—entrepreneurs from Taiwan and Hong Kong—then poorer Chinese, and most recently the Vietnamese rushed to fill the eastern half of the valley.

It was still dark when I exited the freeway. Bounded by the San Gabriel Mountains to the north, the desert to the east, the Whittier Hills—prime earthquake territory—to the south, and by the Arroyo Seco to the west, the San Gabriel Valley's like a shallow bowl into which this hodgepodge of people have been tossed and the whites are trying to float, like crackers, on top of a messy stew.

What had brought Tony Red Wolf out here? I replayed his messages in my mind. Had he called me "girl" like he'd done in jail? Or was he talking about a girl?

The mission was right where the map said it would be. There weren't many cars on Valley Boulevard and none in the parking lot. At one time a string of missions defined Southern California. The untrained priests who had designed and built the mission had seen their work destroyed by earthquakes and fire. Their efforts to buttress the church with stone vaults made it look more like a fortress than a holy place.

The front entrance of the church, however, was unlocked. Although a posted notice promised mass at six thirty, the place was empty and dark inside. The gilt painted edges of carved dark wood beams glowed dully in the light from flickering white votive candles clustered in front of several disinterested-looking saints including Saint Jude. I was pissed off at myself. Of course there was no Tony Red Wolf. I'd suspected his phone call was bullshit from the get-go. I went outside through a door near the altar to look for him. He was probably crashed in a doorway somewhere near Winston Alley.

A brick path led around the side of the mission, which, according to a plaque embedded in the adobe wall, had been built in 1776 and dedicated to the Archangel. Trees and violet-hued flowers smothered the inner courtyard in darkness as the sun prepared for its struggle with the horizon. A round wood-burning stove was labeled and dated. Everything had a sign on it explaining what it had been and how it had been used. A heathen mix of herbs scented the air. The trees and shrubbery grew even denser the farther I went into the courtyard, and it was chilly beneath their leaves.

The path led into a graveyard. Small wooden crosses were jumbled together. I didn't bother to count them. There were too many only inches from each other.

"*Psst.*" A voice came from the back of the graveyard.

I realized I was feeling too hungover to be up this early. I stopped on the path. I usually carry a snubnose .38 in my purse, but I'd left it in the trunk of the car when I'd gotten home the night before.

Tony Red Wolf stepped out of the shadows. He was wearing jeans and a red plaid shirt with the sleeves rolled up. A denim jacket was tied around his waist. His hair was still braided and pulled back from his face.

"Why'd you call me?"

He pointed at the wooden crosses covering the courtyard.

I looked at them again.

"Indians, all Indians," he said. "Once only the Gabrileno Indians lived here. Hunted, made their houses, sang their songs."

I nodded warily. "You called me in the middle of the night to give me a history lesson?"

"They were free people. Connected to Mother Earth. They knew the seasons and the ways of all the birds and animals."

He had to be drunk.

"Then the Spanish came. All we wanted was peace and to be left alone. The priests called us children and forced us to build this church, this impasse of historical knowledge."

"Are you all right, Mr. Red Wolf?"

"Tony."

"Okay, Tony." I heard a noise not far off. A cat or dog in the bushes? "Aren't you going to tell me why you called me?"

"We all lived in peace then. No fighting between our people. The priests made their children drink wine on certain days they said were holy and sometimes then my brothers would begin to fight."

I shifted my purse impatiently on my shoulder. My stomach lining was raw from all the aspirin I'd taken. "You said you were going to need a lawyer and I was the only one you knew. So here I am. I got up in the middle of the night because you said it was important." I paused, expecting a reply, but Tony Red Wolf said nothing. I noticed he was wearing a pair of high-tops made of cheap-looking leopard fabric.

"See, over there." He pointed to the farthest corner edged by the adobe wall to the only place in the courtyard not covered with wooden crosses.

"Yes." My head still hurt and I was thirsty. I wasn't going to humor him much more.

"Common grave. They killed so many Indians they ran out of space to put them. Blood scattered like water. No names. All unknown."

"I'm sorry—"

"I'm telling you this, so you'll understand where we are."

"I got the picture—"

"Where are the graves of the priests slain before their altars?" he muttered. "Don't you feel the air? How it is heavy with disrespect? How it presses down upon us?"

It was growing hot and muggy quickly, considering it was barely dawn and we were in a lush garden. Tony Red Wolf began to walk away down one of the branches of the main brick path. He turned back to see if I was following him.

I stood still. I heard the traffic from Valley Boulevard. Someone honked a horn, someone else drove past playing gangsta rap at full load.

"You came this far for a reason. Your footprints walk this way." He continued down the path.

I sighed. I must have driven all the way out to the San Gabriel Valley for more than a bad cup of coffee and a guided tour of an old graveyard. I followed Tony Red Wolf through the juniper bushes.

"The standing people will watch over us." He pointed at the trees. Finally, he came to a halt at a break in the tall hedge that seemed to form the perimeter of the mission's grounds. He bent down and ducked through the hedge, then held branches back so I could get through also.

We came out into in a deserted gravel parking lot at the back of the mission. Some ten yards away stood a metal trashcan. Two mangy-looking mutts, a shepherd and one that was part Lab, sniffed around the can licking at it. Another shepherd, stretching on its hind legs, nosed into the can.

Tony bent quickly and threw a rock in the dogs' direction. The dogs howled and ran off. Tony motioned me forward. As I got closer I saw a cloud of flies hovering above the trashcan. Like a terrible sick magnet, the smell of blood drew me on.

I stepped back, gagging, and looked at Tony.

He stuffed his hands into his pockets and stared at the trashcan.

A woman's head lay like a discarded cantaloupe on top of the pile of her dismembered body parts. Her eyes were open. Her copper face was round and lightly made up. She had been wearing an unfortunate shade of fuchsia lipstick, or else lividity had already started to set in. She had long black hair that fell like a black veil over an arm and part of her torso.

"It's Shirley Yellowbird."

CHAPTER 3

Blood dripped down the trashcan into the gravel. Through the metal slats of the can I saw the woman's awkwardly bent legs and an arm. The ambiguous twilight seemed to lengthen then shorten the distance to the can. I made myself look at Shirley Yellowbird.

"I guess you're going to tell me you didn't kill her." My voice sounded strangely listless. I took a breath and approached the trashcan. Her severed head lay at a sickening angle across the stem of her neck. I fought back a wave of nausea. I saw the top of her breasts, a half dozen jagged knife wounds rippling the beautiful reddish brown skin. I touched the outside of my fingers lightly to her cheek. Her skin was cool. I'd taken a quickie four-day course in forensics offered by the League of Public Defenders. There was rigor in the small muscle groups. I guessed she'd been dead less than eight hours, probably closer to five or four.

Tony Red Wolf continued to stare at Shirley Yellowbird. His hands shoved in his pockets. I wanted to see his hands. Shirley Yellowbird's right arm was raked with recent scratches and bruised around the wrist and forearm. I stepped away. She'd been grabbed and she'd fought before she was killed.

Red Wolf didn't look up. He felt guilty about what he'd done. Bad medicine. That's why he called me to the mission. Had to tell someone—but now he couldn't leave a witness. Why couldn't he go to one of the priests?

I glanced behind to see how to get out of the lot. I'd known in the lockup of the CCB he was violent, but I'd thought he was just a barroom brawler. I hadn't believed his story about Shirley then, but it had seemed inconsequential. Was this how my life was going to end? The middle of proverbial nowhere with a man I barely knew? What would my parents think? Would Lupe try to find me if I didn't show up at the office? I wondered if he still had the knife he killed her with.

Tony Red Wolf turned to face me.

Throwing my purse to the ground, I dropped into a tae kwon do fighting stance.

Tony jerked his hands out of his pockets and raised them in front of him. "Don't get hysterical on me. I got enough problems without you freaking out." He too glanced around the parking lot. "I didn't kill her."

If he had killed her, he would have just disappeared. I didn't relax my position.

"I called you to show you, didn't I?"

Unless you wanted to look innocent. Then you'd put on a show like this. Someone had seen him with Shirley. It was all becoming crystal clear. When the ground around Tony Red Wolf stopped shaking, he'd need someone to make him look good. Who better than a young fresh-faced WASPy woman attorney instead of some glossy macho hipster with a two-hundred-dollar haircut and an Armani suit that would intimidate the jury? He thought he'd be able to manipulate me and run the show with the same white guilt trip he'd try to lay on me yesterday at the CCB. He wouldn't kill me. He needed me, his court-appointed attorney, to represent him.

Yes! My first big trial. A murder.

He'd seen how effective and comfortable I was in court. I felt myself growing calmer, more self-assured. I've met a lot of guilty people. I eased my stance. I wouldn't tell him it might be difficult to get the court to appoint me again. I wouldn't tell him I'd never handled a murder case before. I wondered if he'd raped her. Murder during the commission of a rape is considered "special circumstances." Death penalty. That would take me out of the bush league fast.

"People will be arriving for mass any minute," I said as the shadows fluttered between us. I needed a confession from him while we were near the body. "Who killed her if you didn't?"

"Dwayne Yazzi," he mumbled. "But there's no time to jaw about this right now. I just wanted you to see what happened to her. See this place. It's going to be important." He motioned to a feather on the ground about fifteen feet away. "Eagle."

"Yeah? And . . . ?" I picked up my purse and wiped it off.

"Person who did this is acting like he has power from the Great One in the Sky. Like it was fate meeting up with Shirley."

I thought I heard a car pull into the front lot where I'd left my car. I didn't want to be found anywhere near Shirley Yellowbird. I could become an accessory after the fact real fast. I felt Shirley Yellowbird's eyes fixed on me in a defiant, glazed stare. "How do you know it was Dwayne Yazzi?"

"Let's get out of here first." Tony Red Wolf cracked his knuckles. His hands looked okay. No cuts, no dried blood under his nails or in his split, dry cuticles. That's what gloves are for.

I stopped myself from shuffling restlessly. I, too, wanted to burn rubber pronto, but I didn't think he'd spill if we split. He'd barely been able to mumble Dwayne Yazzi's name. He could decide he'd acted hastily by calling me and dump me whenever he thought someone else could help him more. He had to feel bound to me by blood. No way I'd let Tony Red Wolf ruin the career opportunity of a lifetime. If he told me he killed her it wouldn't be privileged information unless he actually retained me as his lawyer before the court appointed me, but I wasn't going to share that detail with him. "There's no time left to hide. Almost daylight."

As though on cue the bells in the *campana* tower began to ring. Six a.m.

Tony Red Wolf glanced up at the mountains to the east, where a rim of the sky was starting to turn soft pink. "Thunder's coming."

It hadn't rained in months. "The priests have probably been up for an hour. How do you know none of them saw you in the garden?"

He looked back at the mission. The adobe walls were beginning to glow in the rose wash of dawn.

"Walk out of here alone, someone's bound to notice you. A hungover-looking Indian."

The sky stretched as though about to give birth to the day. Red Wolf shifted from foot to foot. A rooster crowed from inside the garden.

"No one will pay attention to a couple."

Red Wolf licked his lips nervously. "Last night I saw someone cutting Shirley up . . ."

"You were here!" He must have had one or more accomplices. Yazzi? The others took off leaving Tony.

"I was in my apartment watching TV and all of a sudden I saw, clear as day, a man's hands. Holding a knife. Then I saw Shirley. Being cut up . . ."

"How could you see that?"

"I have visions."

Oh great. Insanity defense. "Were you drinking?"

He shook his head. "No. Not then."

"Blazing?"

He looked at me blankly. I'd have to watch the slang. Although he was only eight years older than me, could have been a generation.

"Smoking pot."

He shook his head again, impatiently.

39

"Crack?"

"I have visions. Ever since I was a little boy."

"I don't think most juries believe in visions."

"Do you?"

I shook my head. "Sorry. Not the Easter Bunny or Santa Claus, either."

Maybe I'd end up making law. I remembered from constitutional law that Indians—I reminded myself to call them Native Americans—were allowed to use peyote as part of their religious ceremonies. They even had a special church for it. I couldn't help glancing towards the mission where communion would be taking place. Had Lupe had a Catholic upbringing with this bell tower amid the bones of martyred saints nonsense? I couldn't remember the last time I'd been in a church. I'd been brought up as what my mother called High Anglican and we had communion with wine and paper-thin wafers that tasted like goldfish food.

Tony Red Wolf hitched his jeans up around his waist as though he was getting ready to go somewhere. "I had a vision of you, too. That's why I called you, why I thought you could help me."

I've always wanted to appear in some lunatic's fantasies. I flashed my hand at him. "Later for the mumbo jumbo. So far you haven't told me squat. Besides, once somebody finds her, how's that connect to you?"

"I was with her last night."

How hard it would be to say I killed her/I lost it/I stabbed her so many times I couldn't keep count. I figured this was as good as his confession was going to get until he knew me better. Tony Red Wolf told me he'd been at a bar with Shirley around nine. They had a few drinks and played pool.

"When I talked to you in lockup, you acted like you didn't know her. Was she your girlfriend or not?"

"Used to be. More'n two years ago. I was just hanging out in a bar near downtown—got outta jail around five—when she showed up." He said Shirley was drinking beer with shots of whiskey. Getting drunk and loud. Complaining of a bad day. A guy at Good Samaritan hospital where she was an LVN had been hassling her. "And she was running her mouth she had four hundred bucks with her."

I wondered if the police had ever picked Shirley up for drunk and disorderly and if that's how they recognized her in Winston Alley. "Why'd you and Shirley break up?"

"Argued all the time 'bout nothing."

Shadows between us shrank, expanded, and then grew smaller again as the sun tried to climb above the mountain. I needed to hurry Tony along. "Must have been about something."

He sighed. "She was making it with a couple other guys when she was supposed to be with me. Only seen each other a few times since then. Shirley said she wanted to go to my place. Spend the night."

He told her no. I didn't believe him. Most guys just out of jail would stick their dicks in a melon if they had the chance.

"She started bitchin' at me, like always."

I couldn't block Shirley Yellowbird out of view. I stepped aside so he'd have to look at her while he continued his story. "Stop it. Everyone's staring at you," Tony had said to her in the bar. But Shirley banged her glass on the table. "Fuck 'em." Then Dwayne Yazzi had walked into the bar. Shirley wanted to sit with him and buy him a drink.

"I got mad," Tony said. "Dwayne wasn't a person I wanted to see. Shirley was laughing and carrying on. She stood up like she's announcing something and says 'I'm going someplace better than this dump. You can stay here or rot in hell.' Then she was gone."

A traffic helicopter from one of the radio or TV stations

buzzed by overhead as it flew parallel to the freeway. Tony flinched and we both looked up as it sliced the ambiguous light with gold gleaming off its rotors.

"Was that the last you saw of her?"

He prodded the blacktop with the toe of his leopard-skin high-top. Was there blood spattered among the spots? I wondered how he felt. You'd have to feel pumped after you killed someone. My own throbbing head had cleared dramatically after I'd seen Shirley. "No, I followed them. Figured Dwayne would rip her off. They went up the street to another place. I sat at the bar, watched them for a while."

I asked if they'd seen him.

"Sure. It's the kind of place everyone knows everyone and there ain't no secrets."

The sound of a car arriving in the front parking lot caused us both to look towards Valley Boulevard with a start.

"Dwayne came up to me, told me to fuck off," Tony said more quickly. "I sorta pushed him 'cause he was getting in my face." Shirley jumped up from the table where she was sitting and came running over. She put her hand on Tony's chest like she was going to push him. He grabbed her hand, stepped back and looked at her like she was crazy. "That pissed her off. She started yelling all kinds of shit at me. I turned around to leave and—"

He glanced off into the distance with a bitter look on his face. "She kicked me in the butt. I called her a bitch and said she'd get what she deserved one day."

Sounded like Tony Red Wolf ran with a rough crowd. Had someone from that bar come here with him? Maybe a lot of people had reason to dislike Shirley Yellowbird. She did sound like a bitch and a sloppy drunk to boot. "I suppose everyone in the place heard you say that."

He nodded. He said he went home. It was before midnight.

He tried to sleep, but couldn't. He got up to watch TV, but felt too restless. He went over to Shirley's apartment and saw her lights were off. There weren't any cars he recognized. Dwayne Yazzi's Camaro wasn't there. He sat in front of the building for about ten minutes feeling stupid about trying to spy on Shirley. As he started to leave, Shirley's roommate came home and saw him in front of the building.

" 'Wanted to see if Shirley got home safe.' That's what I told her, but she just looked at me like I was weird. She was with some guy."

That's when he'd gone home, turned on the TV again, and saw the vision.

I looked over at the trashcan. The fingers of Shirley's right hand protruded above the rim of the can.

"You didn't see the man's face in the vision?"

He shook his head. "It was Dwayne. I know it."

"The four hundred dollars?"

He shrugged. "That, and . . . you don't know Shirley. She had a way of making a man not feel like a man."

"Like when she kicked you?"

"In bed. She'd get a guy all hot and bothered, then turn on him so he couldn't get it up. She was a cockteaser. You'd never do that, would you?"

I don't think I blushed, but he made me mad. My life was none of his business. Representing him was one thing, schmoozing another. I turned back towards the hedge and the courtyard and started to walk away. I wasn't sure if he was following me. Then I felt his breath on the back of my neck. He was creeping me out and he didn't seem very sad that Shirley Yellowbird was dead.

When we got to the hedge he surveyed the empty parking lot again. He shoved the eagle feather into my hand. Then he pulled the branches apart for me and I climbed into the shady graveyard. He did this all so quietly I couldn't hear him even though he was right behind me. We didn't say anything, but brushed off our clothing as we hurried through the courtyard towards the lot where I'd parked.

"Surrender yourself. I'll work it out ahead of time with the cops, then go with you." Major wacko, Red Wolf. I couldn't take the responsibility of him on the street and unless I stuck tight to him they'd give him to one of the more experienced lawyers. The typical catch-22, you can't get the case unless you've done a homicide and you can't do a homicide unless you've already done one. Or unless you're working with an experienced lawyer.

Harvey Kaplan, my landlord!

So what if he hadn't been in a courtroom for eight or nine years. He'd been the best. He did the Westlake Maniac case. Not guilty. The Hombly Hills Strangler. Murder in the second, with a parole review in twelve years. The Gower Gulch Rapist, not guilty after hanging the first jury. All of them guilty as sin, although Harvey would never confirm or deny.

It was like riding a bicycle. You never forget. And surely this would tug on Harvey's heartstrings. A Native American with visions. A spiritual brother. A butchered woman was a terrible sight, but he'd done gruesome cases before. The Westlake Maniac had been driving around with boys' heads in the trunk of his car. Harvey probably still had a decent-looking suit. I'd never seen him in anything but jeans, stained t-shirts, and a Dodgers cap. I'd have to coax him into shoes since he only wore sandals. I wondered if I could get him to stop blazing for as long as the trial would take.

"Don't be stupid, girl. I'm not surrendering myself and I'm sure as hell not waiting around for the cops. I'll find Dwayne Yazzi."

"And get him to confess?"

He pushed his hair back. "Shit, I don't know. Kill him

44

myself." He exhaled deeply. "I don't mean that, it's just a figure of speech."

"Okay, then, let's find him if you can prove he killed Shirley," I countered. "I'll give you twenty-four hours. We don't have him by then, I go to the cops. I'm still an officer of the court and I'm not losing my license behind this."

He watched Valley Boulevard without responding.

"How'd you get here? There weren't any other cars in the lot when I arrived." Someone he knew well had given Tony a ride to San Gabriel. Or perhaps Shirley had been waiting for him and he'd hitchhiked out to meet her. I wondered why they'd chosen the mission.

"Got my bike." He pointed towards the east wall of the church. I saw a motorcycle I hadn't noticed in the inky predawn shadows.

A small blue Japanese car squealed into the parking lot. Tony's back was to the car, but he didn't turn to look at it. I worried he'd be easy to identify. A Mexican in her early twenties got out of the car as soon as it stopped, and then the driver, a tall Latino with long dark hair, clutching a prayer book, followed her into the mission. I realized I was the only white person in San Gabriel.

Tony untied the jacket from around his waist and put it on. On the left sleeve an embroidered patch of the U.S. flag was sown on upside down. He turned and walked hurriedly to his motorcycle. To my surprise he put on a helmet as required by law. Then the morning calm and incipient bird songs were splintered by the rumbling roar of a Norton Commando being kicked to life.

I ran to the Chevy. It started up with an answering snarl and I peeled out of the parking lot to follow him onto the freeway.

It was still early enough that the 10 west had not yet turned into a parking lot. I tossed the eagle feather into the glove compartment. I wondered if that nutty bagman who hung around the courthouse, the one who called himself the Messiah of the Harbor Freeway, offered special dispensations such as lanes that are never blocked by overheated cars or never having to drive behind old Chinese ladies, to those who gave him money. I had heard it said that he'd been an attorney until he suffered a nervous collapse.

Doing seventy, Tony Red Wolf moved into the far left lane. I was able to follow him with no problem, but where was he taking me?

We rounded the big curve that took us above Boyle Heights, where the Jews and Italians used to live. Over the donut shop where the mariachis in black and silver *charro* outfits hung outside strumming their guitars and waiting for gigs. Past the Noche Azul Bar, where one of my clients had been arrested for prostitution while pulling a train for a soccer team from Michoacán.

The clock in the dashboard, which had only worked sporadically since I bought the car impulsively, started clicking. It was quarter of seven.

César Chávez Boulevard gave way to Sunset by the nearly obliterated monument at Fort McKlendon marking the Anglo defeat of the Spanish in the battle for Los Angeles, Nuestra Senora de las Temblores de la Porculina. Soon the city would be returned to its rightful owners and English would become a second language. The palm trees would stop trembling and would sway the melodic tropical way they were supposed to.

Tony Red Wolf increased his speed up the rise of the freeway as it broke into downtown and passed City Hall. I swung over a lane so I could keep him in sight.

The sun forced its way above the San Gabriel Mountains. The Los Angeles basin shuddered in the bright light.

Tony Red Wolf cranked the Norton and headed towards Hollywood.

CHAPTER 4

He rocketed off the freeway at Vermont and wove south through the traffic backing up near Santa Monica Boulevard. Cutting off a purple pickup decked with orange flames, I slid across a lane trying to keep him in sight. He raced through the edge of Koreatown, past Wilshire, then threw a left on Seventh. Finally, he slowed down near McArthur Park, where a geyser of polluted water bursts from the artificial lake and dope dealers lounge around Mexican pushcarts that sell slices of watermelon and papaya.

Making a quick turn into an alley alongside a bar called the Bucket, Tony Red Wolf rolled to a stop next to a battered Toyota with a bumper sticker that said "Custer Died For Your Sins." He motioned me to park in the lot across the street.

He waited impatiently in front of a *panaderia* a couple of doors from the bar. He nodded towards the bar as he tucked his shirt into his jeans. "I didn't want you going in there alone."

I nodded, but didn't say anything. There was no reason to tell him about some of the crummy bars I'd been in by myself. Was his solicitousness because he thought I was afraid of him? I wasn't. Not while we were around other people.

"They're not real big on white people. Particularly chicks. There'll be some women in there. You look at any of the men and those broads will fuck you up."

That was sort of a howl. If the women knew how long I'd been without a man, how dispirited my interest in the whole subject had become, they'd probably want to take up a collection for me.

"Whatever you say."

"Just be cool. Indian women are real jealous."

I wondered if he thought women were interested in him. I glanced at him out of the corner of my eye as we walked towards the Bucket. He was a big man. Made you think of being picked up and carried to bed. His black hair shone like obsidian, like Lupe's. His mouth wasn't hard or cruel, as his eyes had been when I'd met him in jail. I couldn't see his eyes, however, because he was wearing a pair of cheap, round black-wire sunglasses with yellow-mirrored lenses. He had no beard but for a tuft of hair below his lower lip. The scar was a nice touch. Maybe women were interested in him. He was an okay-looking guy for a killer.

Tony Red Wolf wrenched open the dented black door of the bar and stepped aside for me to enter. I wondered for a second if this was going to be rougher than that dump, the Pit Stop, near my office where nearly all the young guys were packing.

A strand of red and green Christmas lights was draped over the mirror behind the bar, illuminating the room. The room was long and narrow and dark enough so that the back just seemed to disappear. The bar was on the west wall. Three men and two women sat at the far end. Two more men sat talking at a table shoved between the door and a jukebox that was playing a melancholy Kitty Wells song. It was a real six a.m. kind of place. Nearly everyone was smoking and a gray haze blurred the room.

The door slammed behind me. The narrow ray of sunlight from Seventh Street vanished. They all looked up at me—their faces stern and dark. Kitty Wells's voice faded away. Tony touched the small of my back, nudging me forward.

All Indians. Was this the bar where Tony threatened Shirley?

"Hiya, John, Calvin." Tony nodded at the guys at the table as we passed them on the way to the bar. They stared at us in silence. Tony kept his eyes straight ahead as though not registering their lack of response. He spoke to those at the bar, but they didn't reply, either.

We sat at the end of the bar closest to the door.

"What'll it be?' Tony asked.

I glanced down the bar. Everyone had a beer on deck.

"Beer."

Tony ordered two Buds from the guy behind the bar, an old man with long gray hair in braids. He wore an immaculate white button-down shirt with a silver and turquoise bolo tie. His appearance made me feel better, like he wasn't going to let anyone mess up his bar by starting some nonsense. I reached for my wallet, but Tony frowned at me and laid a five on the counter.

"Is Dwayne Yazzi here?" I whispered.

Tony shook his head and pushed one of the beers towards me. "Working maybe. Works construction sometimes."

"Good, let's go by his crib and check it while he's out."

"Indians move around a lot. Don't know where he lives now."

One of the women called for a beer and conversation resumed.

"You know all these people?"

"Yeah."

"They don't look too thrilled to see you."

Tony took a long draw on his beer.

"You think they know about Shirley?"

He shook his head and said this wasn't a bar Shirley came to.

"Is it because I'm here?"

"Part of it."

"What's the rest?"

Tony Red Wolf sighed and pushed the nearly empty beer away. "My mother was part white."

"And . . . ?"

"That makes me a 'breed. A half-breed. Even though my old man was Choctaw and had a reputation as a rainmaker. Some of them skins"—he nodded towards the crew of drinkers— "think I'm not a real Indian."

I leaned forward slightly and glanced down the bar again to look at them. Two of the men were turned away from me, but one of the women caught me studying her and frowned at me. I pulled back slowly.

"Shirley was full-blood?"

"Sioux. From Rosebud, North Dakota. Came off the rez when she was eight or nine." Tony fell silent like he was thinking about something sad. I picked at the label on the bottle in front of me. My stomach didn't feel a hundred percent yet. Looking at the beer made me feel slightly sick.

"And Dwayne?" It felt weird to ask, like I was some nerdy anthropologist. Tony came back to life and focused on me again. "His people are Navajo. Used to be from Window Rock, but he was born here. Probably couldn't find Window Rock if he had a compass with all points marked east."

I wondered if different tribes got along or if it was like mixing Bloods and Crips. I asked if Dwayne hung out here and what he looked like.

Tony nodded. "Shorter than me, five-nine. Wears cowboy boots all the time so he'll look taller. Big chest and shoulders. Poses around like he's a bodybuilder. Walks that dumb way they do, arms sticking out from his body like an ape."

I laughed. I'd seen plenty of those guys at Gold's. "Everyone here has long hair."

"Indian thing. Cut mine once to get a job. Didn't get the fucking job anyway." He sounded angry when he asked the bartender for two more beers. I picked mine up and drank. It didn't taste good and it didn't taste bad.

Tony told the bartender to give him a package of beef jerky

from the display next to the cash register. Tony opened the package and offered me some. It was pungent, fleshy.

I thought of the pile of Shirley Yellowbird and the smell of blood. I felt my stomach start to turn over again. How could he eat now? One more reason I was convinced he'd killed her. It was getting hot outside. It could boil into the nineties again. Maybe the dogs had come back and tipped over the trashcan and parts of Shirley Yellowbird were all over the parking lot baking in the sun. I started to feel sick and stood up.

The woman I'd stared at earlier looked over at me. Her hair hung free and a silly artificial daisy was pinned on one side to hold it back from her face. She was about thirty-five. She had on a lot of makeup—blue eyeshadow, thick black liner, and clowny pink cheeks—which was too bad because she was nearly beautiful. It looked like she was pretty potted.

"Let's bail," I said. "If you're not going to ask anyone if they've seen Dwayne, there's no point in staying."

Tony shook his head. "We're on Indian time now." He offered the jerky to me again. My stomach rumbled. "There's a right time and a wrong time for everything. Don't worry, when it's the right time, I'll be asking. Looking for the ladies' room?" He pointed his lips towards the darkness.

I made my way past the table with the two guys and then past the group at the end of the bar. I heard a stool scrape across the floor. The door to the ladies' room was painted red.

"Squaws," I read on the door.

Inside was yellow and dirty with a cracked sink. A broken strawberry air freshener lay in a corner. Someone trying to save money had put a twenty-watt bulb, red, in the ceiling, and the room was nearly as dark as the bar. The toilet was in a tiny enclosed closet and I was glad to be able to go inside and have a moment to myself while I tried to sort out everything that had happened so far. Shirley partying and arguing with Tony. The entrance of Dwayne Yazzi. Shirley's big talk about her money. I wondered if Yazzi had robbed her. I hadn't seen her purse at the mission.

Who was Dwayne Yazzi? I tried to piece together Tony's insinuations about him. Was it possible Tony Red Wolf hadn't killed Shirley? He probably lied about going home. He could have been spying on her all along and followed her to the mission. The blood made me think she'd been killed there. Her throat slashed from ear to ear.

I threw up, my knees buckling.

Tony could have been watching everything from far away. Or he could have been right there when she was killed and someone forcibly held him back. Yazzi could have fucked him over on a robbery. He could have been afraid of Yazzi. He could be ashamed he wasn't able to be a real man and save her.

But there was this to be considered: Red Wolf had been insulted while Indians watched him. Later, he came up with the story of the vision so he could be a real Indian, too. I wiped at my mouth with toilet paper. Tony Red Wolf was spooky all right. Yet, I would have to say, certainly courteous towards me, even a bit chivalrous.

Psychopath?

My heart started pounding. If only I could talk to Harvey right now. Some of his most famous clients had been psychopaths, but at this time of the morning he would be at the goofy temple his religious sect had recently consecrated in an empty storefront on Bronson near Hollywood Boulevard. Initially Tony had seemed worried and perhaps sad Shirley was dead. Wouldn't he have been more outraged, more vengeful, if Dwayne Yazzi or some other person slit Shirley's throat? And left him holding the bag. Even though Tony had seen her body before I got to the mission, he hadn't appeared sickened in the slightest by the sight of her in the trashcan. Probably he didn't remember doing it. No, if he didn't remember he would have come upon it as a stranger, seemed more shocked, more offended at the sight of her mutilated body.

He was a stone-cold killer.

If I could show a history of conflict between Dwayne and Shirley, I might be able to plant reasonable doubt about Red Wolf in the jury's mind. I saw myself in front of the jury box, twelve good citizens hanging on every word. Too mesmerized to be taking notes. I'd be able to write my own ticket after his trial. There'd already been a lot of murders in LA so far this year, but none with a sliced-up naked woman. There was also the possible ritualistic nature of the crime, the eagle feather. The newspapers would interview me. I'd mail the clippings to my father.

I heard the outer door open. I flushed so whoever it was knew I was in there. When I came out the nearly beautiful woman from the end of the bar stood in front of the sink. Up close I saw she was in her late forties and not doing too well at it. She was also drunker than a skunk. The door to the toilet almost hit her as I opened it.

"Watch it," she snarled.

"Sorry." I tried to step around her to the sink, but she didn't move. "Excuse me," I pointed at the sink.

She turned and blocked the sink, pretending to examine her makeup in the mirror.

I waited what seemed a reasonable time. Finally she stopped tracing the outline of her lipstick as though she'd been wiping away smudges and stood with both hands on the sink staring at me in the mirror.

"I was just going to wash my hands, if you don't mind," I said.

She didn't answer, but leaned into the mirror to pick her

teeth. "You'll never get your hands clean. You people killed Indians."

I wanted to tell her I wasn't a "you people," that I had radical political ideas and a good heart, but that would sound too wack and I figured she wanted to kick my butt anyway. "Is there some soap over there?"

She picked up a grimy bar of soap from the sink, wrote "GO HOME" on the mirror with it, and then dropped it into the overflowing wastebasket.

"I'm not after any of your men, if that's what you're thinking."

She didn't take her eyes off me.

"Wouldn't even try."

She continued glaring at me.

"You seem like plenty of woman for any man."

There was a moment of dead silence while we stared at each other. "May be old and ugly now, but Norma Elkfoot still too much woman for one man." She hiccupped drunkenly, laughed, and lurched past me into the toilet where I heard her humming a little tune.

I washed my hands, but there weren't any paper towels.

I was glad to see a pay phone between the "Squaws" and the "Braves." I called the office, but the phone rang and rang. I was about to hang up. Lupe didn't usually come in before nine thirty unless she'd had a fight with her mother or Hector.

"Yeah?" Lupe panted as though she'd run to the phone.

"Aren't you supposed to say 'Good morning, Law Office'?"

"Not until I get paid."

"Come on, Lupe, for Christ's sake, this is a team effort. Clients are going to get confused if you don't answer the right way."

"Clients? I'm not sure you have any. If you did, then you'd act like a real lawyer and you'd pay me."

"That's why I'm calling. I got a big case—"

"Whatever you're doing, drop it, get in here. Some guy called wanting an appointment, said he got your name from the county bar referral service. I told him ten. And to bring cash."

"I'm with this guy—"

"A man? Well, that's different. Go for it. If you remember how."

"Would you shut up and listen to me? He's an Indian—"

"Hi ho, Silver!"

"—it's the biggest kind of case . . ."

The drunk woman came out of the bathroom. As she clomped past, she bumped me. It didn't feel like an accident.

"Gotta go. I'll explain it all later."

"Ten. He's got cash."

"Keep your hands off him. Tell him to come back at eleven." I hung up before she could give me an argument.

Tony Red Wolf was still sitting alone at his end of the bar. I wondered if he'd asked anyone where Dwayne Yazzi was. The Indians snickered as I climbed onto the barstool next to Tony. Two more beers were lined up on the bar in front of our seats. "Find out anything?"

"Thought you fell in."

Scratch the chivalrous. He was a loser. I wondered for a second what he'd seen of me in his so-called vision, but I smiled politely.

"We don't have all day. She must have been found by now." I wondered how long it would take for an identification. Was I an accessory after the fact yet? I was either going to be a hotshot criminal attorney or disbarred. "You said last evening Shirley complained about a guy at work who'd been bothering her. Who's he?"

Tony shrugged.

"Maybe he did it." Red Wolf was wearing my patience with

his laconic bullshit. "You don't seem very interested."

He just shook his head and asked if I wanted something different to drink. "Firewater? Know what that was? Watered-down liquor spiked with tobacco and red pepper."

"You better think of as many people as you can who didn't like Shirley Yellowbird," I snapped. "Her own mother. Anyone."

"You think I killed her, don't you?" he whispered. I knew him well enough to know that tone of voice meant he was pissed off.

I'd convict him if I were on a jury. He had motive, opportunity. His lame accusations about Dwayne Yazzi didn't amount to much. Shirley sounded like Ms. Hot Pants, ready to rock and roll anytime, anyplace. Red Wolf knew that about her all along. Rage must have been building in him until it erupted last night. It was revolting that my big break was going to come defending a man who butchered a woman, but there's good reason the statue of Justice has to be blindfolded. Tony Red Wolf creeped me out, but I'm no fool and I can take care of myself. "No, but you have to be prepared when this goes down. That's what you wanted me for, if you didn't kill her, wasn't it?"

Tony scratched at the label on his Bud with his thumb. "Dwayne gets crazy. I saw him stab a Mexican who grabbed a feel off Shirley at a place downtown."

I nodded. Good. Sex-crazed strangers.

"Cut his arm pretty bad," Tony added.

A knife, fine. "Ever tell you about the guy at work?"

"He's from Guatemala."

"She go out with him?"

"Negative. He was just a little creepy guy who bothered her. She wouldn't give him the time of day."

I asked if he knew his name.

"Jose."

"Last name?"

Tony shook his head.

How many illegal aliens named Jose could there be working at Good Sam? Five or six dozen?

The door of the bar swung open. A blast of hot air and sunlight split the room like a mineshaft. Tony looked away from the mirror and the racks of booze behind the bar and squinted into the sun. I turned to see over my shoulder. The door slammed shut. Another Indian, as tall as Tony Red Wolf, but much heavier, paused a few feet away to check the room.

"Hey, Ernie, man, how you doing? Come here." Tony raised his hand in greeting.

The Ernie Little Horse Tony had told me about while he was in jail?

"Bro, what up?" Ernie came over with the barest glance in my direction and did a complicated soul handshake with Tony.

"This is Whitney."

"Hey, man." I stuck out my hand.

Ernie looked at me like I was speaking a foreign language. Damn, I was having a hard time getting it right in here. Tony's lips curled a little like he was going to smile. "Whitney's a friend of mine from work."

Ernie studied my brown linen suit as though it was something inconceivable. I realized I didn't have the vaguest idea what Tony Red Wolf might do for a living. "Well, not exactly, I'm just trying to get into it," I fudged. "See how it works."

He nodded his head then. "Cool. Just lose the suit. You a singer?"

"Don't need two in one band," Tony laughed. "She's a song-writer. Still working in an office 'til she hits it big."

Ernie looked at me like songwriter was code for groupie. "Tony can teach you everything you need to know."

So Red Wolf was a musician. I smiled back and nodded. He

thought Tony was working me for a fuck. "What do you do, Ernie, you a musician also?" In LA a person is his job. You meet someone and the first thing you ask is what they do for a living. After you've talked a couple of minutes you can ask how much they pay for rent.

"Nah, I'm just an ordinary guy."

"Don't believe it for a second," Tony said. He called out an order for a beer for Ernie. "Go on, tell her what you do, man."

Ernie held out his hands, palms down. They were filthy and nicked with cuts, some of which still had traces of blood. I glanced at Tony, but he was turned towards the bar. "What do you think?" Ernie asked me.

That you've used a knife recently. That you have some nasty-looking cuts on your right hand.

"Mechanic," Ernie said.

"Not just a mechanic," Tony added. "A wizard. Taught me everything I know about cars. Guy can fix anything just by looking at it." They went through another round of soul hand-shakes.

Tony had said they'd all been together in Winston Alley the night he'd been arrested. How far back did they go? Chopping up a body would require a lot of force and weight. Even a man Ernie Little Horse's size would have to lean into the job. His hands could easily get cut. They could have slipped on a bloody knife handle.

"Gotta see a man about an iguana," Tony announced, heading back towards the bathrooms.

What had Ernie's relationship with Shirley been? "Always a great skill, fixing cars," I agreed.

"Something you need to know living on the rez. Ever been to the rez?"

I shook my head. I glanced down the hall towards the rest-rooms. I hadn't seen Tony walk past the bar. Had he split? I cursed myself for not noticing where the exit was.

"Junked cars everywhere," Ernie said.

What kinds of things had these two men been into together? "I don't know very much about Indians. Is that okay to say, Indians?"

Ernie looked like he was enjoying my awkwardness.

"I haven't known Tony very long," I continued. Was it my imagination or had the bar grown silent again? Although my back was to them, I felt the two men at the table watching us.

"Meet him in a club?"

"Yeah. In Hollywood," I guessed.

Ernie didn't respond so I figured I was doing better. "Actually I know him from Shirley Yellowbird. You know her?"

"Oh, fuck," Ernie groaned. "The worst fucking bitch on the planet. 'Scuse my English. She a friend of yours?"

"Acquaintance."

"Try to keep it that way. Better yet, get rid of her as soon as you can. Don't return her phone calls. Never loan her money. She'll make your life a living hell. She shows up and the world turns to shit."

"So, she's a friend of yours, too?"

"Worse, I'm stuck with her. She's a cousin, but she's messed me up on so much shit I don't even want to get started on it."

"She's been totally cool with me. Guess all relatives have disagreements once in a while."

"Bitch got me sent to jail about a week ago, you understand what I'm saying? She should do the world a favor and drop off the face of the earth. Die. Disappear. Dust to dust."

I picked up my beer, took a drink, and contemplated my career. Could Ernie Little Horse have killed Shirley? It would be a whole different ball game if Tony Red Wolf were innocent.

CHAPTER 5

"Thanks for the evening," I announced to Tony, who reappeared with his hands in his pockets.

Ernie put his beer to his lips like he was covering a smile. I wondered if Tony knew Ernie hated Shirley. I wondered why Ernie had wanted to give Shirley crack in Winston Alley and why he'd gotten into a fight about it with Dwayne Yazzi.

"Office I work for needs me to come in."

Tony looked at me suspiciously like I was going to bail on him. Did he think I was going to call the police? There'd been a lot of broken treaties with the white man.

"Come with me," I urged. "We'll do lunch."

Ernie Little Horse smirked, undressing me with his eyes like he wouldn't mind snacking off my frame.

"Sure." Tony drained his beer and put the empty on the bar. That was his fourth in less than an hour. "Later, Ernie."

Ernie said it was nice to meet me, which I didn't believe. He strolled over to the group at the bar, said something while nodding in our direction, and there was an explosion of laughter.

Outside, before Tony could argue with me, I told him it was true I had to go back to my office.

"Let's shake it then," he complained. "I got less than twenty-one hours to locate Dwayne and somebody's bound to find Shirley soon." He said he'd follow me on his bike. He didn't look drunk, but he couldn't pass a breathalyzer test.

He seemed unimpressed by my office building and didn't

seem to recognize it. I noticed new black slashes of Seventh Street Locos graffiti by the front door. Sam's, the Thai restaurant downstairs, was deserted. It does most of its business after two a.m., when the bars close in Hollywood. Over the last year it's become a hangout for rockers wanting cheap food and a place to trade news on bookings and upcoming shows. If Tony Red Wolf were a musician he would have heard of it even if he'd never been to it.

Lupe was sitting at her desk in the outer office space we'd created as a reception area, listening to salsa on the radio and painting her nails dark red. She gave Tony Red Wolf the quick once-over and shot me a look like I was out of my mind. She wrinkled her nose as she bent over her polish.

He dropped into the chair in front of her and put his feet up on her desk.

"Would you excuse us a moment, Mr. Red Wolf? I need to speak with Ms. Ramos, my secretary." I ushered Lupe into my office and shut the door.

"Mr. Red Wolf? What is he, a cartoon character?" she laughed.

"*Shhh*, keep your voice down. He's going to be a big client."

"Yeah, how much did he pay you for a retainer?"

"Nothing, it's not like that—"

"Oh great, now you're giving it away." She shook her head. "There's a guy gonna be here in less than ten minutes with three hundred bucks. I'm gonna ask Mr. Red Wolf to wait downstairs so this place doesn't look like a legal aid office." She started for the door.

I grabbed her by the arm. "He"—I whispered pointing to the reception area—"murdered someone."

"Jesus fucking Christ, why can't you just do PI cases?"

"You're not scared, are you?" I asked Lupe.

"Scared?" she shrugged. "You gotta be kidding me. I went to high school with at least five guys who are in state prison for murder. God, I just hate that about you. You're so fucking white bread you think all this *basura*, like him, are exciting. You got everything. You're a lawyer, you went to a good school, you're okay-looking, sort of. You could make all the money you want."

I'd never told Lupe all the specifics about my parents. I'd told her I didn't get along with them and that my dad was a boozer, but I'd never told her how much money they had. If I did, I'd never know if she liked me for myself or for their money.

"Who'd he kill?' she raged. "Don't be telling me it was some woman. He looks like the kind of asshole who beats on women. I can't put up with that shit. If that's how you want to spend your life, that's on you, but I won't work here."

Before I could answer, the outer door opened and closed. Maybe Tony Red Wolf had heard us. I cracked the door. Tony was reading *People* magazine. A white guy stood in the middle of the room.

"What's he here for?" I asked Lupe.

"A divorce."

I groaned. I hate divorces. Clients alternate erratically between maniacally depressed and pissed off. You spend a lot of time on the phone talking to some other lawyer about how to divide up a lot of crappy electronics equipment and unpaid-for Japanese cars.

The first one I'd done, the one that soured me on the entire process, was for a fat woman named Roberta Lewis who worked at the gas company. Her husband was a wacked-out engineer on SSI who hadn't worked for years. He left death threats on my message machine. Said he'd kill us both if she didn't give him their antique tin toy collection. After Roberta was ordered to pay alimony, she was so pissed I'd been unable to collect my fee from her.

Lupe tapped her toe impatiently, waiting to see what I was going to do. I sighed and sat down at the desk composing myself to look professional and understanding. Lupe nodded in approval and sallied forth in mellifluous tones to bring the new client to me.

He'd brought cash, a pile of twenties that looked like they'd just been made. I spent enough time to get the basic facts and his signature on a retainer agreement. Mr. Hayes was a beefy white guy in his mid-forties with a widow's peak, a lot of hair on his knuckles, and Taiwan knockoffs of a pair of Air Nikes. He said he'd selected me from the referral list because he'd specifically asked for a female attorney. His wife had hired a man.

"You got a name like a man."

I smiled and shook his hand when he left, then threw my pen on the desk. Bitch with balls. At your service. I was glad I'd upped the retainer to five hundred bucks.

I waited 'til I heard the front door close before I went out. Tony tossed the magazine aside and stood. I wondered if he and Lupe had spent the entire time in the waiting room without speaking to one another.

"Whitney says you killed someone," Lupe said to Tony.

"Lupe!"

"That's what you said."

"I said possibly killed someone, charged with killing someone—"

"Did you?" she interrupted, glaring at him.

"I haven't been charged with anything," Tony Red Wolf spat angrily, as though accustomed to the use of force in a considerable manipulation of personal history.

"That's right," I hurried to add. "You just knew someone who was killed."

"Who was it?" Lupe demanded.

Tony Red Wolf shrugged. "Lady I used to know."

"I knew it was a woman." Lupe folded her arms across her chest.

"It's none of your business," Tony snapped.

"We're partners," Lupe jerked her thumb in my direction. "I'm her confidential secretary and office manager. We've done investigations together."

I wished Lupe would shut up. She seemed to have no idea yet how important Tony Red Wolf was to my future. I wondered if she'd stay if she knew I thought he'd killed Shirley Yellowbird.

"You don't like it here, find another lawyer," she said to Tony.

Lupe had been on the street long enough to have had some bad experiences. She'd always denied that, but, just as I'd never told her the whole truth about myself, I was sure she'd never told me the whole truth, either.

"Why don't you butt out," Tony said. "Logan's the one I'm here for and I'm not even a hundred percent on her yet."

The thought of Shirley Yellowbird rotting in the sun made my stomach turn again. "You called me," I snapped. "I told him I'd give him a day to find the guy he thinks killed the woman, Lupe. Then I'm going to the police. A day. That's all. It'll be all over the papers by then."

"TV?" Lupe asked fiddling with the bottle of nail polish and trying not to betray her excitement.

I nodded. "There's something I need you to do."

Lupe turned to me triumphantly as though banishing Tony Red Wolf. "Yes?"

"Go out to the San Gabriel Mission." I glanced at Tony Red Wolf to see how he'd react. "That's where the woman's body is. See if anyone's found it yet."

"No way!"

Tony picked up the letter opener from Lupe's desk and began to clean his fingernails.

"You're at the forefront of a breaking story," I urged. "All you have to do is drive by."

She shook her head.

"You don't even have to get out of the car."

"I'm a Mexican so it's my lot in life to do drive-bys?"

I put three hundred dollars in Lupe's hand.

Lupe counted the money quickly. "I'm a secretary," she sniffed. "Not a messenger. And it's a long way to San Gabriel."

I pulled the two hundred I'd been saving for myself out of my suit pocket and handed it to her. "Call in and leave the information on the voicemail. Take the rest of the day off."

Lupe put the money carefully into her wallet. "Just for you, Whitney." She took the magazine Tony had dropped on the table, arranged it neatly in the magazine rack it belonged in, and walked out with her hips twitching.

"She gets like that sometimes," I apologized to Tony when she was gone. "Doesn't mean anything."

"The old prophecies say the white man will come to dominate this continent, but his time in the sun will be the shortest of all the people who will dwell here."

"Pardon?"

"Skip it with the Mr. Red Wolf this and that. I'm not part of a freak show."

"Sorry. I never talked to an Indian before."

"I grew up in the San Fernando Valley, graduated with a degree in government and economics. I ate all the same junk food you did when you were a kid and I went to all the same movies."

"I didn't get to eat junk food while I was growing up."

"That explains a lot about you," he laughed.

"I also didn't have visions. What tribe did you say you are?"

"Choctaw. Take a good look at me. There's only about fourteen thousand of us left."

What would it be like to be one of the last of my kind on

earth? It was bad enough having been an only child. "Didn't your vision tell you where we should look for Dwayne Yazzi?"

"No, but I know a place in Hollywood he hangs out."

I picked up my purse and turned off the lights.

"Don't you have anything else to wear?" Tony asked. "You look like an undercover cop."

I went back into my office and changed into a pair of jeans, a white t-shirt, and tennis shoes I kept in the closet for when I was working late.

"That's better. I'll leave my bike. We'll go in your car."

My gun was in the trunk of the car. I wanted to get it out and hide it in my purse without him seeing it. Imagine the state bar getting a complaint I was carrying a concealed weapon illegally.

Tony Red Wolf had me drive down the Boulevard into the heart of Hollywood where all the theaters and crummy tourist shops are. We left the car on Selma where there was parking because the cops had chased the chicken hawks and boys in cutoffs away.

"I forgot to put my pull-out radio in the trunk." I turned back towards Selma.

"I'll do it for you."

I shook my head and hurried back towards the car.

"You one of those feminists?" Tony grinned. I was glad when he wandered over to examine a wall plastered with fliers about shows and bands. I heard a dove cooing, then the hoot of an owl. I kept an eye on Tony Red Wolf while I got the gun out of the trunk and slipped it into my purse. The owl hooted again. I looked around. There were no owls in Hollywood.

We walked up Wilcox past a Russian market, a taco stand, and a Chinese takeout place. A black queen fluttered by on his way to the newsstand. Hollywood High was just around the corner. Although school wasn't out for the day, a throng of

Latino boys with skateboards and a few girls dressed in short baby-doll dresses and black combat boots stood by a flight of stairs that led down into the cellar of one of the stores. A punk club called the Masque had been in the cellar before I came to Hollywood and the stairs and walls were still splattered with paint and the names of bands.

"Are you in a band?"

"Not right now. Used to be. 'Tinder Wood.' "

I shrugged. "I don't get out much. What kind of music?"

"Hard rock. Blues base. Sorta like Led Zeppelin, but original. I can sing the hell out of the blues. Keyboards and guitar. I'm going to play the Forum someday. Bird calls, too. Did you hear the dove and the owl I did?"

Unbelievable. Everybody in this town is on the verge of being a star. The Forum's one of the biggest concert venues in LA. The Lakers and the Kings play there. You'd think if someone was in his late-thirties he would have already played there if it was ever going to happen. That's the thing I hate about actors and musicians, the insane belief that tomorrow will be a brighter day, but nobody will be any older.

"And in the meantime?"

"Unemployment. Teach some music lessons. Choctaws always been renowned for music and poetry. My great-grandfather toured Europe. Part of a Wild West show. Even went on gondolas in Venice and met the queen of England. And once in a while I get a residual check for twenty-eight dollars from a made-for-TV Western I did about three years ago."

I wanted to ask more questions, but he suddenly lowered his voice. "This is it." He paused outside a small, dark store with a purple candle in a blackened window.

There was no sign anywhere. No credit card advertisements. I looked for the numbers on the black door, but they were painted over with black matte and hard to read. "What is this place?"

"The Crescent."

A bar? Did all Indian activities take place in bars? But I was ready for another drink.

"Don't touch anything." Tony pushed a black buzzer, which I hadn't seen, by the door. "Don't say anything unless someone speaks to you first." He pressed the buzzer two more times in quick succession. I heard the click that meant someone inside had unlocked the door. Tony pushed the door open.

The entire room was illuminated by hundreds of flickering candles. Most of them were white, but to the side of the door was a small, black wrought-iron table with a glass top upon which were several green candles and a basket of business cards. I palmed one of the cards, but it was too dark to read it.

The place smelled like patchouli and something vaguely disagreeable like cloves. I hate incense. It gives me a headache. I was always glad I was born too late to have been a hippie. Hate the incense, hate the tie-dye, the macramé, the strobe lights, and foods with soggy sprouts. I've tried acid and pot, but thought they were overrated. Call me square.

As I looked around, I realized I wasn't in a head shop. Instead of psychedelic posters there were drawings of pentagrams. Instead of roach clips and bongs there were bags of dried herbs and bottles of oil for sale.

I wondered if this was part of Tony's silly rock fantasy. Hail Satan. But what reason would Dwayne Yazzi have to hang around this place bizarrely dedicated to private rituals dictated by personal crises?

Tony mumbled something I couldn't understand, but took to be bastardized pig Latin, to greet a portly white man with a shaved skull and a small black pointed goatee. Six or more silver hoops dangled from each of the man's ears. Although he was over fifty, he had a pierced nose. He was dressed entirely in black—black leather jeans, black silk shirt buttoned to the neck, black velvet cord with a silver Christ on a cross hanging upside down.

Did they need a virgin to sacrifice? I was almost one again.

"Lester," Tony said as if it explained everything. People who give their kids ugly names are practically guaranteeing they're going to grow up to be freaks.

Tony introduced me as a friend. I felt like I was on a bad set for a creepy-crawler movie. Glass jars of the dried herbs covered shelves on the wall behind Lester. There was a jar with a small dried bat in it. Displayed on red velvet in the display case Lester stood behind were several large silver knives for sale.

I thought of the way Shirley had been cut up. The mission. A black mass? It wasn't as funny while I was looking at the knives.

"I wanted to see Dwayne," Tony said. "Where is he?"

"Where you been the last few months?" Lester asked Tony. "We missed you."

"Working like a son of a gun."

So much for the peyote church. Had the Indians subjected to the Christian destruction of their culture rebelled by becoming Satanists? I was impatient to find out what Tony Red Wolf's relationship to Dwayne had been. They'd been banging the same woman. There must have been some sloppy seconds.

"I asked Tony to bring me here," I told Lester. "I want an amulet to protect me."

Tony frowned at me.

"From what?" Lester asked. "It has to be specific so I can custom blend it for you."

It sounded like buying makeup at Saks. Girl looks at your skin under a special lamp and whips up the precise color foundation for you. "From evil-doers."

"You want this powder, oil, or something to wear around

your neck?"

Tony shook his head slightly like I should put a lid on it.

"Around her neck."

"Good," Lester nodded in approval, taking a mortar and pestle from beneath the counter. "That's the strongest. What kind of evil-doers? Bill collectors? In-laws? Lawyers?"

Tony took my hand, squeezing it hard like a warning, but I pulled away from him.

"A woman I know was murdered—"

"Got it. You want death defying. Conquer fear. Vigilance." Lester selected and chopped and ground some herbs and roots. I glanced out of the corner of my eye at Tony. He couldn't believe any of this stuff, could he? I saw the slightest suggestion of a smile on his face and knew that he knew I was looking at him. I felt relieved he wasn't into any of this bullshit. Another crummy tourist shop with things that broke right after you bought them and rings that turned your finger green.

"Dwayne knew the woman. Shirley Yellowbird. Maybe you knew her also." I watched his eyes but there was only dead blankness. I described Shirley.

Lester shrugged as he packed the contents of the mortar into a clear plastic locket.

"It was really horrible, at least that's what I heard. Cut up. Stabbed too many times to count," I said, looking down at the knives on display.

"Thought I should come by and let Dwayne know what happened," Tony said.

I paid Lester. "Do you have a phone I can use?"

He said he didn't ordinarily let people use his phone, but reluctantly pointed me in the direction of his office. The office was even gloomier than his strange emporium. A dark wood desk on which stood a fake Tiffany lamp draped with a dark red silk scarf was covered with papers. Books detailing natural, unforetold, and inexplicable disasters. Next to the phone were two skulls the size of foxes. Rifling through the papers, I used my credit card so my number wouldn't show up on Lester's bill, and I dialed my office.

Lupe had called in her message. "I'm at the mission. All hell's breaking loose. The back lot's marked off with yellow tape. Cop cars all over the place. They're not letting anyone in. A fourth-grade class was making a field trip. A couple kids found the body. I heard the woman was all chopped up in a trashcan." Lupe's voice trailed off for a few seconds. "Jesus Christ, Whitney, you let that guy into our office. I can't believe it. Now you're off somewhere with him. If I don't hear from you within an hour, I'm calling the police." She slammed the phone down.

I called the voicemail back. "Lupe," I whispered. "Don't call the police. I'm at some weird occult store not far from the office." I opened the red accounts book to the last page to see what kind of shape the business was in. I ran my finger quickly down the names and numbers. Dwayne Yazzi owed Lester almost eight hundred dollars. I noticed a duplicate of a week-old invoice for a book on love spells and hexes that had been special-ordered for him. I stuffed it in the pocket of my jeans. "I didn't have time to tell you, but Tony Red Wolf called the office twice from the mission in the middle of the night sounding drunk and saying he needed a lawyer. Told me to meet him there."

I paused to listen to what was going on out in the store, but I didn't hear anything.

"He showed me the body. He threatened her in a bar late last night. A lot of people heard him."

Out in the store I heard Tony laugh.

I lowered my voice. "He says another Indian guy killed her. Dwayne Yazzi. They were both fucking her. We came here searching for Yazzi, but *nada*. I'll call again soon. We're going to keep looking." I hung up, dropped the rest of the papers back on the desk, and caught my breath.

"Dwayne Yazzi?" a man's voice whispered. "Well, you found him."

A muted light clicked on at a table on the opposite side of the room. A surly Indian stood with his arms folded across his chest studying me across the dark space.

CHAPTER 6

Dwayne Yazzi rumbled across the room at me. He was bigger than Tony had said. And good-looking, although his eyebrows grew together across the bridge of his nose and he had the sweaty metal smell guys on steroids have.

"This must be yours." I jerked the invoice from the pocket of my jeans and handed it to him. No point in having him break my hand for it. "You're a romantic kind of guy."

He crumpled the yellow paper and tossed it on the desk. "What happened to Shirley?"

"Was she your lady or Tony's?"

From an ivory stand carved like a dragon chasing its tail, Dwayne Yazzi snatched a crystal ball the size of a grenade. He brought it towards my face, practically into my nose, so fast it made a whooshing sound.

I tried not to blink.

Dwayne pushed it closer, his armbands and amulets clinking together. "What do you see?"

When I was eight years old my folks sent me to Camp Rim Rock in the Blue Ridge Mountains of Virginia for the summer. The counselors told stories at night around the campfire. My favorites were about lost treasures and fabulous gems. The counselors laid thin sheets of tinted translucent paper—green, purple, yellow—over a block of ice they illuminated from behind with a flashlight. Fabulous emeralds, amethysts, and topazes appeared in the dark! All I saw now in the stuffy back room of the

Crescent was the shiny ball and Dwayne Yazzi's hand twitching like crazy in a way that confirmed my thoughts about the steroids. "I got to tell you, I find this whole sorcerer routine really hammy. I thought the Indian trip would be more noble, simpler. Like a single eagle feather."

If Dwayne Yazzi knew about the eagle feather by Shirley Yellowbird's body, he didn't react.

I pushed Dwayne's hand away from my face. "You knew about Shirley before you heard me on the phone."

"No!" The crystal ball turned bloodred.

Dwayne Yazzi's hands trembled even more. "Look. Shirley wants to tell me where she is."

I shook my head. "I've already been privy to one vision today, thank you. Tony Red Wolf's. He saw you kill Shirley."

Dwayne Yazzi shook the ball and muttered at it in a language I couldn't understand as though calling forth the eternal truth, but the red simply ebbed away like dirty water swirling down the bathtub drain. He set the crystal ball angrily on the desk. "That piece of shit Red Wolf. He's been sniffing after Shirley for a couple of years . . ."

More than sniffing according to his story.

". . . you don't know the number of times she called me because he beat her up. If anything's happened to her, it'd be my fault that I didn't take him out a long time ago."

I'd have to check for police reports.

"Hey, girl, we don't got all day," Tony shouted from the other room.

Dwayne Yazzi and I looked at each other. I started towards the door. He grabbed my wrist. I circled my hand fast counterclockwise and broke his grip. "Tough girl, huh? You're going to need it if you're with Tony. He likes a girl who's a challenge."

I cracked my knuckles. "What's your trip? Why are you

75

pretending you don't know what happened to Shirley? She's dead. Chopped up. Looks like kitty food. You were the last person with her."

Dwayne Yazzi looked like he was losing his patience. "Says who?"

"Tony. Last night when he left the bar, she was still with you."

He crossed his arms and smirked at me. "I took her home around one. Kissed her at the door, said goodnight. Maybe somebody came over after I left."

"Oh, man, you mean this all happened because you couldn't get any?" I hooted, hoping I looked a lot tougher than I felt. I had imagined Shirley Yellowbird after midnight, still alive, making love, drinking and laughing.

"If I didn't get any, it's because I didn't want it. I don't fade in the clutch like your boyfriend Tony."

It was too sickening. Dwayne Yazzi telling me he controlled Shirley with his magic mojo. Everyone had sex constantly. Except for me. However I might feel about Tony Red Wolf, this was no time to let him down. I smiled in a way I hoped was mysterious, but satisfied. "I wouldn't say that about Tony. Not at all."

Dwayne Yazzi flashed a condescending smile at me like Tony Red Wolf was an idiot child and I his babysitter. "I've heard all about Red Wolf. And not just from Shirley. Other women along the moccasin trail, too. Red Wolf gives 'em lots of sweet talk, but no follow through. Tony the actor. Even though he couldn't make it in the business."

"He's done a movie."

"He's an extra. A glorified lamppost. His big moment came running from one side of the street to the other yelling 'They're coming, they're coming,' in a movie seen by maybe seventeen people."

"What's going on?" Tony shouted again. He started to walk towards the office.

"Tell him to wait," Dwayne Yazzi ordered.

"Just a minute," I called back to Tony. "You're afraid of him," I grinned at Dwayne.

"I don't want Lester involved in this."

"Fine. Couple quick questions and we'll leave without kicking up any dust here." I was starting to enjoy myself. "When's the last time you saw Ernie Little Horse?"

Dwayne Yazzi started to say he didn't know Ernie, but I just waved my hand wearily. "Winston Alley?"

"Never heard of it."

"Crack crossroads of the world. I saw you there once when I went to score," I added.

"That's how you got mixed up with Ernie," he nodded. "You're one of those girls who likes the pipe. You aren't as skinny as most of them."

I'm not fat! Eighteen percent body fat. "Ernie connects for me sometimes. When he's trying to make an extra buck." I wondered how long it would take to get back to Ernie Little Horse that I was talking trash about him.

"You got him right," Dwayne snorted. "Ernie's so righteous, wants to tell you about the Big Jesus in the sky, your own personal savior—'til he needs money. Then he'd sell you his mother."

"Is this a religion," I gestured towards the store. "Or just a business, too?"

"You raise some interesting philosophical questions. Wish I could discuss them with you, but now the police'll be here any moment. That's why we've had this nice little chat, to give them time to arrive. I phoned as soon as I heard Red Wolf come in."

"Think I believe you'd call attention to this fraudulent enterprise?" I snapped. "What is it, a front for drugs? I can't believe anyone believes in this crap." I rummaged on the desk and picked up a copy of a paperback book entitled *Oracle of the Black Witch*. "Look at this shit. You play it backwards and it gives you secret messages? 'Paul is dead.' "

Dwayne Yazzi grabbed the book from me and shoved me back into the store. I stumbled through the doorway.

Lester looked up without surprise.

"What the fuck?" said Tony Red Wolf, looking quickly past me to Dwayne Yazzi. "Can't keep your hands off the girls, can you, Dwayne?"

"Not into the white ones like you are, Red Wolf."

I was pretty sure I was being insulted. "Shirley's dead," I said. "Tony has an alibi. That's more than you can say, Dwayne." Perhaps I didn't know them well enough to call them by their first names, but I still felt goofy calling them by their last names. It reminded me of being a kid, playing cowboys and Indians outdoors at twilight in the lilac bushes. Once my waist-length blonde hair got tangled in the branches. When my mother brushed it that night, wasps flew out.

Dwayne smiled at us. "I came here last night after I took Shirley home, didn't I, Lester? About one thirty. We talked 'til almost three."

Lester nodded.

Tony Red Wolf laughed. "Lester still trying to get up your butt? You must be letting him. Lester don't give anyone anything for free."

"You calling me a fag?" Dwayne snarled.

Tony shrugged. "Maybe you're a dog. Maybe you sleep on Lester's floor like a dog."

I noticed Lester smile like that was something that would please him.

"You ass wipe," shouted Dwayne. The candlelight bounced off the walls in a creepy way. "You tried to live off Shirley. Take money from a woman 'cause you can't make it on your own."

"Don't have to get dressed up, leave home, carry heavy things around in the sun like you do . . ."

Hands curled in fists, Dwayne Yazzi stepped towards Tony.

"Shirley had four hundred bucks she'd been saving to send her relatives so her kid brother could come out here to go to school," Tony said. "She had the money with her yesterday at the bar. Her purse wasn't with her when I found her last night."

"So now I killed her and I robbed her," snapped Dwayne.

The police would check Shirley Yellowbird's vagina, her mouth, her ass for semen. I glanced between Tony and Dwayne. Had they both done her last night? "Raped, too, maybe she was raped," I prodded, wanting to provoke Dwayne.

Dwayne Yazzi jerked quickly in my direction. "Get her out of my face or I swear I'm gonna hit her. I'm not soft on *wasichus* like you are."

"What did happen to Shirley's purse?" I asked as I pushed forward towards him.

"Ask Tony. She was buying him drinks."

Tony shrugged again. "I left early, remember, lover boy? You, Shirley, the purse were all together."

I tapped my foot impatiently. If he'd called the police, where were they? "I don't want to sound like an elitist, but I can't believe you'd kill someone for four hundred dollars."

I saw his arm go up to swing at me. I dropped back slightly to be ready, but Tony Red Wolf jumped in front of me. He put his arm out to shield me. "Get back, girl."

"You fuckin' 'breed." Dwayne lunged at Tony. Tony shoved him back. Dwayne crashed into the display counter Lester stood behind. A glass beaker of purple liquid fell off the counter and broke. A smelly rose odor filled the room.

"Oh my, my, my," muttered Lester, who seemed excited to see two big men fighting.

Tony punched Dwayne hard in the stomach.

Dwayne bunched up his fists again and caught Tony on the jaw. It rocked him slightly. Tony drew his arms into his chest and kept his hands up to protect his face. He threw one that connected on the left side of Dwayne's face. They scuffled back and forth, two well-matched heavyweights.

Then I heard the distant wail of a police siren. "Come on, Tony. Let's bail!"

With a solid roundhouse Tony punched Dwayne Yazzi, who hurtled backwards into a display of quartzes and tarot cards. "Beat it," Tony panted over his shoulder at me.

I was worried about losing him. Once they threw him in jail all kinds of bloodsuckers in cheap suits would be all over him wanting his case.

The siren wailed.

Lester went to the door and opened it to look down the street. The siren grew louder as it moved closer.

Tony threw Dwayne into a shelf holding sloppy-looking medicine jars of things that looked like roots and fetuses fermenting in rancid brown oils. Jars crashed to the floor, glass and oil splattering everywhere. Dwayne slipped in the oil and had trouble getting to his feet.

Tony leapt towards the door, pushed past Lester, and paused briefly to look up and down the street. I rushed to the door after Tony. Squealing 'round the corner at Selma and north towards the store like it was making its dramatic entrance into a movie, the police car fishtailed, straightened out, then raced towards us. Tony took off running towards Hollywood Boulevard to disappear among the crowds shopping, gangbanging, and having mental breakdowns on the fabled street. The car sped past where I stood with the spooky, dead-white-looking Lester.

I started walking slowly towards the Boulevard, vaguely, like a tourist, hoping to fit into the dazed flow of out-of-towners.

I've always wondered what tourists wanted to see besides Disneyland when they come to LA. Hollywood Boulevard looks like any other economically blighted strip mall. The merchants' faces change, but the merchandise remains the same.

Tony rounded the corner east onto the boulevard running. What had Dwayne Yazzi told the cops? "Murder! Indian guy. He's getting away!" The police car skidded around that same corner to the approval of some German tourists who burst into applause. I broke into a run to see what was happening. I heard the door of the occult store slam shut and a bolt slide into place. When I glanced back Lester was gone and Dwayne Yazzi nowhere in sight.

The police car ground to a stop in a red zone near a crowded bus bench. Salvadorans, a couple of black men, and an old white lady wearing a threadbare fur coat leapt from the bench as a cop burst from the black-and-white. The cop yelled at Tony to stop, but Tony poured on the speed as he pushed through the crowd, which scattered before him.

"Go, go, go!" chanted the crowd. "*Órale,* bro!" shouted a skinny, acne-encrusted teenager in gang colors thrusting his fist into the air in a revolutionary salute.

I pushed through the crowd.

A group of five fat black women the size of linebackers came giggling and laughing out of the Fredrick's of Hollywood lingerie store holding their purchases aloft and dangling pink and black garter belts, feather boas, and enormous gold lamé brasseries to show each other. They didn't see Tony. Tony tried to dodge them, but they took up the whole sidewalk.

Tony knocked one of the women down, then two of the others jumped on him and dragged him to the ground.

"Tony!" I shouted, but my voice was swallowed by the crowd. Before I could get through to the front, I saw the police handcuff him and quickly pat him down. They pushed him back towards the police car. Compliantly, Tony got in. A black cop scowled at the crowd as he shut the car door. His eyes lingered on me for a few seconds. Tony glanced at me, but didn't give any indication he knew me.

"Let him go, let him go!" the crowd chanted. The police car turned on its siren, pulled away from the curb, and made a U-turn back towards the Crescent. The crowd laughed and immediately forgot about Tony Red Wolf.

The police stopped in front of the occult store. The black cop knocked on the door. Lester opened it and the cop went in. I strolled down the opposite sidewalk as though I was headed for the small falafel stand almost directly across from the Crescent. I ordered a Coke.

Lester came out pointing at Tony. "It's him!" he yelled as he moved towards the car. A small group from the falafel stand moved to the edge of the sidewalk to watch. I slumped behind them. "Stole four gold necklaces. More'n six hundred fifty dollars of gold! He said he had a gun. Stole a knife from here a couple months ago." Lester was starting to go hysterical. "I told him never to come back here!" The black cop patted Lester on the arm before he started to take down what he was saying.

The cop asked Lester where the necklaces were. Lester shrugged. "He has them!"

The cop shook his head.

Lester gestured back towards Hollywood Boulevard, his voice tweaking soprano again. "He must have dropped them, hidden them. Maybe he gave them to someone."

I turned back to the stand to order a falafel. I watched attentively as the girl at the grill made it, like I might want to try making one at home myself someday. Eventually I heard the police car drive away. When I turned back to the street Lester was locking the door behind himself and Dwayne Yazzi was nowhere in sight.

I ran across the street and knocked on the door. I called Lester's name. No one answered. I put my ear to the door, but it was silent as a tomb.

I drove east past the LAPD substation on the north side of Hollywood Boulevard. Going around the block once I was able to see, in the front lot, an empty black-and-white with the same service number painted on the side as the car which had taken Tony away. I went back to the office to look for Harvey and to wait nervously for Tony's call. I spilled falafel on my chest and knocked my Coke over on the passenger seat.

Harvey was sitting at his desk reading a fishing magazine and smoking a joint.

"I didn't know you liked fishing."

"I don't." He tossed the magazine into the trash, rubbed his eyes, and stretched. "I just like knowing other people are doing what they want. The world would be a better place if more people did what they wanted."

"Cool, that's sort of what I wanted to talk to you about. Something I want to do."

Harvey nodded. He absentmindedly offered me the joint. I shook my head. "Sorry," he mumbled. "I forgot. Sure you don't want to try it? It's real good. Mexican. I got it from Lupe."

My Lupe! "Lupe gave it to you?"

"Sold it to me. But at a good price." Harvey nodded again as though reminding himself of something.

Selling drugs out of my office. What else was she up to behind my back?

"I asked her if she could get me some. It's not like a regular thing. She's a good girl."

I shook my head warily, afraid to find out any more. "I want you to help me with a case—"

"Sure," Harvey agreed, relieved his slip about Lupe was

forgotten. "Take any of my books you need. Did they give you a felony?"

I nodded.

"Great! Burglary? Robbery?" Harvey examined the joint with satisfaction before taking another big hit. I waited a long time for him to exhale. "A rape?"

"Perhaps."

"Far out. About time." He smiled at me proudly.

"It's a bit more than that—"

"All right, Whitney! Way to go. Assault with a deadly weapon?"

"Murder."

Harvey choked on his smoke. "You can't, you're not ready—"

"That's why I want you to help me."

"Research?"

"Go to court with me—"

"No."

"—we'll be co-counsel."

Harvey tossed his joint on the desk. "You know I never go to court."

"But you could. You're the best. Always have been, always will be."

Harvey pried himself from his chair and got up to get himself a drink of water from the cooler in the corner. He didn't look at me. "I told you before why I don't go to court."

I shut my eyes. Harvey had told me that he'd been threatened with disbarment and criminal prosecution about nine years ago for allegedly threatening a witness who was later killed in what looked like an organized hit while he was representing Artie Lowe in a triple murder case. I was in high school then, but I knew who Artie Lowe was. Even in Maryland it was news. Artie Lowe was Vegas. Harvey hadn't fought any of it—he just disappeared off the front pages, left his handmade Italian suits in the closet, and turned to the nutty Temple of White Light Exalted.

I could barely bring myself to say his church's name. I saw his fellow church members slipping in and out of his office on official business. Harvey seemed content to write wills, set up trust funds, or call insurance companies if any of them got into fender benders. An unusual number of them did get into car accidents and I'd wondered if they were running some kind of insurance scam or if they were just so blissed out they couldn't pay attention to traffic.

I opened my eyes. "Harvey, I need you. The court won't give me this case without you. It's an Indian guy, Native American . . ."

Harvey drained the glass and put it back on the shelf still without looking at me.

". . . real spiritual . . ."

"I like you, Whitney, but I don't think you're cut out for this. Getta job with the public defender if you want more felony experience. Or think about going back to Maryland. To your family."

CHAPTER 7

I flopped onto my couch, clicking on the TV to see if there was any news about Shirley Yellowbird. Shirley was blasting from all channels. A picture from her Belmont High yearbook showed a pudgy, bespectacled girl with ratted hair and *chola* makeup—brows plucked almost to nothingness then painted up in a high artificial curve, heavy black eyeliner, and mascara, a thick line of dark brown outlining her lips that were colored in with chalky white lipstick. She must have been trying to fit in with the Mexican girls. Judging from what I'd seen of her face and hair in San Gabriel, she'd gone back to a simpler, more natural look. A return to her roots.

I flicked the remote between channels. I was limp as a rag, still in my shorts and halter. I'd gone to Gold's in Venice after I left Harvey and jerked weights for nearly three hours while I tried to put my racing thoughts in order. What was Tony telling the police? If they'd charged him, he should have called me. I'd checked my messages every half hour. Another lawyer could be holding his hand already.

Shirley had a mother and an older brother, but they hurried away from the cameras and into their apartment building. It was impossible to tell which of the numerous anonymous streets near Belmont and Varrio Loco Nuevo it was located on. I flipped to another channel.

"She was such a good person," cried one neighbor into the camera.

Shirley had been identified by fingerprints. No mention of a purse. The newscaster said she was twenty-four. The same age as Lupe.

"She knew a lot of bad people," said another neighbor, a trendy girl in her early twenties dressed in black. She refused to speculate on who killed Shirley or why. She was probably holding out for a book deal.

The police weren't releasing any information about the time of death or the murder weapon. They did say she'd been dismembered. The news team looked pleased. Dismemberment is good for ratings. The anchor said they had a suspect in custody. I held my breath.

A photo of a man flashed on the screen. He had short hair and was in a Navy uniform. "A Native American male in his late thirties—"

Tony? The man was young and skinny. I glanced at the eagle feather I'd left on the coffee table.

"—identified as Tony Red Wolf—"

How could being taken in for questioning on a robbery have led to Shirley Yellowbird? Had Red Wolf freaked and confessed? Or had Dwayne gone to make an additional statement? A knock on the door interrupted my thoughts. I got up impatiently from the couch and flung the door open.

"Tony!"

He stepped inside my apartment, closing the door behind him. He glanced over at the TV.

"—being held for questioning."

Tony walked over to the TV and knelt in front of his image on the screen. He stared at himself for several seconds before turning the TV off.

The police wouldn't have released their only suspect so early in the investigation. Unless they didn't have enough to hold him. Or his story had checked out.

Tony Red Wolf stood and glanced at the coffee table where a nearly empty beer bottle stood dripping onto the dark oak. "Got anything to drink here?"

I went to the refrigerator and brought back a beer that I shoved into his hand. "The cops let you go?" I wondered why that hadn't been on the news.

"Someone anonymous—Dwayne, I bet—called in while I was being questioned about the so-called robbery. The white guy, Ehrndt, left the room. When he came back he started asking questions about Shirley."

"You tell them about Dwayne?"

He shook his head. "What do they have on me? Squat. Told 'em I knew Shirley, I drank with her in a bar, and I left her in the bar. I know Dwayne did it, but I'm not giving up his name 'til I can prove it."

It was quarter of eleven and I was feeling wiped out. I wondered if he'd told them I was his lawyer. I was struggling with his story. I couldn't believe they'd let someone bail out on a murder with a mutilated corpse. Bail on a 187 would be five hundred thousand dollars, a million probably. No ten percent security. It would have to be cash or property. And who could Tony Red Wolf possibly know who would have posted that for him?

"You didn't tell them about Dwayne?" I shook my head in disbelief.

"Man's name means something. For some of us, it's all we have." He stood calmly in front of my bookcase examining a half-dead philodendron.

"How'd you know where I live?" My address and phone number are unlisted.

He shrugged. "Nice place. Not too much junk. 'Love of possessions is a disease among them.' Sitting Bull said that."

"Come on, goddamn it, how'd you get here?"

"Don't believe me? Want a more exciting story?" he muttered. "I escaped."

"Impossible!"

"When Ferguson, the black guy, went out of the room for a while, I told the white one I'd give him a blow job." Tony grinned. "I got down on my knees—"

"Bullshit."

"Told him to close his eyes . . ."

Tony saw the troubled scowl on my face and softened somewhat. "Then I changed into a hawk and flew here."

"Let me get this straight, you're at the Hollywood substation, with a couple of cops, you change into a hawk, and fly out of the interrogation room?"

He nodded. "Actually, I had to change into a cockroach to get out of the cop shop, then to a hawk. And I'm sure glad I did. I like your outfit." He threw me a thumbs-up which I ignored.

"The cops were watching all this?"

"Of course not. The rules of ordinary reality apply. I waited 'til they turned their backs, poof, into the cockroach, etcetera, etcetera."

Grabbing and finishing my beer, I slammed it on the table. "Am I your lawyer or not? Make up your mind. If I'm not, you got no reason to be anywhere near me. If I am, you have to tell me everything. The truth."

"I told you the truth about the vision, about being able to shapeshift, and you don't believe me. So I try to tell you in words and ideas that you understand. I tell you because of the vision. Because the Great Spirit tells me to. Not because of the laws of the State of California or your license or any of the stuff they taught you at UCLA."

He hadn't been in my office, only the waiting room, so he couldn't have seen my framed diploma.

Did he imagine I had the television on all the time and my brain had been irradiated by too many alpha waves? That I was some pathetic New Ager who painted rainbows on my walls and talked to crystals? Or just that I was a stupid twat?

He picked up the dying plant. "You must have a brown thumb. Get me some water."

I clumped back into the kitchen. Less than twenty minutes it should take the cops to find me if they wanted to. Check my name with the state bar, run a DMV on me. How had Tony known where I lived? I tried to remember if I'd left my purse on the bar, but I was sure I hadn't.

Without another look at me, Tony took the water I brought him and poured a few drops onto the parched soil. I sat down on the couch. He was creeping me out. If Harvey wasn't going to help me, wasn't I just flirting with criminal prosecution and disbarment? Tony hadn't given me a cash retainer and he hadn't actually told me whether he'd killed Shirley Yellowbird or not.

From his shirt pocket Tony took a small bundle of sage tied with a red string. He lit the sage with a plastic disposable lighter. A warm, sweet, pungent smell filled the room. He waved the clouds of smoke from the burning sage over his head, face, and heart. He turned to the north and closed his eyes. He turned in all four cardinal directions while muttering to himself in some guttural language. Opening his eyes, he saged the philodendron, then walked through the apartment shaking smoke at all the walls and windows. He returned to the living room and sealed my picture window and front door twice with smoke.

"Very impressive," I felt like saying, but there'd been something so sincere and unselfconscious about the way Tony Red Wolf held the blazing herb that I kept my mouth shut.

"Okay, that's that. You'll be safe here," Tony announced after a brief silence and another look around my apartment. "Followed you when you left Winston Alley."

I saw a hawk in the sky that afternoon. Tony would still have been in the lockup at the CCB. They don't process people out that quickly. He was guessing about Winston Alley.

"I'll sell you to the cops in a sweet second if I have to. You never gave me a retainer so nothing you've told me is privileged."

"What about at the mission?"

"So far you gave me a feather and bought me three beers. I'm not your lawyer and I don't want to be. What happened to Shirley Yellowbird makes me sick." This was going to play bigger in the news than I could have hoped, all this weirdo shit. Like the Manson trial. "If the cops arrest you, they can also get a warrant for me. Aiding and abetting. Accessory after the fact. As for your *escape* . . ." I shot him a look that I hoped conveyed my disbelief. "I don't know if you're guilty or innocent and I won't represent you unless I know."

He reached into his pocket. Could he have the knife?

I visualized kicking him in the throat as he bent forward.

He pulled out some grimy twenties and thrust them towards me.

"Did you kill Shirley Yellowbird?"

He leaned forward, dangling the money.

"Did you kill her?"

He grabbed my wrist and with his other hand folded my fingers around the cash. "No."

He stepped away. The money felt hot and sticky in my hand.

"You didn't kill her?"

"There's a lot I don't remember. My great-great-grandfather had a dream. I can't remember it." He sat down on the couch next to me. He smelled sweaty.

"What about last night?"

He tapped his fingers rhythmically against the beer bottle. "When I was five, people from the Bureau of Indian Affairs came to the rez, snatched me from my parents, and took me to a government boarding school. They cut your hair off and don't let you speak your language. English only. I met this other kid there, a Choctaw, and we'd talk Choctaw to each other. One afternoon they caught us. Beat the bejesus out of us. That night, he hanged himself."

I got up from the couch and started to pace around the room. "I don't want to hear your life story. Besides, you told me you lived in LA."

"Came here when I was twelve," he continued as though I hadn't spoken. He said after the Second World War the government started a relocation program to move Indians off the reservations and into the city. "Boom time. We were supposed to find jobs in construction, aerospace, factories. Not my old man, though."

I was momentarily distracted from worrying about how he'd gotten out of police questioning. From his tone it sounded as though he hadn't liked his father. I could relate to that.

"They gave us one-way train tickets. I'll never forget the day we arrived. The air smelled like oranges. My father got a cab. Told the driver, a white dude, to take us to Hollywood. My old man saw every movie ever made. Wanted to be an actor."

"Forget the movies. They didn't let people of color work in them anyway," I added despite myself. Lupe had told me that often enough.

"Not many. Some stunt work. Most all the speaking parts were played by Armenians and Italians with big noses. He just got a few bits, nothing steady. Had to go to a factory in Bell Gardens making mattresses."

I glanced at the clock in the kitchen and the minutes ticking away. I was mad if the cops had let him go and I was worried if he'd escaped. Even though I didn't want to get caught on the streets with him, we had to leave so I'd have more time to sort out what was true and what wasn't. He could tell me the epic saga of his life if he was locked up. I'd use it at the penalty phase of his case if I lost at trial. Why was it so hard to get him to focus?

Schizophrenia. Did he have voices talking to him, interrupting his train of thought? Before I left the apartment with him I needed to know exactly how crazy he was. "That picture of you in the uniform . . ." I gestured towards the television.

"You paint yourself with vermilion. You wear a fine war shirt. You look at the good-looking girls. You look at the young women whose husbands have no war honors. They look back at you." He shrugged. "I was a seventeen-year-old punk. Came from people who used to do the scalp dance. Choctaws even fought in the Civil War. So I joined to serve and protect my country."

I couldn't tell if he was being ironic. He finished his beer and without asking walked into my kitchen. The refrigerator door opened and closed. "Want one? You're almost out," he called. "We'll have to go buy some."

"Why don't you just fly over there and do that?" I muttered beneath my breath. Even though I've had everything I ever wanted, I have a problem sharing food. I can't stand to eat in the Chinese places where you have to share plates of food with other people. I'm always afraid I won't get enough. I'm sure one of those overpriced shrinks in Century City could make a lot out of that. "Vietnam was over."

He came back into the living room. "Don't guess you ever noticed that only white people pace around their houses. Sit down and relax, Whitney. And you don't have to pretend like you don't booze when you're with me."

"I don't drink much."

He shook his head. "You're stocked better than the Bucket."

"In case people come over."

He shook his head again. "I don't think many people come over. It feels lonely in here."

"So now you have a psychology degree!"

"I saw an empty bottle of Southern Comfort. You have a party last night?"

"I'm not on trial here, you are," I almost snapped, but kept a lid on. "You don't seem like the kind of guy who wants to wear a uniform and be told what to do."

"Wanted to see the world."

"The Navy? You come from oppressed people. The Battle of Little Big Horn—"

"Don't give me any of that 'in the spirit of Crazy Horse' shit all the white wannabe injuns mouth."

"What about AIM and Wounded Knee?"

"I was fifteen. Tried to hitchhike to South Dakota. Got as far as Fresno before the cops picked me up and sent me home."

I asked him what he did in the Navy. "Technician? Radar?"

He showed me the inside of his left forearm where a butterfly was tattooed. "Helps elude bullets. I was in the SEALS."

Right. And I was Clarence Darrow. He had a lot of wacky fantasies for a guy his age. But so do a lot of men. That's what keeps Hollywood in business. Movies about exploding buildings, submarines with nuclear bombs commandeered by Russian agents. The end of the Cold War had left a void in Hollywood.

He said he came back to LA when he was twenty. Got his college degree, cut his hair, and bought a suit. Held a series of mediocre jobs his first year out of school. He either quit or was fired from all of them.

"Gotta keep on the move. It's my Indian blood makes me restless."

He wanted to be an actor. He worked out everyday. Grew his hair long again. Worked as an extra. Joined a rock band. It was easier to get a gig at a club and make thirty bucks a night.

Where he met Shirley three and a half years ago.

"But Shirley's restless, too. Wanted a guy who made more money than I did, so she started going out with them. One thing leads to another and pretty soon she was doing crack. I'm sure she met all kinds of people then."

"Dwayne Yazzi?"

He nodded. "Shirley was never an addict. Just liked to party. Dwayne's dealing. He's not above fucking up someone he thinks has done him wrong."

"Shirley must have been dealing, too." Ripped him off or tried to cut into his business.

He shook his head. "I would have heard."

"Was she involved in that occult shop? They're a—?"

"Coven. That's sort of aggrandizing it. She wouldn't have anything to do with it. Made fun of Dwayne behind his back."

"Would he kill her for that?"

"If she said it to the wrong people."

"Who are the wrong people?"

"Some black guys from Compton who control the crack into downtown. Shirley could have been shooting her mouth off while Dwayne was making a buy or setting up a deal. About how powerful Dwayne is, how he's got the magic. They could have thought Shirley and Dwayne were disrespecting them."

I nodded. "We gotta find Dwayne if you think you can prove he killed Shirley." I started to get up from the couch, but Tony pulled me back so I tumbled onto his lap.

"Get your hands off me," I pushed him away. "Don't ever touch me again."

"Okay, okay. Sorry."

"I met you in jail where you talked to me like I was shit," I exploded. "I do you the courtesy of meeting you in the middle of the night, you show me a sliced-up woman, your ex-girlfriend who you'd been trying to spy on, you try to dazzle me, or scare me, with some horseshit story about flying like a bird—"

"I know it's a lot to ask, but the vision—"

"Did the vision tell you to paw me?"

"No—"

"Did the vision say to touch me?"

"Well—"

"If the vision told you to touch me, get the fuck out of my house right now or I'll call the cops myself."

Tony Red Wolf slumped comfortably against the couch cushions. "You wouldn't be able to do your first murder trial then. Your first felony so you can stop spinning with all those lame misdemeanors."

"You don't know what you're talking about! I've done felonies."

Tony Red Wolf shook his head. "Nope, not yet. But when you do, you'll be good at it."

"How would you know what I've done?"

"It's all just the way Charley Lomas showed it to me. Plus the way you act in court. Sort of nervous and overeager. Most people wouldn't notice it, but I did. Like you're not comfortable in your own skin."

I jumped up without speaking and got a beer. I glared at him from the opposite side of the room. "Who's Charley Lomas?"

"Medicine man." He put his feet up on my coffee table. "Don't worry," he said. "Really, hardly anyone notices it. They just think you're a little . . ." He paused for the right word. "Formal. I like it, though—it's sort of cute, endearing. Shows you have a soft side and a sweet heart."

I drank some beer and continued to glare at him although I spoke in a cool, measured voice. "Don't waste your time trying to psych me out. It's not going to work. I think you're crazy. I won't be surprised when I look into this a little more to find out that you've been in the nuthouse. Where was it? Camarillo?"

"I've never been locked up!"

"Metro? When did it happen? When you got out of the Navy? When you got fired from your thirteen hundredth job? When you couldn't make it as an actor?"

"I wasn't in the hospital!"

"Clinic, rest home? What did they call it?"

"I wasn't in anything except the Navy."

"Hmm, oh this is tough, let me see if I can figure this out. You were in the Navy, you wanted to have an exciting life, prove you were a real, red-blooded Indian warrior . . . and you were a fucking dishwasher in San Diego for three years."

"I was in Cambodia." Red Wolf stopped as though inspecting the air that hung between us and regretting his words.

"Big deal. The war would have been over by the time you were in the Navy," I grinned victoriously.

Tony Red Wolf shook his head. "There were still U.S. incursions into Cambodia in seventy-four. Secret operations. SEAL teams. I was there 'til the middle of seventy-six."

"In the spirit of Crazy Horse?"

He cracked his knuckles and shook his head.

"Wonderful," I sneered. "Here you are, this oppressed person of color, one of the last of your people left in the world, and you're over in Cambodia killing other people of color?"

"I must be nuts if I'd think of putting my life in your hands." He got up from the couch, brushed past me, and took the last beer from the refrigerator.

I looked at him across my kitchen, which now seemed unfamiliar to me, as though everything in it had been rearranged. "You need my help. So from now on you're following my directions. First, you're getting your hair cut before we leave here so you won't stand out so much."

"I'm not cutting my hair."

"For Christ's sake, grow up."

"It's my spirit. It links me to my people."

I reached into the drawer that held my silverware near the stove. I kept a pair of scissors there for opening boil-in-the-bag frozen food. "Sit down." I pointed towards my dinette table. "I don't have any more time for this hocus pocus way of the native shit."

He crumpled the beer carton and threw it in the trash on top of the empty Southern Comfort bottle. "You know what, I think the vision's wrong. Dead wrong about you. The police believed and you don't. If I did have a case, I wouldn't want you handling it. You're just another white bitch with no soul."

I heard the door, which he'd sealed twice with smoke, slam behind him.

CHAPTER 8

I dropped the scissors back in the drawer. My father's always been right about me. I can't make it as a lawyer. Don't have the personality for it. I felt ashamed thinking about my nervous quaky overeager behavior in court. Like a cocker spaniel on speed. No wonder I couldn't get enough work. I was probably the punch line for every joke in Division 40. I'd end up outside the Criminal Courts Building like the Messiah of the Harbor Freeway, wearing a dirty sheet and annoying people with jobs.

My membership in the National Lawyers Guild would be revoked for culturally abusive behavior. Even if I didn't believe Tony Red Wolf, he was a human being. No color lines. No Jim Crow. I felt awful. And he was the most important client I'd ever had.

I felt like having a good cry. Instead, I opened the bottle of Jack Daniel's.

If the police had let Red Wolf go after questioning him, what had he told them? That he'd been with Shirley last night—many people had see them together; but he wouldn't have told them that after midnight he'd gone to her apartment uninvited. He must have told them about Dwayne Yazzi. Were the cops looking for Yazzi now, too? I also wondered if the cops had shaken Shirley's roommate down yet.

I partied with Jack a while, poured the rest down the sink, and went to bed alone. When I woke up it was after six. The twenty-four hours I'd given Tony were nearly up. It was my duty to go to the police.

I couldn't guess where he'd gone, but the police report I'd received in court had his address. I didn't think he'd be there, but I might find some record of Shirley's address so I could go talk to her roommate. It's a free country. Fuck the police.

From my bedroom I grabbed a pile of suits and silk blouses I needed to drop at the cleaners, threw them on the backseat of the car, jumped in the Chevy, and cranked a Solomon Burke tape. If I hurried I could get to the office by the time Harvey wafted in from early morning services at the newly consecrated Temple of the Weird Bullshit.

I hit Wilcox and slowed to look down the street to the occult shop. Harold Wilcox, one of the city's original founding fathers, had been a devout Methodist and wanted Hollywood to become a model of Christian virtue. There was no sign of activity; Dwayne would have taken off. He'd probably had enough of Lester's leather trip. I wondered if the people at the bar where Dwayne had been with Shirley would confirm he'd been the last person with her and I cursed myself for not getting the name of the place from Tony Red Wolf earlier.

One of Harvey's endless loops of bootleg Dylan rocked the hall as I ran up the stairs to the office. Harvey was kneeling on the floor, wrestling open a large cardboard box.

"Finally got a computer." He hoisted the equipment onto his desk.

"Know how to use it?"

I was surprised that Harvey immediately got it connected and on. He punched the keyboard a few times, bringing up an image of a golden locust—sometime symbol of his renegade religious group. Other times the symbol is a neon mandala or an orange triangle. I don't know if this means the church has an evolving theology or if it's just a way to stay one step ahead of tax collectors.

"Harvey, you ever known anyone who had visions? I mean, personally known someone you thought was reliable? A vision that wasn't drug induced."

Harvey nodded without looking up from the screen. "My wife had a cousin who used to communicate with the spirit of her dead father. He gave her stock tips. One day, clear as light, she saw a blue screen and on it the invention of the microchip. This was years before it was invented. She put five thousand dollars in it. Became a multimillionaire and moved to Miami."

"Your wife." He'd never mentioned her before. I could imagine the Harvey before me as one of the greatest lawyers Los Angeles had ever known, because I used to read about him in the newspapers. But not as a husband. Not even with a woman.

"She's in Encino now, probably not so far from where you live, with her fourth husband. A urologist."

"When did you get divorced?"

"About the time I stopped practicing law."

She must have left him when he was threatened with disbarment.

"Hey, this is pretty easy." Harvey hit another key and brought up some text on the screen.

Watching Harvey hunched over the keyboard reminded me of my father who, though he had an office and a secretary, liked to use an old manual typewriter for some of his correspondence. I always wondered who he was writing to. One of the women he'd had affairs with? "Did you and your wife have any children?"

Harvey typed in more commands. His actions were so deliberate I understood I wasn't to ask again. I asked if he'd be able to access information such as DMV or criminal records. Harvey shrugged. "I'm just a beginner."

I told him about Tony Red Wolf's unannounced visit to my

apartment and that I wanted any information available on him—military records, tribal registration, birth certificate. I didn't tell him about the vision Red Wolf said guided him to me.

"You're beating a dead horse. They'll never give you a murder case. They'll give it to one of the big dogs." He named three attorneys. I was surprised he knew their names and that he kept up with what was happening at the CCB.

I wished I'd brought the eagle feather with me. It might have evoked powerful sacred images for Harvey, holy dreams of untainted blue skies, or whatever it was he was seeking at his church. "They'd give it to you."

"That's the past."

"You could still do it."

"I told you no. I've made a vow and renounced the world." He changed the screen to a squawking game of intergalactic war.

"Don't you miss the action, Harvey?"

He'd already forgotten me. He raced the spaceships across the screen, blowing them up with loud explosions. I went to get Tony's police report. Maybe Harvey would at least try to run through the computer and find out something about him.

I didn't expect to see Lupe, because her car hadn't been out on the street, and she didn't expect to see me. She moved hastily to hang up the phone when I came in.

"It's okay. Don't worry. Call again if you need to," she whispered. I waved my hand at her feeling dispirited. Probably some toad with premature ejaculation and a filthy apartment full of sticky wads of toilet paper. I slumped into the chair opposite her. Maybe she could teach me the phone game. I had no viable career as an attorney without Tony Red Wolf.

"It's not what you think," she said with shiny, angry, dark eyes. "That was Bob Hayes. Your new client. The divorce. Remember? You met him yesterday morning."

I slumped farther into the chair and nodded in a dull, vacant kind of a way. An endless life of divorces and drunk in publics stretched in front of me. "Did he need some 'HOT BOX TALK'?"

"He needs a restraining order. His wife keeps calling his new job and raising hell. That's all we need, for him to lose that job before we finish his case and he finishes paying us." She licked her lips with excitement. "A restraining order has got to be worth three or four hundred bucks, right? Maybe five hundred."

"Yeah," I mumbled.

"Snap out of it. What's wrong? I saw that creep Red Wolf on the news. Isn't this what you've always wanted? To be bad to the bone. To know a killer."

"He blew me off. Didn't like my attitude."

Lupe nodded her head as though she wasn't surprised. I told her that he'd been released by the police and had come to my apartment.

"You invited him over?" Lupe looked at me with distaste as though I was a giant *cucaracha.*

"Just showed up. I don't know how he knew where it is."

"He followed you. Creep."

I stopped examining my nails. I didn't like being caught in a lie by Lupe. "No, he said . . ." I sighed and told her the whole nutty story about turning into a hawk, his escape, and then argument we'd had.

"Good riddance. He's nothing but a fucking con artist," Lupe snorted. "Don't worry about a thing. I been taking care of business. Look." She pulled a form out of the typewriter and held it towards me. "The restraining order. I borrowed a book from Harvey about how to fill it out."

"That's really great. I'm proud of you, Lupe."

"Don't you want to look at it? See if it's correct?"

"Sure." I sat up in the chair. Why should I make her life

miserable? She needed this job and I'd pledged to help her. If things got any worse, if my career continued its freefall into the toilet, I'd call my folks for money. I wouldn't have to tell Lupe where it came from. I could say it was an appointed case I'd had while she was in jail and that the county was just getting around to paying me. I glanced at the restraining order. Although there was a thick dot of white-out in the upper left-hand corner, her typing had improved. "Did you spell this right?" I pointed to the wife's name. Tran Ving Hom.

"I copied it carefully," she said, sounding miffed. "She's Cambodian."

"Cambodian! Tony Red Wolf said he was in Cambodia in the Navy SEALs."

"That just thrills the pantyhose right off me."

"Why can't you understand how important he is to me? You've done a good job, but I'm sorry, I just can't get excited about it. I need this murder trial. To make a name for myself. I don't want to be living on crackers and peanut butter for the rest of my life."

We heard men's voices outside the door. She frowned as she glanced at the empty appointment book.

Someone knocked at the door. It had to be the cops. But they wouldn't have bothered to knock if they had a warrant.

"Come in," I said impatiently.

It was the same two guys who'd taken Tony into custody on Hollywood Boulevard. Dressed in slacks and sports coats. The white guy Tony called a Nazi had deep-set hooded eyes and wore a light brown jacket the color of old bologna.

"Whitney Logan?" he asked. "Tony Red Wolf's attorney?"

I nodded. Tony and I could sort this out later. The west was settled by desperados and I'd sworn I wasn't going back home.

He identified himself as Detective Erhndt and introduced the other as Detective Ferguson. I was getting nervous with the formalities. "Ms. Ramos, my secretary," I countered.

Had they seen me in the crowd when they arrested Tony? I thought Ferguson had looked directly at me, but he gave no sign of recognition now.

"Where's Red Wolf?" Erhndt asked.

"According to the news he's being held for questioning," I said.

"I saw it on Channel Five," Lupe added.

"Not anymore," said Ferguson. His jacket looked expensive and he wore a Gucci tie with it.

"You mean there wasn't enough evidence to hold him?" Lupe cocked her head and smiled at Ferguson as though he was the only person smart enough to know the answer to the question.

Erhndt and Ferguson exchanged a look. I caught Erhndt examining my diploma and state bar certificate to see how long I'd been in practice.

"Tony Red Wolf's a fugitive from justice," Erhndt said.

Tony had told me the truth. "Does that mean we can't rely on the news on TV?"

"How about *Sesame Street*?" Lupe asked. "My little boy watches it all the time." I shot her a quick glance so she'd shut up, but she bit her lip slightly, as though she really needed to know.

Erhndt ignored her, but took one of my business cards from her desk and studied it before patting it carefully into the inside pocket of the brown jacket. "If you know his whereabouts, Miss Logan, you're advised to report that to us forthwith." He handed me his card. "We'd consider it an aiding and abetting situation if you didn't."

"I'll have to check with my malpractice carrier."

Erhndt frowned at me like he couldn't decide if I was a smart-ass or an idiot. I wasn't sure myself.

"I wonder why he didn't call me from jail," I mused. "I'm

sure you read him his rights and gave him a dime for the phone, isn't that so?"

"Of course," Ferguson snapped. He must have been getting bored with his role as the good cop.

"I haven't seen him for a couple of days," I said. "Just the news on TV last night. I don't understand how he could have become a fugitive from justice if he'd been taken into custody. You're the ones who arrested him, aren't you?"

They didn't answer.

"Wow!" Lupe exclaimed. "That's exciting. But if he's gone, doesn't that mean you screwed up?" She focused an apologetic little grin on Ferguson.

"Lupe!" I snapped.

"Well, I'm sorry," she sniffed. "But that's what it means, doesn't it?"

Ferguson got up from her desk. I saw a fat vein throbbing at Erhndt's temple.

"I'll call if I hear anything." I, too, smiled apologetically.

They turned to leave without replying. Erhndt stopped at the door to fix me with an angry look. "You do that. Aiding and abetting's a felony. I don't know if they taught you that in law school or not."

"You got my promise."

We heard them clumping down the stairs, then it was silent.

Lupe exhaled loudly. "Ohh, it's so exhausting being dumb."

We looked at each other across the desk for a second, then burst out laughing.

"I'm so tired I think I need a nap now." Lupe grinned contentedly.

"Nope, we got somewhere to go."

"We? You. You go wherever you want to play detective."

"You stepped in it this time, homegirl."

"I didn't do anything."

" 'Like I explained, aiding and abetting's a felony.' " I dropped my voice in a rough imitation of Erhndt.

The grin faded fast from Lupe's face.

"You knew Tony had been at my apartment. You should have told them. And it's not like you kept quiet, you were talking crazy to them. Yep, you've aided and abetted like a pro. I bet your probation officer, Mr. Collins, would think so, too."

"You wouldn't."

"No, I wouldn't, but they would. Collins will be on you like flies on a popsicle if they haul you in for questioning."

"Shit."

"Precisely."

"I have to go home and fix lunch for Joey."

She'd never done that in her life. I doubted she knew how to make a peanut and butter jelly sandwich. "Your mom's got his rice and beans on the stove."

"Fuck."

"I'm sorry."

We picked up our purses. I told her we were going to Tony's apartment to look for Shirley's address.

"Oh, goodie," Lupe sneered. "Bet he's got a swell bachelor pad. Collection of beer bottles on the windowsill and some pictures ripped outta *Hustler* taped on the wall."

I took Tony's file off my desk, where it had been covered by some loose papers. "There has to be something at his place that'll help me figure out where he's gone."

"A trail of breadcrumbs?" Lupe turned off the lights and locked up.

"I am sorry. Really."

Lupe tossed the office keys into her purse. "One more thing. I don't like it when you call me a pro. I don't like the way you say it."

"You know that's not what I meant."

"I'm just as good as you are."

Better, Lupe. You are a much better person than I am. I scribbled Tony's address on the back of a crumbled receipt from Saks that was in the bottom of my purse, then pushed his file under Harvey's door.

Tony Red Wolf's apartment was a single on Orange in a four-story building capped by the top of a red pagoda. Red and black columns stood to either side of the door. Grauman's Chinese Theatre was only a block away. To the north a Japanese mountain palace dominated the view. Lupe and I sat in the Chevy looking at Tony's building. I'd kept a careful watch for Erhndt and Ferguson in case they'd been waiting for us outside the office, but the coast was clear and they'd probably gone Code 7 to get something to eat.

"I hope Tony Red Wolf's gone back to wherever he's from," Lupe said angrily.

The rez. Had Tony left LA? I quickly told Lupe what little I knew about the reservation. She seemed massively disinterested.

"Pretty wacky, huh?" I said indicating the building.

"You don't have any idea where we are, do you?" Lupe snapped. "That's Loretta Twimbly's house. All the stars, Mary Pickford, Clara Bow, Valentino, came here for parties. It was beautiful before those trashy people like Tony Red Wolf came along. They should all go back to where they came from."

"The Native Americans were here before any of us."

"Save it for the jury." She got out of the car.

"You got something against Indians? Ever known any?"

Lupe shrugged. "What are they but people who couldn't make it as far as Mexico?"

His apartment was on the third floor overlooking the street. Lupe said once all of these streets had been an open movie set. Cowboys raced their horses down the streets screaming and shooting up palm trees. The hall was gray and festered with black smears along the walls as though throwing furniture about was an indoor sport akin to ancient Scottish hurling. No one answered the door. It was locked. I'd picked locks a couple of times, but it was iffy work, and noisy, so I'd gotten a universal key from a locksmith out in Van Nuys. I hadn't used it yet and didn't know if it worked or whether I'd been hustled for fifteen bucks. I was about to try Tony's door when a muscular, tan, good-looking young man of no more than nineteen came up the stairs.

"What are you doing?" he asked. He brushed his hair, which was frosted blonde in the front as though the sun had kissed it away from his face. He wore cutoffs, a tight t-shirt, and construction boots. Lupe gave him a quick once-over. He looked like a hustler.

"Looking for a place to rent," I said. "A guy out front told us he thought this one was going to be empty soon. He said the man living here was charged with a murder and had disappeared."

"Yeah," the young man said. "Far out, huh?"

"Unbelievable," I said. "Did you know him?"

"Sure. Indian guy named Tony Red Wolf."

"I saw him on TV!" I gasped. "Remember, Maria," I nudged Lupe. "We saw him on TV."

"Just this afternoon," Lupe added without much enthusiasm. "He looked like a bum."

"No, he was a cool guy," the young man protested. "Hung out with me sometimes and played guitar. Didn't complain if friends of mine came over."

"Did he come on to you?" Lupe asked.

"No!"

"I'm not trying to make you uncomfortable," Lupe said. "I'm not suggesting that you're—"

"I'm a hundred percent queer and proud of it," he snapped.

"Tony, he liked women."

"There's no accounting for taste," Lupe offered in an effort to placate the young man.

"Did women like him?" I asked.

He turned to me. "Yeah, I guess so."

"Did you see any of them here with him? Like Shirley Yellowbird? The one who was on the news?"

"Never saw any women with him. And I don't think he killed that one."

"Why?"

"I don't want to get involved with anything. You might be cops."

"I know you've had a lot of experience spotting plainclothes cops, haven't you?" Lupe said. "First, you look at the shoes, right? Plainclothes, their shoes are always shined sharp, but the heels always real rundown."

"I don't know what you're talking about."

"Athletic clothes that are never quite the right brand. I been on the streets, too." She put up her hand to forestall his protest. "You've never been wrong before, have you?"

"No," he admitted.

"Well?" she said. I guess she wasn't going to tell him about her arrests.

"Old guy I know, a businessman, was visiting me last night. He was telling me another boring chapter of his life story so I was listening to Tony playing guitar on the other side of the wall. When the old guy left I went next door to Tony's to see if he had anything to drink. He played me a new song he wrote."

"You sure he didn't go out?" I pressed.

"What's with all these questions? You said you weren't cops."

"I'm a producer. Made for cable movies. *All My Secrets, Lola: True Story of an American Soldier, Consider This, Ms. . . . .*"

I was ready to go on inventing titles when he interrupted. "I saw that one! It was really good." He smiled. His teeth were disarmingly white. Cosmetic bonding. But I saw he hadn't had the money to get the bottom row done yet.

"Thank you. I wrote that one, too." I returned a gracious smile.

"Hey, you must know lots of people in town. Kip Turner, nice to meet you." He grabbed my hand and pumped it a couple of times.

"Enough to get a few movies made, get my friends bit parts once in a while . . ."

He preened. "Got anything in the works now?"

"This interests me," I gestured around the hall. "I can smell story. What time was it you saw Tony Red Wolf?"

"Twelve, twelve thirty."

"And he didn't leave his place?"

He shrugged. "I went out again around three. His bike was still there."

Tony had told me the truth. "This place would be too small." I nodded at Lupe, who looked more than ready to go. "I'll keep you in mind."

Lupe looked as though she was about to say something to him, but changed her mind. She fished in her purse, pulled out a couple foil-wrapped condoms, pushed them in his hand, turned, and walked down the stairs to the street.

CHAPTER 9

An innocent man's life was in my hands.

Tony Red Wolf had been safe at home in his apartment when Shirley Yellowbird was killed. It was just as he'd said. I had to find him. Convince him I believed him. Apologize. And now I'd have enough ammunition to talk Harvey into helping me. I hadn't shown enough real enthusiasm. No inner flame illuminating me. I could do all the work. He was probably afraid I'd nag him about blazing. All I needed was Harvey propped up in the courtroom with me.

Lupe hurried past the Chevy towards Hollywood Boulevard. She strode purposefully in her high heels, her miniskirt straining against her ass. Cutting through a full parking lot, weaving her way between dirty rental cars, she headed for the Chinese Theatre.

She looked around the courtyard of the theater with displeasure. I knew what was coming. There used to be a thirty-foot dragon above the pagoda-like entrance. The lobby had been nearly all red. There were bronze and crystal pagodas on the sides of the screen. The bathroom faucets resembled dragons. "Didn't that guy seem a little too insistent that Tony was in his crib during the exact time in question? Alone?" Lupe demanded.

"What's your point?" I barked in return, starting to feel claustrophobic. The courtyard was packed with tourists oohing and ahhing, snapping pictures, and jostling each other aside.

"We don't have all day. Ferguson and Erhndt are probably going to toss Tony's place this afternoon. If they haven't already."

"Shirley could have been with him. He could have killed her quietly," Lupe said. "Strangled her, put something in her drink, then suffocated her, shot her with a silencer—"

"How would he have gotten her out to the mission on his bike if she was already dead?"

"He drove her car, abandoned it somewhere. Then came back to Hollywood for his bike before he called you. You don't even know it's his bike. He could have stolen it in San Gabriel after driving her car there."

"That trashcan at the mission where I saw Shirley Yellowbird looked like a slaughterhouse. Blood everywhere. She was killed there. I saw it, you didn't. Why are you fighting me on this? You better hope I can prove he's innocent, the way you mouthed off to the cops."

"He gives me the creeps." She went directly to the footprints of Rita Hayworth. "Ay, Marguerite," she sighed and took several deep breaths as she gazed lovingly at them.

"Fine, he's weird," I said. "You don't like him, I don't like him—"

"You don't? Sure didn't look that way."

"What are you talking about?"

Closing her eyes, Lupe stepped carefully into the footprints. "You were practically holding his hand in the office."

"I was not."

"Fawning all over him. 'Oh, Mr. Red Wolf,' " she mimicked. "Practically creaming your pants."

"You're sick," I said, but I was thinking about tumbling into Tony's lap. I'd rather liked the way he steadied me with his arms for an instant. "Let's jam. We can't risk bumping into Erhndt and Ferguson here."

She didn't reply. A few seconds later her eyes flickered open.

"Okay, I feel better. Just being near that psycho's apartment made me feel dirty." She looked around disapprovingly at the tourists as she made her way out. "Haven't seen this much polyester since the sofa factory in my area had a fire sale a couple years ago." She frowned when she heard a teenage girl ask who Tyrone Power was. "The sexiest man ever created, you idiot television viewer," she growled at the startled girl. "Lana Turner, Hedy LaMarr, Marilyn," she muttered like an incantation as she parted the crowd. "What kind of woman was Shirley that she'd be with Tony Red Wolf?"

In the car I told her Tony said a Guatemalan guy at Shirley's job was harassing her and we were on our way to check the *vato* out. I floored the car away from Tony's, across Franklin, then down to Third.

"Another suspect? It's gotta be reliable information if Tony the Hawkman told you," she sneered. I wished I'd left out that part of his story. Examining the well-kept mansions, she fell silent as we drove through Hancock Park. It was hot and she let her arm trail out the window to catch a breeze.

Good Samaritan Hospital sits on the edge of Varrio Loco Nuevo. It is strikingly devoid of style and a greasy gray, but some famous people have died there.

"Guy's named Jose."

Lupe sniffed her disapproval. "You don't know his *apellido?* Then we'll have to go to the cafeteria. Sooner or later everyone has a cup of coffee."

We bought some of the black water they were calling coffee and sat near the door. People surged in and out of the cafeteria. It seemed nicely balanced—Asians, blacks, Latinos, Anglos.

"Any Guatemalans?" I asked. "How about him?" I pointed out a handsome man across the room.

She shook her head. "Too tall. From Michoacán. Jose's going to be *indio.*" She examined her coffee with its sickly skim of powdered milk floating on the surface, then put it impatiently down on the Formica table. "You know what this stuff'll do to your skin?" She got up and went over to the desserts in the cafeteria line. I saw her flirting with the guy who was arranging slices of pie. She was back in a few minutes juggling slices of lemon meringue, strawberry, and chocolate cream pie. "There's about twenty Joses, but the one who worked with Shirley's an orderly on the third floor." She demolished the chocolate pie, looking satisfied with herself for this information.

It was quiet on the third floor. Although most of the rooms had open doors, curtains were drawn around the beds.

"Feels like dead people," Lupe whispered.

The nurses' station was vacant. A sad-looking arrangement of red carnations with a wilting balloon that said "I LOVE YOU" stood on the counter. I peered into all the rooms, but saw no orderly. Only old men with tubes in their arms.

A fat nurse came around the corner. "Who are you looking for? You have to check in here."

"We checked in downstairs," Lupe said.

"You have to check in here again. Hospital rules." She waddled to the computer behind the counter of the station. Why do so many nurses look like they're going to drop dead of heart attacks? I told her I need to see Jose Garcia.

"He can't have visitors while he's working."

I flipped my wallet open to my bar card. "His immigration attorney."

She frowned.

"You want him sent back to Guatemala? Maybe killed?"

She sighed. "I haven't seen you." She sat down and foraged through her lunch sack.

We made our way then down the corridor of the east wing, which was similarly silent and empty. At the end of the hall was a large supply closet and although the door was closed, we heard a whisper of salsa inside. I knocked. The volume of the music went down. I knocked again. "Emergency! Room 342A!"

We heard the door being unlocked. Lupe and I looked at each other.

The door cracked open. I smelled weed.

"I'm on lunch break," a man said.

"Jose?" Lupe purred.

The door opened slightly. A man in his late twenties, short, stocky, dark, with straight black hair cut in layers designed to make his face look less round, squinted at us. His left eye was blackened and he had scabby scratches on his left cheek. "You look like shit," I said. "What did Shirley do to you?"

He didn't answer so I glanced at Lupe as if to ask if she thought he spoke English.

"*Conocemos* a Shirley." I felt embarrassed by my pronunciation and didn't speak Spanish much around Lupe.

"Who's Shirley?"

"Tony RedWolf's my boyfriend," bristled Lupe. I felt a twinge of jealousy that I shook off quickly.

"Never heard of him," Jose shrugged.

"I heard you're supposed to be Shirley's old man."

"*Y que?*"

"Shirley's telling people she's going to take him away from me."

"Write a letter to *Dear Abby*," said Jose, trying to close the door. Lupe wedged herself in against it so he couldn't shut it.

"Tell her Sad Girl's looking for her." With both hands Lupe threw down some local gang signs that made Jose look troubled.

"That's right, girl, you tell him," I added, but they both ignored me. Jose must not have known Shirley was dead.

"Fuck it," said Lupe. "This guy's useless. Can't even stand up for his woman. No wonder Shirley's trying to take my man."

"We'll go to that bar," I said to Jose. "The one she hangs

out . . . what's the place, man?"

"If she's there, I'll whip her butt myself," Lupe said. "If not, I'm gonna tell my homeboys to come back and kick the shit out of you."

He tucked his shirt in his pants in an effort to look more alert.

"My homies'll rearrange your face. Permanently. You'll have to blow snot outta your mouth. It won't be no sissy little scratches like those." Curling her fingers like claws, she tore at the air in front of his face and hissed like a cat.

"Oasis," he said, edging away from her hands. "Near Third and Normandie."

"You better be telling *la verdad* or you'll be making a horizontal inspection of the emergency room," Lupe added. "That'd be too bad, 'cause you're kind of cute."

He dropped his gaze.

"Hasta luego, chulo." Lupe sauntered away from him.

We were getting close to Shirley. The scratches on Jose's face were less than forty-eight hours old.

"Harvey told me you sold him some weed." I unlocked the car door for Lupe.

"I didn't!"

"I don't care what you do as long as you don't do it at my office."

"It's not like it's a dangerous drug," sniffed Lupe. "Look at Harvey."

"Precisely my point. The court's not going to appoint me to do this murder case unless I have an experienced co-counsel. I need Harvey."

"Find somebody else. Somebody more on the ball. You think I want Harvey involved if my tail's on the line?"

"Harvey's one of the greats! The Mulholland Murderer. The Holmby Hills Hitman . . ."

Lupe yawned. "Ancient history. Besides, he never leaves the office. I think he's, big word—afraid to go outside."

"Agoraphobic. I can talk him into it. I think Harvey sees me as sort of a daughter."

"Like your own father's done so much for you," she muttered, looking away.

I started the car and pulled carefully away from the curb. The Chevy doesn't have power steering and parallel parking is a son of a bitch. I didn't want to talk about my father. "Just out of curiosity, where'd you get that dime bag you sold Harvey?"

"I never told you about my cousin, Luis?"

I shook my head.

"Part of my family's from Michoacán. My father's side. Luis is like my thirtieth cousin twice removed."

"He's a drug dealer?"

"Entrepreneur. Pyramid sales."

"Lives here?"

"Crosses the border a lot."

Here everyone is a border crosser.

Third at Normandie is an area with lots of Filipinos, but mostly Mexicans and Central Americans. On the corner was a bright pink hut with pictures of dancing shrimps and crabs painted on the sides. *Mariscos.* Next to it a small TV repair shop and beyond that a squatty place painted black with messy red lettering.

The Oasis.

"How come we never get to interview anyone any place nice?" Lupe pouted. "The Polo Lounge? The bar at the Beverly Wilshire? I was there once for New Year's Eve. On a date. It was swell. I wore a black dress and had my hair up with a little bit of glitter on it. Silver. Nothing flashy."

Inside, the Oasis was pitch dark, illuminated sporadically, like an afterthought, by blue lights. It was empty except for a bartender and a lone male figure at the end of the bar. I ordered a Corona, Lupe a martini. "Don't bruise the gin," she snapped at the bartender. She carefully wiped off the stool before sitting down.

I paid for the drinks with a twenty and pushed the change back to the bartender. He nodded amiably. He was a Mexican in his late thirties, with a white t-shirt that said "Cancun" riding up on his beer belly.

"Pretty quiet today," I said.

He nodded again companionably.

"I'm looking for an Indian guy named Tony Red Wolf."

The bartender shrugged and wiped at the bar as though he'd discovered some new spots on it. If I ever redecorate my apartment I'm going to paint everything with the shiny black paint used on bar counters: I'll be able to clean the entire place with a sponge. "Can't help you."

"Six feet tall, sort of skinny, long black hair."

"Lots of people come in here, can't remember them all."

I took a sip of the beer. It wasn't as cold as I like it. "How about a woman named Shirley Yellowbird? My height." I got up and stood back from the bar so he could see me. "About thirty pounds heavier."

He shook his head, turned his back to me, and started polishing some glasses.

"Hey, blondie," the drunk at the end of the bar whispered. He was a *chinito*-looking Mexican who'd turned his head over his left shoulder to watch me.

This is the kind of thing I hate about men. They think they can come on to anyone, that you're going to be thrilled because they've got dicks. I walked back towards the barstool I'd been sitting on.

"Come here, blondie, I wanna tell you something," he slurred. I tried to think of a useful phrase in Spanish and decided *come mierda* was right. I was just about to tell him that when he said, "I know Shirley."

I turned to him.

"Come down here and buy me a drink and I'll tell you what you want to know."

Lupe snickered with disgust and muttered, "Glad I'm out of that business."

I told the bartender to give him another of whatever he was drinking. "Make it scotch," said the drunk. The bartender poured a shot and set it down angrily in front of the guy. I picked up my beer and sidled down to the barstool next to him. He was small and smelled awful. Like he didn't change his underwear often enough. He had a gold front tooth, which I figured was the most expensive thing he'd ever own in his life. He took a pack of crushed cigarettes from his pocket and offered me one. I shook my head; he shrugged and lit one for himself.

"You know Shirley? Indian woman, about my size—"

"She got some nice titties," he cackled. "Big as melons. Firm and round. I don't like no little saggy titties—"

"How do you know her name's Shirley?'

" 'Cause that's what everybody calls her," he cackled again. "Sometimes they call her Yellowbird. I'd like Shirley to open her wings and fly away with me—"

"When's the last time you saw her?"

"Take me back to her nest . . ." He picked up the scotch and drained it. He looked at me expectantly. I snapped my fingers for the bartender and pointed to the now empty glass.

"Last night?"

The bartender interrupted with the fresh drink. The drunk took an appreciative pull from it. "Sure, Shirley was here last night. Most every night. If Shirley'd open those wings for me I'd eat her pussy so good, so good—"

"What time?"

"—she'd think she was flying in heaven." He laughed and reached for his drink.

I grabbed his wrist. "Tell me what time she was here or this party's over right now."

He looked at me in surprise as though examining me for the first time. "Eleven thirty, close to midnight. She was here with that *maricón* Dwayne."

"And Tony Red Wolf?"

He shrugged. "Never heard of him."

I described Tony, but the drunk only shrugged again and picked up his drink, which he attacked with relish.

"Did she leave with Dwayne?"

"Yeah, and I bet she was hotter than a pig to fuck after the fight—"

"What fight?"

"Do you like to fuck? Are you a good fuck, blondie?"

"The best. I fucked the pants off ten presidents and three of the Rolling Stones. Who was in the fight?"

He looked at his glass as though surprised to see it was now empty *otra vez*. He looked at me expectantly again.

"Jesus Christ," I snapped. I glanced around for the bartender, who didn't want to meet my eye. "Hey, buddy, bring the bottle down here." He shuffled over and sullenly put the half-empty bottle on the counter between us.

"That'll be twenty-five dollars," he said, not removing his hand from the neck of the bottle.

"She'll pay you." I gestured towards Lupe, who shook her head at me and mouthed "no."

"Pay him," I ordered. "We'll settle up later. When I get to an ATM."

Lupe swore, ripped her purse open, and threw some bedraggled-looking bills down on the bar. She got up from her barstool and irately punched in a song selection on the jukebox.

I poured a drink, but held onto his glass. "The fight . . ."

"Shirley and Dwayne were sitting back there," he pointed to a dark corner of the room. "This little *pendejo*, don't know his name, comes in . . ."

He licked the corner of his mouth with a raspy-looking tongue and reached for the drink, but I blocked his arm. "Guatemalan?"

"Yeah. Starts yelling at Shirley. Called her a bitch. Then he takes out a lot of money. I heard him say three hundred dollars. He threw the money down on the table and floor in front of her. Said 'I give you money. Why don't you want to be with me?' "

From the jukebox the voice of Vicente Fernandez filled the room. The drunk looked away from me, let out an ear-shattering whoop, screamed "Que viva México!" and tried to wave at Lupe, who ignored him.

"And then Shirley . . ." I prompted him.

"Shirley laughed, 'cause she's a *cabrona*. Said, 'Go home little boy.' Dwayne laughed 'til he almost piss in his pants." He made with another of his dirty cackles. "Shirley gets up from the table and gets on her knees, picks up the money that's down there, and then she reaches out and unzips this guy's pants like she's gonna give him a blow job—" He looked up at me. "You suck cock? You like to suck cock?"

I picked up my beer bottle, wrapped my lips around it, and gave it a short, but incredible, hose job. Then I drank the rest of it in one thirsty gulp. I couldn't believe I'd done that. Even the drunk looked impressed. I felt Lupe watching me disapprovingly. "And then what?"

"She reached inside his pants, felt around, and says, real loud, 'There's nothing in there. I can't find it!' The little *guatemalteco* tried to hit Shirley, but Dwayne got up and punched him in the eye."

"Did Shirley scratch him on the face?"

"Maybe. It happened pretty fast. She's yelling at Dwayne, 'Hit him, hit him again.' So he does. The little guy falls on his ass. Then Dwayne takes the rest of the money from the table and hands it to her. Shirley laughed and put all that money down there between those big jugs of hers. The *guatemalteco* left then."

I stood up.

"Don't you want to talk no more?"

I shook my head.

"Want me to eat your pussy?" He wiggled his tongue at me.

I took my purse from the bar and nodded at Lupe, who'd been leaning against the jukebox watching us. As she picked up her purse and we made to leave, the door opened. Another man came in.

It was Ernie Little Horse.

"What are you doing here?" I asked.

"Working at a garage down the street. Come here this time most every day. Ain't that so?" he asked the bartender, who grunted back in acknowledgement.

"You want a drink?" I asked. Lupe clutched her purse protectively.

"Let me buy you one." I introduced Lupe as my friend Maria. The drunk shouted at us a couple of times, but we all ignored him.

I thanked Ernie and asked if we could sit on the opposite side of the room. He returned with the drinks, smiled at Lupe, and sat down next to her. Lupe snuggled towards him, looking happy. He asked why we were there. I told him Tony and I had an argument and Tony left me. I didn't know where he was, but Tony had told me this was a place he hung out sometimes.

"Never saw him here," Ernie said.

"Maybe he comes at a different time than you do," I suggested. The drunk started to laugh hysterically at something, then broke off, suddenly muttering to himself.

Ernie shrugged. "Don't think so. I live near here. Tony doesn't."

"He told me he has a friend named Dwayne Yazzi. Know where he is? Maybe they're together."

"Dwayne?" Ernie looked surprised. "Evil motherfucker, that Yazzi. 'Scuse my language," he nodded at Lupe. "He's a demon worshiper. Fornicatin', dopin' motherfucker. I'm a Christian man, myself. He works at the slaughterhouse in Vernon. Probably messes with the dead animals. Takes their hearts for that black magic crap he's into."

I had another horrible flash of the carnage in San Gabriel. "You see the news about Shirley Yellowbird?"

He shook his head.

I didn't believe him, but told him she'd been found murdered and that I didn't know any more about it. "Far out, huh?" I waited to see if he'd say anything, but he just picked up his glass and tipped it towards us as a toast.

"Who do you think killed her?" I asked. "You didn't like her, but from what you've said a lot of people didn't like her."

"List's too long to name 'em all," he agreed sanguinely. "There's always been a lot of talk about Shirley. Bad things happen wherever she goes. Almost like she's walking with a black cloud, like she's upsetting even the spirit world. Stirring up all kinds of things."

"Like what?"

Ernie shrugged. "Grandmother Coyote, the Whirlwind, Skinnywalker."

"What's a Skinnywalker?" asked Lupe.

"Looks like a man, like someone you know, but isn't. Walks through walls. Kills people and disappears into the air."

I felt the hair on the back of my neck stand up.

"Ugh," Lupe sighed in exasperation. "You don't believe in that stuff, do you, Ernie? I thought I had it bad with Bleeding Jesus and the Holy Ghost."

They looked at each other for a second, then laughed together. The Episcopalians I'd come from were a pretty lame-ass group, I decided. I laughed, too, and we settled back to drink and talk about the weather.

CHAPTER 10

Lupe shifted restlessly in the chair and swayed drunkenly closer to Ernie Little Horse, laughing at something he'd whispered to her. She put her hand on his biceps as though to steady herself. She wasn't much of a drinker, but she'd only had two martinis. Hadn't even finished the second one yet, just kept stirring it with the double olives, which she periodically hoisted from the glass to suck on. "You're the best storyteller!" she laughed. "You must keep your girlfriend up all night. Unless you're busy doing other things."

"I don't have a girlfriend."

"Don't put me on. I could fall in love with a guy like you. I'll bet you have more than one girl, don't you?"

He shook his head. "No one. I swear."

She wasn't going to try to sell him a blow job was she? "Refills, anyone?"

Ernie pushed his glass in my direction without looking at me. I got up feeling unwanted and handed the empty glasses to the bartender. The drunk was crashed at the end of the bar, and it smelled like he'd pissed his pants when he passed out.

"Let me guess their names. Tina? Linda? Connie?" Lupe was giggling as I sat back down at the table.

He laughed, too, pleased with her game.

"Patti? Yvonne? I don't want no man who's already got a woman." She gave him a dazzling smile. "Maria?"

"I'd like to have a girl named Maria if she was as pretty as you." He reached for her hand, but I shoved a Rusty Nail into his meaty paw. Ernie Little Horse must have been the one who'd given Indians a reputation as bad drinkers. Vodka and Kahlua should speed-shift him over the edge. I guessed he'd smoked some crack before he met us. He was talking fast as he slurred his words.

Lupe traced his hand with a long nail painted bloodred. "Shirley?"

"No!" He smacked his hand on the table.

"It's not illegal to love your cousin," I said.

"Watch your mouth."

"You're getting all crabby," sniffed Lupe. "That proves she was your sweetie."

"It's not good to speak of the dead," he warned.

"Well, excuse me," Lupe drawled. "It's not my fault if your girlfriend croaked."

It was getting old buying drinks for horny guys with B.O., and I was starting to feel cranky myself. "She was murdered."

"I don't know anything about that."

"Nobody said you did," Lupe snapped. "You don't have to fly off the fucking handle." She reached for her drink, knocking it slightly so some of the greasy gin slopped on the table. "Fuck you if you can't take a joke." She stood as though to leave. "I thought you and I might have a little fun, go out back, but you're acting like a real pain in the ass, lying to me, saying she's not your girl. Whatta you think—I go with anyone. I'm a whore or something?"

"I'm sorry."

"Prove it," Lupe said, brightening a bit. "If she wasn't your girlfriend, drive me over to her house right now and swear there, right in front of it, that she wasn't. Then I'll be your lady and we'll get this party back on track."

He chugged the runny remnants of his drink and stood, hitching his pants up. "Car's out front."

Lupe smoothed her miniskirt around her hips.

"See ya when I see ya," she crowed at me. I saw her eyes were clear and sharp and sober.

The Chevy, bright red though it was, was parked five cars behind Ernie Little Horse's pathetic green Buick, but he didn't seem to notice me slip into my car and pull into traffic after them. I saw Lupe in profile laughing, turned in the car seat attentively towards him. How many tricks had she pulled the drunk routine with? I followed them to Portia Drive near the intersection of Sunset and Echo Park Boulevard. To the left I caught a glimpse of the lily ponds in Echo Park Lake and looming above them the twisted parapets of Aimee Semple McPherson's temple built in the twenties. Streaks of pink and yellow neon twinkled from *tiendas* half a block ahead, but Ernie turned left up into the hills above Sunset. Three blocks later he slowed to a stop and pointed to a squatty-looking red two-story apartment building with metal screens across the windows.

Lupe jumped out of his car, slamming the door and yelling something I couldn't hear—but imagined meant "screw off," because he gunned the engine, then tore off, leaving her in the middle of the street, a wisp of black smoke trailing behind him. "That's it. Front upper left," Lupe grinned as I pulled up. "Roommate's named Angela."

The news media had decamped, leaving trampled Starbucks white and green Styrofoam coffee cups in their wake. Erhndt and Ferguson? Had they already been there? I broke a thin branch off the fluttering acacia by the side of the building and headed for the front door.

Lupe took a breath spray from her purse and spritzed her mouth. She passed me the spray. "Keep it."

"Little Horse didn't do anything to you, did he?"

"Want to check me for hoofprints?"

Outside the door of Shirley's apartment someone had placed a candle in a glass jar and its flame illuminated a picture of the Virgin of Guadalupe painted on the glass. I knocked. We heard footsteps, then the metal cover over the peephole clicked back. I composed a slight smile of apologetic sadness on my face.

"Whatta you want?" asked a brown-faced woman.

"Angela? We worked with Shirley at the hospital. We wanted to find out if there's going to be a funeral."

"I don't remember Shirley saying anything about a white girl."

"I'm one of the nurses from the ER. She only worked there a few times."

The woman turned her attention to Lupe.

"My friend. From billing."

"Why didn't you call if you're a friend of Shirley's?"

"Didn't know the number. Just met her over an emergency tracheotomy a while ago. Her first trach. Few of us had a couple of drinks together afterwards. Guy on the Hollywood freeway slammed into the center divider, steering column went through his throat. Blood spurting everywhere. Doctor cut through the thyroid, cut up the cartilage rings—"

Angela looked away as though it made her sick.

"But Shirley was cool. She—"

The peephole cover slammed shut.

How well had Angela known Shirley? Best friends or just two people splitting the rent?

The door opened. Angela Valdez was about Lupe's size, but big in the hips. She had messy long black hair pulled carelessly into a ponytail at the top of her head. Although she was only in her mid-thirties, it looked like she'd squandered her youth at a disgraceful pace. Her face was creased and wrinkled. I always expect brown skin to hold up much better than my thin white skin. I am, after all, the descendant of bog dwellers.

"Catholic?" Lupe pointed at the candle.

Angela shook her head. "Not Shirley. I'm just trying to cover all the bases."

"I didn't know if it was right to bring flowers," I apologized, handing her the acacia stem. "I would have liked to have been able to get to know her better. Is Shirley's family arranging the funeral? I don't know them."

"Neither do I," Angela shrugged. "Shirley wasn't very close to them. She made her own family."

"Kids?" asked Lupe.

Angela shook her head again. "People she knew over the years. Different tribes. They'll be putting on her funeral."

"Can you find out if it would be okay for me to go?" I asked. "Only one I ever met was Ernie Little Horse."

Angela Valdez opened the door. "How do you know Ernie?" Looking startled she stepped away from the door and I took it as an invitation. I got a better look at her as I stepped inside. She had a butt like a sagging back porch.

The apartment stunk of cigarettes and there was an overflowing ashtray on a table in front of a black vinyl couch. The rest of the room was furnished with shiny cheap Early American imitations. The two women must have been very different to have come together with such disparate pieces. A framed picture of Jesus stood on an end table; a gold Buddha next to the ashtray was surrounded by paperbacks about reincarnation.

She motioned towards the couch. Lupe sat down gingerly. A bookcase was shoved against the wall and I leaned against it. *To Hell and Back, I Was Satan's Slave, Caught in the Crossfire* were crammed on the shelves, along with numerous similar redemptive volumes all of which smelled like they'd come from a used bookstore. "Wherever Shirley is, she's at peace now," I offered, deciding the books were Angela's. "Guess the police have been here to talk to you. They have any idea yet who killed Shirley?"

"I don't like cops, but they do good sometimes," Lupe said.

Angela continued looking worried. "You haven't told me how you know Ernie."

I hesitated, trying to create a credible explanation. "One night her car wasn't working and she called him to help her . . ."

Angela frowned.

"Shirley didn't tell you?" Lupe interrupted.

Angela picked up a pack of cigarettes, but tossed it back down impatiently as though she was smoked out.

"She didn't want to call him," I quickly invented. "While we were waiting she told me they didn't get along very well. I offered to let her use my Auto Club card, but she was real stubborn about doing things her own way." Angela's back was to Lupe and I saw Lupe moving her hands like she was balancing a scale, like the believability of my statement could go either way. I knew I was on safe ground, no one but people from the Westside buy Auto Club memberships.

"Yeah, stubborn was her middle name," Angela said finally.

Lupe made a large gesture of wiping her forehead in relief and it was all I could do to keep from grimacing at her to tell her to knock it off.

I shrugged. "As soon as I saw he was going to take care of the car, I went home. Seemed like a nice guy."

"He didn't mention me?" Angela touched her face reflexively and tentatively as though she was afraid of what she'd find there.

"He hit you?" I blurted out.

"I was married to him. Still am."

Lupe put her finger down her throat and made like she was throwing up. Then she leaned into the conversation. "Did Shirley know he hit you?"

"They hated each other. She knew what he'd done and she helped me get away from him. She went with me to get a restraining order, but he still came around here all the time." Angela fell silent. "I never called the police on him. But Shirley did about a week ago. Restraining order covered both of us. Sent him to jail." She looked embarrassed. Or perhaps she felt responsible for Shirley's death.

Lupe stood and put her arm around Angela. "You don't know if you want him back or not, do you, girl? That's hard. Been there, too."

Had Lupe been there? When I'd seen her in jail earlier in the year, she had a bruise on her cheek which she never explained.

"He came here the night before last. Around midnight or twelve thirty. Pounding on the door. He was loaded."

"And you didn't call the police?'

Lupe frowned at me like I was an idiot.

"Shirley told me to, but I didn't . . . I yelled at him to shut up and go home, but he just kept banging on the door. Shirley opened it and he tried to push her so he could come inside."

Lupe patted Angela on the shoulder.

"I locked myself in the bathroom. Then it got real quiet and when I finally came out, the front door was open and they were both gone." She picked up the cigarettes again, looked miserably at them, lit one, and dropped the match on top of the stinky pile in the ashtray.

"Which cops were here about Shirley?' I interrupted. "A black guy and a white guy? At the hospital they were asking questions like she was some trashy slut."

"They said that about Shirley?" She pushed aside the ashtray, picked up a business card that had been shoved under it, and handed it to me.

Ferguson's.

"I told him Ernie had been here and said he'd kill Shirley if she didn't get out of his way. You think they're looking for him?"

I nodded with relief, hoping this would draw the cops off Tony.

Angela dropped her head into her hands and began to cry. Lupe and I looked at each other. "There, there, there," I said awkwardly. "You'll have time to cry later."

"Is Shirley going to be cremated?" Lupe asked Shirley.

"Buried. That's what her people believe."

How long would it take the coroner to complete an autopsy on all the little pieces of Shirley Yellowbird?

"Pick out something beautiful for her to be buried in," Lupe said.

They wouldn't try to sew her together, would they? Closed casket. "Her favorite dress," I added. "You know which one it is, don't you? You must have known her better than anyone."

Angela stopped snuffling and motioned us to follow her into Shirley's bedroom. It was painted yellow and an unmade queen-size bed took up most of the room. Shirley's sheets were pink and had been washed so many times it was more a suggestion of color like sunset on a cloudy day. Angela opened the closet that was full of bright flimsy dresses. The floor of the closet was a jumble of shoes tossed about. I shuddered. Cheap shoes depress me. An orange plastic shopping bag was tossed on top of the shoes. "She just bought this. I don't know why she didn't hang it up or take off the tags. Maybe she was going to return it." Angela pulled a red Lycra minidress from the bag.

"Gorgeous," murmured Lupe. "Perfect for the afterlife."

I wondered if Lupe's idea of heaven was a salsa club in Pico Rivera.

Angela looked in the closet for a moment without saying anything, then closed the door. "I still can't believe she's dead." She looked hopelessly around the room, then brightened as she pointed to a dresser I'd already noticed. It was the kind you'd expect to see in a high school girl's room complete with a mirror with photographs stuffed around the frame and curling at the edges. The top of the dresser was littered with costume jewelry, bottles of knockoff perfumes, barrettes, and a dirty hairbrush.

"Take something," said Angela.

"No thanks, it's really not necessary," I said, my fingers itching to touch something of Shirley's.

"It's the Indian way. A giveaway. Take something to remember Shirley by."

I looked at the jewelry. It was all plastic and paste except for a red coral necklace with silver handworked beads and a turquoise ring with a large irregularly shaped stone. I picked through a tangled pile of necklaces. Beneath the pile lay a silver earring carved like a feather. I skimmed the dresser for the mate, but it wasn't there. I'm no expert, but I was sure it was an eagle feather. The great silversmiths were Navajo. Like Dwayne Yazzi.

"That's a nice picture of Shirley," I tapped one in which she was alone, posed on one of the living-room chairs. The other photos showed Shirley with people I didn't recognize. None of Dwayne Yazzi. Or Tony Red Wolf. "Thought she had a boyfriend. Dwayne Something."

"Yeah," Angela agreed absently. "He wanted to marry her about five months ago, but she told him no. Look, I found a photo that was strange. I was looking through the drawers of this dresser yesterday after I saw the news . . ."

What had she been looking for? Something she didn't want the police to find.

". . . it was in the bottom drawer, turned upside down." She bent over and opened the drawer and brought out a five-by-seven color print of Shirley standing with an older woman. They had their arms around each other's waist and were laughing. The older woman was in her early sixties. She had shiny, stiff black hair ratted and combed in a curly flip arrangement with bangs trickling towards her thin, precise black brows. She was Indian, but didn't look like she was related to Shirley. Perched on red high heels, she was short and slender. She had nice legs and okay tits. Beyond that she could have been anyone on earth. The women stood on a plot of grass. To their right were several palm trees. Behind them and to the left was the corner of a log cabin, logs burnished a theatrical reddish brown.

"Shirley's mother?" I asked. I'd seen her on the news and this woman was ten or twelve years older. "She mentioned her a few times."

Angela shook her head. She took the picture and hesitated slightly before placing it back in the drawer. She didn't want to put it here, but she didn't want me to know that. She'd move it when I was gone. "Is Lucille coming to the funeral?" Angela asked.

"Uhm . . ." Who was Lucille? "I'm sure she will when she hears about it."

"Can you tell her when you see her at work?"

"I'm off for a couple of days, but I could—"

"Shirley's friend Lucille left Good Sam five months ago. Went back to Texas."

"I must have her confused with—"

"Who are you? Shirley never talked about her mother. They didn't get along. You don't know Shirley."

"I do, but not well."

"How come you're asking all those questions about the cops?"

"I'm a reporter from the *National Enquirer*. I'm able to offer you five thousand for an exclusive."

"You're no fucking reporter. Put that earring back."

"I could try to get you seventy-five. Your picture with the story naturally." I felt Lupe edging towards the door and then, reflected in the mirror I saw her dip into her purse and pull out a tape cassette, which she waved at Angela. "I've got everything on tape!" Lupe exalted. "I'm wired. I got a recorder in my purse." Angela swiveled towards Lupe, but Lupe ran out of the room and through the living room. The door slammed.

"Get the fuck out of my house," Angela Valdez screamed. "I'm calling the cops and telling them about you." She tried to grab the earring from my hand.

I blocked her arm. "I need this. To help Shirley." Then I shoved her hard enough so she fell on the bed. "Chill out."

I pounded out of her apartment and caught up with Lupe in front of the building. Was Angela watching us from her living-room window? Would she call the police? "That cabin in the photo, I've seen it before, when I get off the freeway when I'm coming from home. It's across the street from the Hollywood Bowl."

Lupe nodded. "It's the Hollywood Museum. Cecil B. DeMille's place. First studio in Hollywood. Used to be on Vine. City bought it and moved it. I bet less people go there in a year than to that stupid 'Ripley's Believe It or Not' place on the Boulevard in a day."

Angela's street was silent.

". . . first movie made there was *Squaw Man*."

"Fascinating," I muttered, checking up and down the street. "I'll have to go there someday."

We got in the car. I hung a U, made a rolling stop at the bottom of the hill, and greased my way into traffic on Sunset. I had to find Tony. He was probably worried that the twenty-four hours I'd given him were up. Probably thought I'd gone to the police already.

A buzzing noise interrupted my thoughts. Lupe fumbled in her purse and pulled out a pager. "So my mom can call me about Joey," she said defensively.

"That happens all the time, I'm sure."

"You could buzz me if you needed to." She frowned at the number displayed. "It's Hayes, our divorce client. Pull over so I can find out what he wants."

I drove into a mini-mall parking lot and went into a liquor store and bought two coconut popsicles and a pint of Jack Daniel's while she was on the phone.

I handed her a popsicle when she got off the phone.

"He's wacked out. He's down in Long Beach in front of their condo. He's been trying to get in to talk to her and she's throwing furniture over the balcony at him. He said he doesn't care if the cops come and take him away. He's got two grand on him in case that happens. He wants you to come down there to bail him out if he needs it."

"You go. You made me take his case." I pulled out of the lot and back onto Sunset.

"He seemed like a nice guy and he brought cash when he said he would," Lupe said.

"Great. I should have fucked him."

"Fuck you." Lupe tossed her popsicle angrily out the window. "You're a real fucking asshole sometimes."

"Ladies, ladies. Calm yourselves."

Lupe screamed as she swiveled around to the back of the car.

I looked in the mirror.

Tony Red Wolf sat in the center of the rear seat with an amused smile on his face.

CHAPTER 11

"Pull over," Tony ordered.

"How'd you get here?" Lupe demanded. "Don't give me any of that flying horseshit."

He laughed. "Sounds like Whitney's been telling you some wild stories. That was just a crazy little something I made up to dazzle her while we were having a few drinks. At her place."

I jerked the car to a halt at a bus stop. "How the hell did you get here?"

"Piece of cake. I was in a cab, coming down Sunset to Shirley's to find out what's happening. I saw the Chevy. Hard to miss. Bright red—"

"Like blood," Lupe interrupted in disgust, but he didn't even look in her direction.

He reached over the front seat to the paper bag with the Jack Daniel's in it. "You mind?' He cracked it open and took a drink. "Told the cabbie to follow you and climbed in back while you were in the store. Snuggled in among your silk shirts. They smell good. Like you."

"Too bad the cops haven't caught you yet," Lupe screamed at him. "Motherfucking slimeball."

"Get out of the car," Tony scowled at her. "I gotta talk to Whitney. Alone. If she wants to handle a case this big."

"Whitney says you killed that girl."

"Shut up, Lupe," I snapped.

Lupe swiveled towards me with a cold, hard look. "Don't you ever—"

"Need an interpreter? Tony and I got to talk." I glared back at her. "Now get out of the car. Or are you intentionally trying to fuck things up for me?"

"I'm not going to tell you again," Tony growled at her while waving a hand in my direction.

"Ohhh, a big man like Ernie Piss on His Horse Foot," Lupe drawled. "So, you don't murder women, whatta you do, just hit them?"

"I never hit a woman in my life."

"I don't believe you," I said. "I think you've hit a few, like Shirley. But I don't think you killed her."

He looked at me in surprise. "You don't?"

"Not since I talked to the guy who lives next to you."

Lupe grabbed my arm. "Turn you on that Tony might bat you around a little? Did your old man mess you up so much, you think this is how men are supposed to act?"

I picked Lupe's hand off my arm. "Leave my father out of this. He might be a crazy son of a bitch, but he's my old man. If anyone's going to talk shit about him, it's going to be me."

Lupe put her hand on the door handle. We looked at each other across what seemed a great distance. "You lied to me! You said you were going to turn Red Wolf in to the police in twenty-four hours. Now you got me mixed up in this, and with the cops."

Tony leaned over the seat, put his hand over hers, and forced open the door.

I will not crawl back to my old man with my tail between my legs. "Get off my back. Go try taking care of your kid for a change. You're in my way."

"You're a selfish bitch." Lupe put one foot out the door. "If you're not back by six tonight, I'm going to call those two cops and tell them everything I know about Tony."

"Don't worry, we'll be nice and cozy by then. Better friends than we are now," Tony said.

She got out of the car and walked away. Tony got in the front seat. I drove off angrily without a glance at her.

"To Long Beach," said Tony. "We could do with some good sea air, the sound of the waves, walking barefoot in the sand."

"You're real cool for someone the police are looking for." I didn't tell him Angela had threatened to call the police about me. I had no idea whether she had or not. She'd seemed upset enough to do it.

He leaned over and touched the vertical wrinkle between my eyes. "So much worry. The white man's burden." He slumped comfortably back in the seat. "The Chinese say it's a sign of liver damage." He passed me the bottle.

I took it from him and took a drink. "Kip said you were home after midnight—"

"Right about the time Shirley was killed," he agreed.

"You never told me how she was killed."

He shrugged. "That happened before the vision came."

"Come on, there has to be a beginning, a middle, and an end. Or is Indian time too special for that kind of rigid structure?"

"Only Charley Lomas and the Great Spirit know the beginning and the end."

"Terrific. Let's make an appointment. Who do you think'll be home now?"

"You don't believe in anything, do you? Nothing bigger than you? Nothing more than this middle you call your life?"

"Jack Daniel is a great man. I can do without the rest of this bullshit." I picked the bottle up from the seat between us and took another drink. "Who's Charley Lomas?"

"Medicine man."

I asked where he was.

"The ghost hotel."

"That's the name? Where is it?"

"Could be east of here. Or west. Covered with stars and palm trees."

The desert. Charley Lomas lived out in the Mojave. I'd passed a Morongo Indian reservation once on the way to Palm Springs for a two-day seminar on criminal practice.

"What are we waiting for? He knows who the killer is."

"He won't see us. That's part of the vision. You and me. That's the way it's supposed to be. You know there's something special between us, don't you?"

I wished I hadn't been so cavalier with Lupe. I glanced at my watch, a few minutes past two. "Your neighbor said when he went out at three thirty your bike was gone. You could have left as soon as he left your apartment. Killed Shirley. Convince me. I have to convince a jury."

"I was in my apartment till after three. Kip left around two. He'd been waiting to hit the street."

"You could have left your place after Kip. You'd still have two hours to meet Shirley and kill her. Then call me."

"Kip didn't tell you about the little hissy fit he had out in the hall with the Filipina chick who lives on the other side of him?"

"Must have slipped his mind."

"It was after two, close to two thirty or quarter to three, the bars had closed and the Filipina—calls herself a dancer—came waltzing in with two big black guys. Guess she was going to do some face dancing . . ." Tony eyed me sideways to see if I had any reaction, but I was just starting to get buzzed enough to be cool. "The black guys were being real loud. Kip yelled at them and started to talk shit to them. They would have fucked him up, but I went out in the hall and that was the end of it."

"Seems rather important for him to forget to tell me."

"That's what friends are for. He's probably hoping the cops come back, make a big fuss over him, he'll tell them he last saw me at one thirty, the chick'll agree with him. She doesn't want them knowing her business. The cops thank them and they think the cops won't hassle them in the future because they've been good citizens."

I nodded. "Makes sense." I wondered if Lupe had gone back to the office or if she'd quit. Maybe she'd never speak to me again. I'd call her before six, ask her to go see Kip again. I asked Tony what he did then. He repeated that's when he'd tried to go to sleep, saw the vision, jumped on his bike, and rode out to the mission. Hence the call to me. There was something to cover nearly every minute. Seen outside Shirley's around midnight, left, Shirley arrived home. Ernie Little Horse came over and Shirley disappeared with him. After that Tony's time was covered, more or less, by the people in his building. Should I be worried by the details he kept adding?

"You can't expect people like Kip to tell the truth unless there's something in it for them," he said, cutting in on my thoughts. "I was brought up to be strong. Among my people, in the old days, the boys, as young as four, were taught to endure pain. They were pinched or shoved into nests of wasps. Learned to play rough and dodge arrows."

I told him about the photo Shirley hid in her dresser. "Who's the woman?"

He shook his head. "I'd have to see it. Could be several people. Woman she calls Auntie. Knew her from sings in Bell Gardens." He explained sings took place every fifth Sunday at a church. "First, Bible class and a worship service with praying and hellfire. Singing. Then a big feast. The women cook for days. Chicken and roast pork, *tash-lubona*—a corn and hominy soup—Jell-O salads, all kinds of cakes and pies."

I realized I was hungry. I couldn't remember when I'd last eaten.

In the afternoon, he said, Indians come from all over, different tribes, to sing gospel songs. A large proportion of the early relocatees had come from eastern Oklahoma, Cherokee, Choctaw, Chickasaw, Crees, and Seminoles. "Then they sing the specials, like church songs in Choctaw."

It must have sounded good to hear his own language.

"Met Shirley there, if you can believe that."

I asked what he'd been doing in church.

"Gets lonely being an Indian. Even though this is the biggest injun town in the country. Don't like to drink everyday. Get tired of the bars. My folks were church people."

"What happened to the Great Spirit?"

"Easier for a lot of people to accommodate themselves to the surrounding reality. Join the oppressor's church. Fundamentalist usually. Damn shame, I might have made a good Unitarian."

Tony RedWolf had the gift of gab. I like that, being as shy as I am. It was what I liked about Lupe.

I said I thought Indians didn't like to get their pictures taken. It stole part of their soul.

"You crazy? This is Hollywood." He gestured out the window towards a dilapidated movie theater showing two features for a buck fifty. "The woman in the photo might have been Edwina Jones. She's a Creek married to a black guy. Runs a drop-in counseling center Shirley went to a few times a couple years ago." He scooped up the bottle and looked at it thoughtfully before taking another drink. "Pretty brave of you to be alone with me. Knowing all the bad stuff you do about me."

"I've known lots of guys who've been in jail."

"Never had any of them in your car, though."

"How'd you know that?"

He shrugged. "I know a lot about you. Only child. You're no

daddy's girl. You drink too much. Don't feel comfortable with many people. Your people have money, plenty of it."

"That's not true."

"Don't start to go freaky on me. I don't have to be psychic to know these things. You got an open bottle in the car, you got pissed at your friend when she mentioned your father, you got manners, but an old junker car—sort of an affectation—like people have when they don't want folks to know they got money they didn't have to work for." He put his hand on my knee.

I shoved it away. "And you're—"

"When I was a kid, fourteen or fifteen, I was in a gang with the 'cans in my hood. That's all there was, Mexicans. They were my *iksa,* my clan. Lil Sleepy, Dopey, some good guys, but Christ, those names. Why not Brave Dog? Little Lightning? Young Snake? No pride, no sense of the long resistance. All using drugs. That's why I joined the Navy so young. SEALs because it was the baddest. I might not have been as big or strong, but I could hold my breath underwater all day, swim like a fish, and I didn't care if I lived or died."

"But you thought you were so much better than everyone else."

"It was a girl. I had a little Mexican girlfriend and as soon as I went to the Navy she wrote me a Dear Juan letter. Started humping some idiot named Oso who worked at the gas station. Guess he did a better lube job than I did back then."

"You don't have to go into detail."

"Swallowed a bottle of aspirin to kill myself, but it just made me stay up for three nights playing the Stones *Sticky Fingers* album."

I laughed although I didn't want him to think he was making any points with me.

"Thought we were going to hang out in the Philippines playing war games and spending our money on hookers." He fiddled restlessly with the bottle. "Cambodia was a big surprise to me."

"Ought to be like old home week for you then down in Long Beach. Biggest Cambodian community in the country," I said.

"You don't understand what I did there, do you?"

"Saw *Apocalypse Now*."

"They made us kill people. Even women."

I didn't think Tony Red Wolf was funny anymore, but I didn't believe everything he said anyway. I got off the freeway at Cherry and ended up doubling back towards Anaheim Avenue.

A five-block area between Cherry and Orange was full of Cambodian restaurants, jewelers, and beauty shops. I heard music. It wasn't Latin, but had a cha cha beat. A fat Mexican woman at a bus stop danced by herself, swinging her arms as though she was trying to fly, while Cambodians and a few Salvadorans looked away or grinned in embarrassment.

Hayes's wife lived a quarter of a mile away in an inexpensive-looking townhouse with a "For Sale" banner hanging from the roof. Leaning against the side of a tatty black Japanese four-wheel-drive, Mr. Hayes was staring sullenly at the balcony on the first floor. Above it a white couple leaned over their balcony, cans of Miller lined on the wooden railing. It looked like we'd arrived during a seventh-inning stretch. I parked behind the four-wheel. I hoped Hayes wouldn't notice I'd been drinking, but he looked like he'd already had a few himself. I felt Tony stiffen almost imperceptibly as though he knew there was going to be a fight. Great, two hotheads on my hands. I snatched my Lakers cap off the backseat and thrust it at Tony. "Do me a favor. Tuck your hair up inside it. I don't know if these people saw you on TV." He turned the hat in his hands, examining it, but put it on without comment. I got out of the car. "Mr. Hayes, what's going on?"

"Call me Bob."

"Bob," I agreed. "This is no way to be handling things,

particularly if you're going to the trouble of applying for a restraining order against your wife. Sends a mixed message, know what I mean?"

Bob looked questioningly at Tony.

Did he know who Tony was? Had he seen the news? I realized that half the time when the TV news showed a black suspect—either in a photo or police I.D. sketch—I couldn't remember enough about the person to be able to make an identification. I hoped Hayes had the same problem with Indians.

A Cambodian woman appeared on the first-floor balcony. She was petite, with long black hair, creamy brownish lipstick for a natural look, smoky eye makeup. An Asian dream fuck. Soft, retiring, compliant.

She heaved a framed picture into the street. It shattered at Bob's feet. It was their wedding picture. "Go away, mothafucka," she screamed in a voice straight outta Compton.

Bob laughed. "That's right, baby. You got something else for me? A big kiss? Throw me the key and I'll come up and get it. Bitch changed the locks on the door," he whispered as an aside to Tony.

Tony nodded impassively without looking at Bob. He couldn't take his eyes off the woman. Tony the ladies' man. Why did it bother me?

Another photograph came hurtling over the balcony and broke at Hayes's feet. The couple on the second-floor balcony hooted and laughed. Bob looked up angrily. "You want to come down here?"

A third photo flew into the street, striking Hayes in the knee before it touched down. It was a picture of the Cambodian babe feeding him cake at the wedding. He screamed and ran across the street to his balcony. "That's it, you cunt. I'm gonna come up there and smack the shit out of you."

I ran across the street, Tony right behind me. "Bob, this is not in your best interests," I yelled, but Hayes hurled himself at the balcony, caught the ledge, and pulled himself up towards his shrieking wife. He fell over the wall and onto the balcony. He backhanded his wife and she fell, screaming, towards the sliding glass door that must have led to their living room.

Tony threw himself at the wall and pulled himself up across the ledge, jumping onto the balcony. He grabbed Bob, spun him around, and threw one big punch. Bob went down like a brick building hit by a ton of dynamite.

"That's okay, baby-san," Tony said to the still screaming Cambodian woman. "Him no make trouble, no trouble." Who wrote this dialogue? He sounded like a horrible movie.

"Get off my balcony before I call the police."

"No problem, no worry, mama." Was he going to offer her a chocolate bar or a pair of hose? He pulled Bob to his feet. "Let's go, pal." Bob looked back and forth between his wife and Tony. He half jumped, half stumbled, off the balcony to the ground.

Tony bowed to the woman. "No problem." Had he spent his entire time in the military in whorehouses? He jumped from the balcony, strode past Bob without looking at him, and got in the car. "Let's go."

"But I need to talk to—"

"We gotta go." He was bent over with his head nearly touching his knees. Had he hurt himself?

I started to the car and headed back towards the freeway. I'd lost a client. Would he want his retainer back? It was already spent. I glanced over at Tony, who was still hunched over. "What's wrong?"

He didn't answer, but his shoulders were trembling in uneven spasms. The back of his neck was drenched with sweat. I heard his teeth clattering as though he was freezing cold. "What is it?" I started to pull the car to the curb and stop.

"Keep going. Faster," he groaned.

I looked over at him uneasily.

"In Cambodia, we . . ."

Another spasm of shaking tore through him.

"That was her. Back there. That woman." He lifted his head slightly, then dropped it in his hands the way a child does. If he can't see you, you can't see him. ". . . didn't just kill them."

"What are you talking about?" I didn't want to know.

"They tortured some . . . a woman."

"Tortured? A woman?" I repeated hollowly.

"I . . ." He looked sideways up at me. His face was wet. I wanted to look away. I wanted to go home and take a long hot shower and scrub my skin off.

"I did something so wrong I can't ever be human again." He moved closer and dropped his face in my lap. I could feel his hot face through my jeans.

"I was barely seventeen. Point man. Middle of the night when we came upon her . . . deserted hamlet . . . sitting on a big straw basket with a top on it. We'd heard there were explosives and thought she was going to kill herself to blow us all up—"

"You don't have to tell me."

"I was scared. Sarge said to make her talk so I—"

"Tony, don't—"

"They strung her up and used her for target practice. I couldn't stop them. There was nothing in the basket but a pile of old silk clothes."

He nuzzled his face deeper into my crotch and the tears soaked my jeans. My hand, like a cat on its way home in the dark on a night with no moon, found his hair. I pulled the cap off his head and stroked him until he was quiet.

CHAPTER 12

It was late afternoon. The sun was molting into an acrid orange in the west. Tony sat up and fiddled with the radio without speaking.

"I'm going over to Vernon. Where Dwayne Yazzi works," I announced.

"Last I heard he worked construction in Hollywood."

"Ernie Little Horse says different."

"Ernie!"

"Why does that surprise you? I thought you knew everything."

"Charley Lomas knows everything." He took another swig of Jack Daniel's. He offered it to me, but I shook my head. "Ernie tell you about Dwayne while I was in the john?"

I nodded. I didn't want to tell him yet about my drinking party at the Oasis. "From the way he tells it, the two of them are great friends. You said they got into a fight in Winston Alley."

"More than once. Ernie used to be married to this little Chicana named Angela. Angela left him and rented a place to share with Shirley. Dwayne was always going over there. That's how he met Angela."

"While she was still married to Ernie?"

Tony nodded. "He was sniffing around, pretty soon they're making honey." Tony switched off the radio and looked through my cassettes. He put in a tape of B. B. King recorded live in Amsterdam. "You think we're all savages running around in loincloths screwing nonstop?"

"Running around in Levi 501s screwing nonstop." I tweaked the left knee of his jeans. "Shirley was making it with Dwayne?"

"Dwayne, Dick, and Harry. Everyone but Long Tall Sally and Ahab the Arab."

Most of the traffic was headed south, but it was still a squeeze north towards downtown. "I went to Shirley's apartment. I met Angela." I waited for some reaction. He'd go nuts. He'd know I was still trying to check up on him.

Tony nodded thoughtfully. "Good girl! I knew you were a smart one. Charley said I had to let you figure out some of this for yourself. That's the secret, our combination, how our paths come together."

I scooped the eagle feather earring from the pocket of my jeans and dangled it in front of him. "This was Shirley's. I couldn't find the mate. Navajo, isn't it?"

"Good guess, crumbcake. It's Navajo all right. Dwayne wears an earring, but I've never seen this one. Usually a turquoise stud. He does like to give the ladies little presents, though," Tony snorted. "A pair of earrings and he could have Shirley eating out of his hand."

"Don't you like to give the ladies little presents? Ladies like them." I quickly inventoried the gifts men had given me. A Nancy Drew mystery that I already had from a boy in the fourth grade. A scratchy pink sweater that was too small and I was embarrassed to exchange from a junior high school football player. The best had been a gold-plated bracelet from a guy I went out with when I was a senior in college. I didn't know where it was.

"Don't have anything to give but my heart. If I gave you my heart, would you take care of it?"

"I lose things pretty quickly."

He examined the cassette's cover art. "1985. You been taking care of this for eleven years. Still have it."

"Got it when it came out. I was sixteen. That's when I started listening to the blues." Sitting in my bedroom on a summer afternoon, the window open, looking out at the sun playing on the Chesapeake Bay and my father's sailboat, the *Lovely Lady*, moored at our dock. It had been nearly two days then since I'd spoken to my mother or father.

Up ahead I saw Boyle, my exit, and flicked on my turn indicator.

A gold Peugeot two car lengths in front of me slammed on its brakes. I hit my brakes. My foot went all the way to the floor. I tapped the brake pedal again and it slapped the floor again. Without thinking I threw my arm across Tony's chest as I jerked the Chevy into the next lane.

"Downshift," said Tony.

A beat-up old station wagon with a green plastic trash bag over the rear window rumbled past, the driver screaming "Asshooole!" I ripped the car into low. Two tired and wary-looking kids in the back of the wagon threw me the finger.

I pumped the brakes again. Nothing.

"Head for those bushes," Tony said, pointing out some inhospitable-looking shrubs on the far side of the off ramp. I turned the wheel again and cut the ignition as I slid through the space between a van and a Mercedes.

"Geronimo!" Tony screamed and grabbed the wheel turning it harder to the right.

The car spun sideways. I must have closed my eyes for an instant because the next time I looked the car was facing up the off ramp. A gas truck followed by a line of honking cars roared towards us. The Chevy smacked into the bushes.

Tony climbed out, waving the gas truck on. Panting, I put my head down on the steering wheel. I heard Tony open the hood. I felt my arms and legs. I was intact.

"Somebody loosened your brake cable." Tony climbed back into the car. Ernie Little Horse, the mechanical wizard? Perhaps he'd seen me get into the Chevy across the street from the Bucket. Perhaps he'd only pretended to not see the car parked on Sunset. Perhaps that's why he'd come into the Oasis. But what would have been his motive before we'd talked about Shirley? I wondered if Tony could have loosened the cable.

Vernon is filthy and the air smelled like blood. The Farmer John processing plant took up a couple of long city blocks. Jolly little pink pigs cavorted with happy nineteenth-century farm boys along the painted walls of the plant. Some of the pigs were three-dimensional so it appeared they were escaping over the tops of the walls. Although the driver side of the Chevy was crunched in, as I cruised along at thirty-five, the trees growing in front of the painted walls merged into a pastoral scene that made me want to whistle zippity-do-da. I'd heard that the artist responsible for the murals had fallen from a scaffold to his death while painting.

We parked in a lot marked "Employees Only." At the personnel office a scrawny, flat-chested young blonde in a miniskirt knew immediately who I was asking for. She scowled possessively when she told me Dwayne Yazzi was a part-time worker and that he wasn't scheduled to be in that day. Tony and I retreated down the hall as though we were going back to the parking lot, but instead exited through a side door we'd noted, marked "Plant."

We walked down a corridor until we came to a changing room. Tony made a quick recon inside the room. "All clear." He closed the door behind me to stand guard in the hall. Alone in the locker room I found a bin of bloodstained uniforms. I tucked my hair up into an encrusted soft white hat and pulled a pair of pants and a shirt over my clothes. I grabbed an extra set for Tony.

Tony held the bloody clothes I handed him in front of himself like they made him dizzy. He shook his head.

"Then wait for me out in the car."

He tugged the clothes over his jeans and t-shirt.

We continued down the hall. Various safety notices were posted along the wall. Through a series of viewing windows I could see that at the stations we passed there were no women working.

"So much for women's rights," I complained to Tony. "They're probably all stuck in fat rendering and sausage making." We must have come in near the beginning of the line. To our right were pig sounds and then a space of relative quiet as the hogs were gassed unconscious before they were killed.

"In the old days," Tony said in disgust, "we rode after the buffalo, exchanged furs for German silver to pound into ornaments or sheet metal to file into arrowheads. Now Dwayne's a piggy roper."

We passed a series of immense vats where the animals were scalded and dehaired. The viscera were removed into sloppy piles that made me think again of my first sight of Shirley Yellowbird. The hogs were refrigerated overnight and cut by butchers the next day into wholesale pieces, which went on down the line to shipping rooms.

"Too bad you don't have a clipboard," Tony said. "Makes it look like you have something to do. Old military trick."

I told him when we went in with the workers that I'd follow his lead. I didn't tell him I'd never had a job until I opened my office. Tony walked up to a guy standing around in a supervisory kind of way. "Hey, man. We're just on a break. Need to see Dwayne Yazzi right away."

"Ain't here."

"Tell him—"

"Ain't been here for two days. Tell him to look for another job."

A man nearby laughed. "Dwayne's got better things to do. He's probably out at his granny's."

Tony asked the man if he knew where that was.

"Huntington Park. Fifty-seventh near Boyle. Place looks like a Taco Bell."

Tony thanked the guy.

We hurried back down the hall in the direction from which we'd come. As I started for the locker room Tony grabbed my hand and pulled me through a door marked "Emergency Exit." I expected an alarm to go off, but the door merely clicked solidly behind us. We found ourselves outside on an end of the building far from where we'd parked. We stripped the filthy uniforms off and threw them in a Dumpster.

"Never thought I'd be getting your clothes off this way," Tony said.

I looked around, orienting myself. "When you were at my place, telling me your wacky story, I asked you if the vision said you were supposed to touch me. You said no. I like you better than I did then, but that doesn't mean you're getting any from me," I said over my shoulder as I headed for the car.

Tony caught up with me. "Dwayne doesn't have a granny. Not here at least. All his people are still back in Arizona."

It hurt to look at my battered Chevy, but it started without a problem. I touched the brakes gently a few times in the lot before venturing out into traffic. "Shouldn't I go to a garage?"

He shook his head. "I fixed it for the time being. It's not far to Fifty-seventh."

Fifty-seventh near Boyle was working class, residential, and downbeat. Dwayne's Camaro was in front of an adobe-colored apartment with faux columns and an imprint of a mission bell above the entrance. I headed for the front door, but Tony motioned me over to the side of the building. The ground-floor windows were nearly shoulder high to me. We prowled from window to window. I expected someone to shoot at us, but it appeared no one was home in the building. Then from a window on the south side of the building we heard Stevie Ray Vaughn and his band Double Trouble coming from a cheap sound system.

We crept closer.

Lacy pink curtains were tied loosely back. On a king-size bed shoved against the opposite wall, a naked man slammed into a moaning woman. It was quite rhythmic, though much faster than Stevie Ray Vaughn's electrified Texas blues. Tony and I stared at the thrusting buttocks without looking at each other. The last time I'd had sex, in a motel room with a stockbroker, had seemed more like a slow waltz.

Tony glanced at me. He seemed aroused, resentful and amused at the same time. The action hero in front of us, long hair flowing free and back glistening, was Dwayne Yazzi.

The woman put her hands on Dwayne's shoulders and he slowed down and pulled out of her. She turned to her side. She had long gray hair and was old. Nimbly she got onto her hands and knees with her butt towards Dwayne. He moved to mount her like a dog, but his dick went soft. She glanced back to see what was happening. Dwayne stroked himself, but didn't get any harder. She murmured his name and reached for him, but he was concentrating in a troubled way on his penis.

I nudged Tony in the arm and we made our way to the front door of the building and through the main hallway towards the apartment we calculated to be the pleasure palace.

I rang the bell. When no one answered, I rang it again. Then, a third time. I heard Dwayne padding angrily towards the door.

"Who's there?" he barked.

"UPS," I said.

"Leave it."

"Needs a signature."

Dwayne threw open the door. He wore a pair of jeans that hung on his hips. "You?" he said eyeing me with disbelief.

"Always thought you were a motherfucker," said Tony, stepping into view. "But this takes it to a whole new level."

"Who is it, baby?" called the woman from the bedroom.

"No one," Dwayne replied over his shoulder. He glared at Tony. "Thought you were in jail."

"Cops didn't have enough to hold me. I gave 'em your name."

"Who's your lady friend?" I asked. "Didn't take long for you to transfer your affections once Shirley was dead."

Dwayne started to close the door in our faces. Tony shoved him aside and I pushed my way into the apartment. In contrast to the soft pink feminine harmony of the bedroom, the living room was painted a light tan and the furniture black or dark green. Pictures of Indians and tepees, buffalo, big clouds, and gurgling streams covered the walls. Several framed black and white headshots of an Indian man in costume and stills of the same man in westerns stood about on end tables and on a small desk. I sat down on the couch. "Comfy."

"Dwayne, what's happening?' the woman called again. I heard her get off the bed and a closet door open.

Dwayne looked towards the bedroom with annoyance.

"We can be out of here in a few seconds without having any problems with her"—I nodded towards the bedroom—"if you come with us now."

"Talk to the cops," said Tony. "If you're innocent, they'll let you go. This is America."

"You owe it to Shirley," I said.

"Who's Shirley?" The woman padded into the room.

She wasn't as old as she'd looked at first. Twenty years older than Dwayne. She was nearly five-eight, slender, but tanned for decades that had left her skin a ruined map. A white woman. She was barefoot, but wore a rose-colored chenille robe.

As little as I may know about men, I know two things. Never put a TV in the bedroom and never wear chenille.

"Old girlfriend," Dwayne grunted.

"Dead girlfriend," I added.

The woman looked back and forth between us. She looked questioningly at Tony and said something in a language I didn't understand.

Tony answered and she nodded. "But I'm Choctaw," Tony added. "Only know a few words of Lakota."

"We don't want to disturb your home, but Dwayne either needs to leave with us or I'm going to use your phone and call the police." I quickly explained to her what had happened to Shirley Yellowbird and that Dwayne had been the last person seen with her the night she was murdered.

"Dwayne was here with me." The woman tugged the belt around her waist more firmly closed.

"What time did he get here?"

"Midnight."

"Funny, I've already talked to two people who say they saw him after midnight."

"They were wrong."

"One was Shirley's roommate," I said. "Angela. I couldn't tell from your back window if you were practicing safe sex. I hope so. Dwayne's been fucking at least two women besides you. Angela and Shirley."

I saw her stiffen.

"In the past, perhaps," she murmured. "Before he met me."

I shook my head.

"Shirley! That was more than a year ago. I never touched Angela. She's lying," he pointed at me.

"Doesn't it make you wonder what else Dwayne would keep

secret from you?" Tony interrupted. "Look, lady, I got no problem with you. I knew this guy, Henry Tall Bear." Tony tapped one of the photos. "A good guy. When I was a kid he used to volunteer and teach an acting workshop for Indian kids on Saturday mornings. I went there for almost two years. He was a good man, generous. If you knew him, your life's been blessed."

"He was my father-in-law."

Tony nodded. "One of the original members of the Indian War Paint Club in the twenties."

She smiled.

"I never knew his sons," Tony continued. "They were much older than me. I'm sure they were good men, too. You want to make whoopee with Dwayne, that's your business, but I need to honor Henry Tall Bear and tell you who Dwayne is." He looked at Dwayne. "He's a drug dealer, a womanizer. I don't know if he's taking money from you . . ."

Her smile faded, but she didn't stop looking at Dwayne.

"I can prove he killed Shirley Yellowbird," I heard myself say.

"How?" she demanded.

"He was at her house the night she was killed. He'd given her a pair of silver earrings. Like eagle feathers. One was found next to her body," I lied. "The other's missing."

The woman frowned. "If I say he was here with me, he was here with me."

I got up. "You'll swear to that in court?"

She nodded.

"Then we'll leave." Instead of going to the front door I turned down the hall towards the bedroom.

"What are you doing?" the woman shouted. "You can't go in there." I heard Tony push Dwayne into a corner and then a chair scraping along the floor and toppling. I ran into the bedroom. Nothing. I heard picture frames hitting the ground and shattering. I rushed into the bathroom. On the sink counter was the silver earring.

I ran back into the living room holding it out in front of me like a bloody knife.

Dwayne and Tony were rolling on the living-room floor. Tony was on top and about to pin Dwayne's arms when Dwayne kicked him and broke free. Dwayne staggered to his feet and bolted through the front door.

The woman screamed and Tony told her he was sorry.

I ran after Dwayne but his car was already racing away down Fifty-seventh. I yelled for Tony, but by the time he appeared Dwayne was out of sight.

I stopped at the nearest pay phone and called Lupe. It was nearly six. She must have been sitting next to the phone.

"I'm okay," I said excitedly. "Dwayne Yazzi was just here, but he got away from us. Don't worry about me."

She didn't say anything.

"I'm sorry about what happened this afternoon," I added.

She cleared her throat but still didn't say anything.

"Let's talk about it. When I see you." I glanced back at Tony who was sitting in the car.

She hung up on me.

I saw Tony get out of the car and wander towards the back of the store I was parked in front of. Was he going to pee? Men are like dogs. I had to pee, too, and if he could just wait a minute we could go to a McDonald's and take care of peeing and eating. It annoyed me.

Several moments passed, but Tony didn't reappear. I walked to the back of the building, but he wasn't there. I ran to the car again, but he wasn't there, either. I looked in the market, then outside again, and called his name. He was gone.

I rushed to the pay phone again and grabbed it from a pregnant woman who was just about to dial a number. "Sorry, it's an emergency." She mad-dogged me, but I turned my back to her and dialed the office again. "Tony split again. He's told me about a medicine man named Charley Lomas. Supposedly Charley Lomas knows who killed Shirley."

Lupe groaned. "You're not going to fall for that B.S., are you?"

"Tony won't tell me where the medicine man is, just some nonsense about him living in a ghost hotel."

"I know where it is!"

I turned back to see what the pregnant woman was doing. "He said it used to be covered with palm trees and stars—"

"I know where it is," Lupe insisted.

CHAPTER 13

The Alexandria Hotel on the southwest corner of Spring and Fifth is a welfare flop. On weekend nights *greñudos y roqueros,* long-haired Mexican rockers, came to see punk-ska bands like La Tumba del Doctor Horror in one of the ballrooms, or so Lupe told me when I met her out front the next morning.

"How do you know this is the place?" A half dozen people stood blocking the entrance as they gathered around a hastily constructed shell game being run by a tall-gaunt Mexican.

"There's a palm court. All the stars stayed here. Sarah Bernhardt. Some presidents, too. Theodore Roosevelt. Charlie Chaplin called it the swankest hotel in town.

I looked at her doubtfully.

"King Edward the Eighth."

"And the ghost?"

She nodded. "A lady in black."

The red carpeting was tattered and the Victorian remodeled lobby grimy. Only the marble columns which remained hinted at the luxury Lupe had described.

The desk clerk must have thought I was a social worker. He told me Charley Lomas was in room 1145. He glanced once at Lupe in her tight jeans and high heels exploring the faded lobby, but if he was going to say something he must have decided it was a waste of time to try to control the clientele.

The elevators were located past what had been the main dining room. Lupe, pointing inside, told me Chaplin, Douglas

Fairbanks, and Mary Pickford had formally announced the creation of United Artists there. "Mary Pickford, she played a Mexican. *Rosita.*"

I admitted I'd never seen it. Lupe shook her head.

She wanted to look around more. To see the Peacock Room where glamorous tea parties had been held, but I told her I had to find out fast from Charley Lomas where Dwayne had gone.

"I don't know why you're so certain Dwayne killed Shirley," Lupe argued. "Even if I believed Red Wolf was innocent, she disappeared with Ernie not Dwayne. Why would Dwayne want to kill her? You think it was a robbery?"

"Shirley had at least seven hundred dollars with her when she left the bar. I didn't see a purse and I don't think the cops did, either."

" 'Cause Tony has them," Lupe snapped. "This is a hell of a time for you to fall in love or get an itchy pussy, whichever it is."

I told Lupe about the mate of Shirley's earring. I told her about the widow I'd found Dwayne with that afternoon. "He was riding her like they were in the final stretch of the Triple Crown. She's way into Dwayne—enough to commit perjury— even though he lost it on her and went limp."

"Older woman? Bet he's already tapped her for all the money she has."

I shrugged. "The knife's personal. It was someone who loved her. Dwayne. He's been with a lot of women, but Shirley's the only one he ever asked to marry."

We got into the elevator. The door closed, but opened again. A strung-out-looking white guy got in. He called us "Ladies," then hocked a big loogie on the floor, although the two events did not seem connected. He got off on the third floor.

"They used to have spittoons here. For gentlemen," Lupe muttered angrily.

"Please, can't we go anywhere without you giving me a lot of attitude? I didn't ask you to come. You could have just told me where the hotel was." I bit my tongue. Things still weren't smoothed out between us.

"Another trashy loser," Lupe continued as though she hadn't heard me. "Like your Charley Lomas. Medicine man, my ass. I bet we find him shooting up."

"Why don't you go back downstairs and do some more sightseeing?"

"Oh no," Lupe crowed. "I want to see just how nutty you're going to get with this tribal hocum pocum. Why don't you give yourself an Indian name? How about Fast Running Water?"

"Knock it off."

"Fluffy White Cloud."

The elevator doors opened at eleven. The hall was dark and dusty. It smelled like piss with a faint undertone of industrial cleanser. Fake candles were attached to the wall every fifteen feet, but most of them were missing the top orange flame-colored glass lightbulb and some of the light fixtures were missing altogether. I wondered how the hotel could permit this; somebody was bound to get hurt and sue.

I turned left to look for Charley Lomas's room. A gust of cold air blasted me in the face. I glanced up looking for a fan, but there was no fan. A scent of lavender filled the air. The false candles flickered.

A woman dressed in black from head to toe stood at the far end of the hall. She wore a hat with a veil. I couldn't see through her, but she wasn't solid, either.

"Do you see that?" I whispered to Lupe.

"What?"

The woman moved forward, gliding, her dress from the beginning of the century whispering along the floor, then she disappeared through the wall.

I hurried down the hall where the woman had vanished. I touched the wall. It was a real wall.

"That woman felt so sad," I said.

"What woman? There aren't any ghosts. Thought you didn't believe in ghosts." Lupe looked paler than I'd ever seen her.

"Perhaps the hotel—"

"You think this fucking place would spend the money for special effects for the tourists? They don't even have goddamn air-conditioning."

We marched bravely down the hall in the opposite direction, looking for Charley Lomas's room. I knocked on his door. It was answered almost immediately by a woman in her early sixties. The woman in the photo that had been hidden in Shirley Yellowbird's dresser.

"Yes?" she chimed.

"I'm looking for Charley Lomas. I'm a friend of his friend Tony Red Wolf. I need to see Mr. Lomas."

The woman squinted at Lupe, then at me. "Who are you?"

I gave her one of my cards. "Is he in, please? It's an emergency."

"No, he's not." The woman inspected my card while I inspected her. She wore creamy mauve eyeshadow and red lipstick. "Why don't you come back later?"

Lupe put her hands on her hips. "We don't have time to come back. And my friend doesn't want to stand around the hall."

"I saw a ghost," I blushed.

"Really?" said the woman, opening the door and peering down the hall. "I don't believe in ghosts. I've heard of the ghost, but never saw it. Come on in, you can sit down and wait for Charley and tell me about the ghost. I've always wanted to see one." She opened the door. "I'll make some tea."

The room was small, but neat. Nothing more than a bed

covered with a green bedspread, a chest of drawers, two green plastic chairs, and a black and white TV, which was attached to the ceiling like in a bar.

Ignoring our hostess, Lupe stared up at the TV. *The Maltese Falcon* was playing. Lupe watched for a few seconds. "That's Gladys Henry." Lupe pointed to the screen as though this was something important to know.

I nodded without interest.

"It's Gladys George," said the old lady as she set a kettle of water on a hot plate. She took several pinches of strange-looking tea with purple flowers and dried stems and put it into an ivory-colored porcelain teapot.

Lupe shook her head. "Gladys Henry."

"Gladys George."

"I know everything about this movie," Lupe argued. "I've seen it a million times."

"I saw it when it came out."

"Yeah, and you've forgotten," said Lupe. "That was a long time ago. Ancient history."

I glared at Lupe, but she didn't notice.

The kettle whistled. The old woman set out three saucers with matching cups. "Gladys George. Had the title role in the earlier *Madame X*. 1937."

Lupe frowned.

The old woman took the kettle off the hot plate. "Oh my dear, I'm out of sugar. Would you mind going next door and borrowing some?" She handed Lupe a chipped glass.

"I don't want any tea," Lupe said.

"I do." I dropped my purse on the bed.

The old woman opened the door for Lupe, closed it quickly behind her, and locked it. She turned to me with a smile of triumph. "Gladys George went on to do *Detective Story*."

"I wouldn't know about that, ma'am."

She handed me a cup of the tea. It was stinky. I put it to my lips and pretended to take a sip.

"It won't hurt you, it's good for you."

I took a swallow. It tasted like licorice and mud.

Lupe pounded on the door. "The guy next door told me to fuck off."

The old woman ignored the knocking.

"Whitney!"

I took another sip of the tea. Lupe's voice sounded like it was coming from far away. She knocked a couple more times. "I'll be in the lobby." I heard her walking away, then the chime of the elevator and the elevator door closing.

"That girl's going to end up in trouble someday." The old woman drank her tea. "Alone in a country where no one knows her."

I had no idea what she was talking about, but her raspy voice worried me.

She set down her tea. In one smooth movement she peeled off the wig she was wearing. She had short gray hair, cut up above her ears and parted on the side. Gold-colored earrings framed her face and yet there was something coarse and full about her chin and jawline. I glanced down at her hands.

"I'm Charley Lomas," she said. "I've been expecting you." She got up and went into the bathroom. I heard the water running. She returned; a rather small old man with sagging skin and vestiges of mauve shadow around his eyes.

"You were the woman I saw in a photograph with Shirley Yellowbird."

He nodded. "I've known Shirley nearly five years. Since she was twenty."

"In the photo, your dress and hair—"

"Shirley knew."

"You always dress in drag?" I couldn't help myself.

"When I'm alone. Or among friends. Sometimes when I go shopping."

"Does Tony know?"

He nodded again. "I met Shirley through him. It wasn't so easy for him, though," he laughed. "He thought I was a woman."

I imagined some horrible situation. Tony groping Charley Lomas in the backseat of a car.

"At a bar, dancing." Charley Lomas smiled as though he'd read my mind. "Tony tries to be good to women."

"But you're a man."

"I'm a woman in a man's body." Charley Lomas touched his mouth lightly.

I put my teacup down. My face felt hot. I felt dizzy. "I'm sorry. I'm having a hard time with this. Not that you're a man. It's just all so secular. The drag. Going to dances. I thought you were a medicine man. Aren't you supposed to be like a priest?"

"I don't like small boys."

"Don't you have to fast—?"

"God, yes. I have trouble staying this size."

"I mean special offerings and sacrifices, celibacy."

"I have to honor life and remember there are differences between people."

He told me he had known when he was twelve that he would be a medicine man, and that he was homosexual. "Among my people, we are between heaven and earth. That is how we can talk with the Great Spirit."

"I don't believe in the spirit world. I have a hard enough time understanding how TV works."

"You saw the ghost. There are spirits among us," he insisted. "They move on the strength of their own memories. Some good and some bad. The one you saw, it was sorrow killed her. It doesn't matter what name you call them. Thunderbird, Whirlwind, Skinnywalker."

"Skinnywalker."

Charley Lomas nodded. "Some people say Tony Red Wolf is a skinnywalker."

"Is he?" I wanted a glass of water, but was afraid to ask for it. I was afraid it would be dosed, too. I already felt like there had been something very crafty in the tea. "Is Tony Red Wolf evil?"

"Do you know what makes a good man?" Charley Lomas began to sing softly. At first I thought he was chanting, but then realized it was a Supremes song.

What did make a good man? My ex, Bill Peters, had been a good man, sort of. Until I found him with another woman. "Honest, hardworking, not afraid to go alone to buy Tampax at the supermarket."

"A good man doesn't kill. Unless it's to protect his family."

"You must know Shirley Yellowbird's dead. I saw her. Mutilated. An eagle feather was near her body."

He nodded. "This has all been told when the great skies were clear and there was no wind. Eagle represents Thunderbird, master of storms. An eagle feather might be given by a warrior to represent an act of bravery. Or someone who wishes to send a message to the Great Spirit does so with an eagle feather."

Who would think it was brave to kill her? "Tony told me you knew who killed her. And why. He said you knew the future as well as the past."

He shrugged. "When Indians become like white men, you can't trust them."

"Are you saying Tony killed her?"

Charley Lomas put his hands on his knees, but I couldn't tell if he was examining them or the green floral pattern of his dress. He looked up at me. "It is right to bring tobacco to a medicine man."

"I don't smoke."

"You have come here unprepared, unwilling to be taught

anything. In our tradition I have three days to decide to take you as a patient."

"I'm not sick. I just want to know if Tony Red Wolf's a murderer."

"You're here because this is about you. Not Tony."

I tried to get to my feet, but felt too heavy to move. I glanced up. The incomprehensible plot of *The Maltese Falcon* was beginning to make sense. I must be stoned.

"You only want Tony to make you famous. You want Tony to be your father."

"I already have one father too many," I snapped. I was starting to sweat.

Charley Lomas shook his head. "Your father is not a father."

"I'm not here to talk about him. Look, if you won't tell me about Tony, tell me about Dwayne Yazzi. I think he killed Shirley."

He asked me why. I repeated the same things I'd told Lupe. He listened without reaction and didn't speak for a while. "Dwayne lives too fast. Drives too fast. He will die behind the wheel of a car."

So will .08 percent of the population.

"With you."

I shook my head trying to clear it. "Are you trying to scare me off?"

Charley Lomas poured himself another cup of tea. "Don't your philosophers say free will distinguishes us from the other animals?"

My head was starting to pound and the funky gardenia perfume Charley Lomas was wearing was beginning to annoy me. I asked how well he'd known Shirley. "It sounds like she was no good—"

"I'm accustomed to the pain and loneliness one must endure to acquire knowledge. I knew Shirley as well as I can know anyone. You don't know why she was killed," he interrupted.

"Tried to play too many people."

"Shirley told only three lies. She told Dwayne she loved him. She told Angela Valdez that Ernie Little Horse had cheated on her with another woman."

I sat forward in my chair. "And she told Tony Red Wolf she didn't love him!"

"Now you think he killed her? Or do you imagine you can trick me into telling you what you want to know?"

"I don't know." I put my head in my hands. The room was spinning. "I can't figure out where Shirley went when she disappeared from her apartment with Ernie Little Horse."

"Close your eyes. Tell me what you see. Sometimes dreams are wiser than waking."

"I don't think—"

"I didn't tell you to think, I told you to close your eyes."

I closed my eyes. I could hear my own breathing. It sounded ragged and nervous.

Charley Lomas hummed off-key.

I saw a long stairway surrounded by trees and littered with eucalyptus leaves.

Charley Lomas drummed his fingers on the table.

There were houses nearby on either side of the stairway. The stairway descended down to a sidewalk. I saw myself walk down the stairs. I looked up and saw the stars. I looked down. A pool of blood stood at the foot of the stairs.

I might have screamed out. When I opened my eyes, Charley Lomas was nodding in approval.

"Where is it?" I asked.

He didn't answer.

"Near Shirley's apartment, isn't it?" I guessed. I took his silence to mean I was correct. I stood up to leave. "There was a fight. Shirley was forced to go to the mission."

"In the old days when the warriors who had killed or scalped came home from battle they had to camp on the outskirts of the village for four days and purify themselves with fasting, singing, and frequent bathing before they could rejoin their people. This is no longer done."

I thought of the guys, bearded, dirty, and hungover who stood at the freeway on-ramps holding signs that said "Vietnam Vet Please Help." "Tony lied about having been in Cambodia?"

Charley Lomas shook his head. "Our warriors may count coup. It is brave to do so . . ."

I saw the seventeen–year-old Tony Red Wolf proud in his uniform, listening to Jimi Hendrix, hanging on the words of the older guys who were bragging.

". . . and to kill the enemy. But Tony . . ." Charley Lomas sighed as though in pain. "Killed an innocent woman."

"He tried to stop the other men from killing her."

Charley Lomas shook his head.

CHAPTER 14

Shaken, I went downstairs. I decided not to tell Lupe what Charley Lomas had said. Who was he anyway? Some flighty broad in garish eye makeup. A confused old man living on SSI. If I didn't have any proof about Tony, I wasn't going to spread rumors. I found Lupe sitting in the Peacock Room toying with a portly Salvadoran in a plaid sports jacket.

"Gotta call Harvey." I motioned her towards the phones on the opposite side of the lobby. I was relieved to find him in his office still playing with his new computer.

"Tony Red Wolf's his real name," Harvey announced before I could tell him what happened. He sounded faintly impressed, but whether by what he'd found out or because he'd been able to operate the computer I wasn't sure. "I was able to get some info on him. Not much. No birth certificate or driver's license, but he did have an honorable discharge from the Navy." The year he told me corresponded with what Tony had told me.

"Was he in the SEALs?"

"Can't tell."

Next I called the UCLA law school to find out what kinds of Indian civil rights and community groups existed in LA. The Salvadoran kept creeping closer, but Lupe had lost interest in the game. At the multiservices Indian Center a woman with a soft voice answered the phone.

"We don't give out information on our clients," she said when I told her what I wanted. "But you could leave a message and if

172

that person is a client we'd give it to them. What's the name?"

"Tony Red Wolf."

The woman fell silent.

"Do you know where I could find him?"

"If he's not back in jail, you could try the powwow tonight," she said finally, as though glad to be absolved of any responsibility regarding Tony. I got the information from her about the powwow and hung up feeling confused. Details of Tony's story kept matching up, but there was still the unmistakable feeling no one liked him.

It was nearly seven when Lupe and I got in her car and I asked her to drive me back down to Long Beach to Cecil B. DeMille Junior High School.

"Did I tell you it was DeMille who made *The Squaw Man*. He was only twenty-two."

"I don't know if I should believe you anymore. The old lady at the hotel said you don't know beans about the old movies."

"I may have missed a bit player," Lupe pouted, "but I know what I'm talking about. I got celluloid in my blood. Did I ever tell you I had a great aunt who was a cook for Doris Kenyon? *Pawn of Fate, Counsellor at Law, Blonde Saint.*"

The junior high parking lot was rapidly filling with vans, pickup trucks, and beat up old cars as I pulled in. I looked for Tony's bike, but didn't see it.

"Let's just try to blend in with the crowd," I cautioned. "If Tony's not here, then we want to find out what people are saying about him—might help me figure out where he's gone."

She parked the car, checked her makeup, and tucked her form-fitting t-shirt into her jeans wearily. "What you say, homechick. But can I at least get something to eat?"

The air smelled like tacos and hamburgers, and I realized I was hungry, too. I couldn't remember if I'd eaten. Lupe guided me towards a food stand selling hot dogs outside the gymnasium. She ordered one. I shook my head and got a Coke and some fry bread smeared with honey from the cafeteria instead. I was probably through with hot dogs for life. I paid at the door for us to get in the gym. Drums beat slowly. Several security guards, Indians in blue windbreakers, stood around the door, and as I glanced over my shoulder I noticed several more patrolling the parking area.

Inside, forming a ring around the gym floor, were the tables and displays of traders selling bead necklaces, t-shirts with wolves and buffalo painted on them, and round woven hoops which I would later learn were called dreamcatchers. The perimeters of the basketball court were staked out by drums. A steady stream of Indians wandered into the locker rooms. They reappeared: Nikes replaced by beaded moccasins. Lakers tank tops replaced by buckskin shirts. Baseball caps that said "Metallica" replaced by porcupine and horsehair roaches and feathered headdresses. In the girls' locker room the women exchanged miniskirts, faded carefully ripped jeans, and sweat suits for beaded, elk-teeth-yoked dresses of buckskin, satin, and Pendleton wool.

It was nearly eight. I scanned the crowd for Tony, but didn't see him. Dancers began assembling at the far end of the gym. An elderly Indian man stepped to a microphone on the opposite side of the gym. I wondered why Charley Lomas wasn't here and why he hadn't told me about the powwow. The old man repeatedly urged all dancers to gather at the locker room door for the grand entry. The tinkling of ankle bells filled the air as dancers strode to their positions. The women drew shawls about their shoulders and made final adjustments to their heirloom dresses.

A red-wool-sheathed, otter-decorated curved coup stick was hoisted triumphant from its protective case by a man in buckskin leggings. He took his place at the head of the line that was forming. The drums became more insistent. A chant rose.

"All stand for the grand entry."

Lupe and I stood near the wall. The spectators who were crammed onto the gym bleachers and in lawn chairs surrounding the dance area got to their feet. Removing cowboy hats and truckers' caps, men stood respectfully. Women hoisted small children and stood. A silence fell upon the room.

"Everybody up. Everybody up. It's powwow time!"

A young woman in a gleaming ornate elk-skin dress and the man in buckskins who carried the coup stick stepped forward with deliberate dignity, followed by a hundred or more dancers. In single file they proceeded around the circumference of the gym.

The audience resumed their seats and there was good-natured jostling and buzzing as friends, relatives, and acquaintances were proudly pointed out. I searched the gymnasium again for Tony as I made my way through the crowd. The emcee intoned the names and tribal affiliations of the powwow officials. The head singer of the host drum group chanted a song honoring the flags of the United States and California.

An old man was brought to the microphone to lead the opening prayer. He raised a fan made of white feathers to the sky and began to chant in his tribal language. The audience stood again, holding their hats by their sides and placing their hands over their hearts. It was a solemn moment, but I guessed that only a few in the audience actually understood his words.

The old man returned to his seat in the dancers' circle. The head male dancer and his attendants placed a banner, the American flag, and the otter staff at the speakers' podium. The dancers surged onto the dance floor. Old women carrying babies. High school boys with long hair. Overweight girls with shawls trailing behind them. Toddlers with feather bustles taped onto their diapers.

"What makes you think Tony's going to be here?" asked Lupe.

"He's a 'breed. A lot of the Indians don't accept him because he's not full-blooded. I bet he wants to participate in these events to prove he's a real Indian." As I watched the dancers on the floor I tried to imagine Tony in regalia with feathers and skins. I found the image rather intoxicating.

"I got another call from Hayes. The cops showed up after you left, but they just gave him a talking to instead of picking him up on the TRO his wife took out against him. Makes you feel real safe, doesn't it? He wanted to know who Tony was and why you brought him with you."

"And you told him?"

"I told him you use a bodyguard sometimes because you're used to working on high-profile cases."

"He believed that? He didn't recognize Tony from the news?"

Lupe shook her head. "I'm sure Tony was just another nigger to him. What are you going to do if you find Tony tonight? Get smart and call the cops? We could take him to Parker Center ourselves. You'd look like a hero instead of a fool. Or a felon. While you're talking to him, I'll hit him over the head." She opened her purse and gave me a peek at a pair of handcuffs.

"When I was upstairs with the old lady, she was the same one I saw in the photo with Shirley—"

Lupe nodded impatiently. "I never forget a face."

"She was a he."

"*No me jodas!* Usually I can spot them. He was good. Indians don't have much facial hair. Probably used Max Factor pancake," she mused, more to herself than to me. "Drag queens and old ladies love Max Factor."

"While I was talking to him I had a vision."

Lupe put her hand on my forehead. "Are you ill? Since when do you have visions? Why don't you just 'fess up, you got stoned."

I shook my head and told her what I'd seen.

"It's the Laurel and Hardy stairway! In *Silverlake*. It was in one of their movies. They try to push a piano up the stairs."

"I bet those stairs are in the street behind her apartment. Someone pushed Shirley down the stairs. Or there was some kind of fight there."

We walked to the end of the basketball court. I wished I'd bought another Coke because I was starting to come down and my mouth felt like a sand pit. I wondered if Tony would have the nerve to come here. Not only was he, like Dwayne Yazzi, still being sought by the police, many of the people here probably thought Tony had killed Shirley. I turned randomly to a woman standing next to me. "I heard about that girl Shirley Yellowbird on the news, did you know her?"

The woman shook her head.

"Do you think the guy they showed on TV, Tony Red Wolf, killed her?"

Looking annoyed, she took a step away from me.

"Sorry, guess that was a dumb question. Really a shocking thing," I apologized. I heard Lupe cough and out of the corner of my eye glimpsed her jerking her head towards the opposite side of the gym as though we should beat feet.

"Whoever killed her wasn't human," the woman said moving away to join her friends.

Lupe grabbed me by the arm. "You want to get us scalped here tonight? Look around. There's maybe ten white people here. I'm a little better off because I'm part Indian."

I looked around the gym. She was right. There were few white people, some watching the dancers, some buying things at the traders, and several dressed up like Indians. "You never told me that."

"I'm not one of those phonies who's going to tell you my family came from Spain and never touched one of the natives.

My people fucked everyone. I'm *raza*, but I'll be damned if I'm going to stick dirty feathers in my hair and wear that tacky-looking jewelry." She pointed out an obese white woman wearing her hair in braids dragging an aqua shawl as she stomped heavily around the edge of the dance floor.

I was watching the woman when I saw Tony standing at the far end of the bleachers nearly hidden beneath them. I moved quickly, with Lupe following me. He watched me make my way towards him.

"I was beginning to think you wouldn't be here," I said before he had the chance to speak. "Pretty shitty, cutting out on me like that in Vernon. Did you turn into a bird again? A chicken?"

"Aren't you ever going to let me live that story down? I don't know where Dwayne is. I thought he must have gone back to Hollywood so I jumped on a bus. I figured you'd have to go get your car fixed and I didn't want to lose any time."

"Not even time to tell me what you were going to do?"

"I'm sorry. I had an anxiety attack," he mumbled. "Maybe my thinking's not as good as it should be right now."

"You're a jerk," I snapped. "And if you think I'm going to wait around like some kind of ninny while you get your head screwed on straight—"

"Okay, kids." Lupe threw her hands up. "This is no time for a lovers' spat."

Tony laughed and shook his head. "I had a hell of a time getting in here. People looking at me, whispering and pointing. Saying I'm a killer and that I'm an apple—red on the outside, white on the inside. I thought Dwayne would be here. He never misses one. He's a powwow person." Tony explained that Indians who wanted to be with Indians had two basic choices. "You're either a church Indian or a powwow Indian. The two don't mix much."

He said he'd met Shirley at a church sing. "Does that mean

Shirley didn't go to powwows?"

"She was powwow, but she loved to sing and that's the only reason she'd go to the church sometimes."

For an instant I thought of the two of them singing together and I fought a strange jealousy. "Must be a lot about Shirley you haven't told me. How safe is it for you to be here?"

He shrugged and pulled a half pint of whiskey from beneath his shirt. I wondered how he got past the security guards with a bottle. "See the elk-skin dresses. The elk spirit helps the women find someone to love." He pointed out some dancing men clad in spectacular double bustles, roaches, and beaded clothing as they executed fast, intricate dance patterns. Tony explained they were fancy dancers—the most flamboyant of the Southern Plains dances. "The center of the circle, where the host drum is, is the most sacred space. Listen, it's like a heartbeat." He quickly pointed out the other areas. The dancers moved between the host drum and another circle of guest drummers. "It gets less sacred and less Indian as you move away from the center. I need to dance tonight."

I shook my head in exasperation and glanced at my watch. Nearly nine thirty. "I don't want anyone to see you. Wouldn't Dwayne be here already if he was coming?"

"Oh, no," groaned Lupe, looking past me.

Ernie Little Horse strode towards us with an angry frown plastered across his face. He was dressed in tan cords and a yellow t-shirt with a medicine wheel drawn on it. "Thought I'd seen the last of you bitches," he snarled in our direction.

"What have I done to deserve such a shitty life?" I heard Lupe mumble.

Ernie Little Horse grabbed her arm. "You owe me an apology, you cunt. Dumping me in the middle of the road after you tell me you're going to do me."

"Fuck off." Lupe shook her arm, but he didn't let go.

179

She raised her other hand to slap him. Tony pulled Lupe out of the way and pushed Ernie Little Horse in the chest. "Leave the lady alone."

"She's no lady. She's a cunt."

Some kids on the bleachers looked down. "Fight, fight!"

Tony pushed Ernie again until they were under the bleachers.

"Is that why you killed Shirley? Sex?" I taunted Ernie as I pushed in near him. "Bet you raped her. To punish her. She wouldn't let you see Angela." I got closer until I felt his breath on my face. "Your wife told us you were at their apartment that night. She said Shirley left with you. She never saw her again."

"He killed Shirley. Everyone knows it," Ernie said.

I glanced around worriedly, but the crowd seemed still to be focused on the dancers.

Ernie Little Horse broke free of Tony. The two men glared at each other, then Ernie stepped away and strode back out towards the dance floor.

"Are you okay?" Tony and I asked at the same time.

She nodded as she looked at Tony. "Thanks. And you, girl, you're crazy. I'm going to get something to drink." She started away from the bleachers, too. "Oh fuck. Here comes the award for best costuming."

I looked in the direction she'd been headed. Ferguson and Erhndt, in the same suits we'd seen them in earlier and looking like cops, strolled through the crowd as though with no deliberate destination.

I watched Tony as he spotted them. He didn't look as troubled as I would have expected. I wondered why not. Would the other Indians who'd seen Tony shield him from the LAPD?

Ferguson munched on an ice cream sandwich. The Indians who parted ways to let them pass avoided eye contact with them. No one else was eating so I figured it must be prohibited. The drums came to a halt. The emcee introduced the powwow princess and said she would lead a ladies' choice dance. Women laughed and men hooted with pleasure. A new stream of people surged around Ferguson and Erhndt onto the dance floor.

Lupe took Tony by the hand. He looked at me in surprise. "I can't dance," he protested.

"Doesn't look that hard. One two three stomp—"

"I been drinking. Not supposed to dance if you've been drinking."

"It's not like I'm all into you now that you got rid of Ernie, but you'll have a better chance of getting out of here with me than with blondie." She jerked her thumb in my direction. "She's set on being your lawyer, least I can do is give her a fair shot. Getting arrested here isn't going to help anyone."

I said I'd meet them in the parking lot in ten minutes.

Tony followed Lupe to the dance floor and I saw him pull her towards the center drums as though to hide among the other dancers. He ducked behind a tall, stooped man wearing a pair of Crow moccasins with wolf tails on the heels. I wondered why he was going towards the sacred drums if he'd just said it was wrong to do so.

Ferguson and Erhndt moved closer in my direction through the crowd. Ferguson spotted me and came towards me. I thought of running, but made myself stay where I was. "Ms. Logan," he hailed, from about fifteen feet away.

"Looking for Tony Red Wolf?" I asked.

Ferguson nodded.

"Me, too. He's sure made a problem for me. Will you call me if you find him?" I grinned at Ferguson like a schoolgirl.

Erhndt shoved his hands in his pockets looking pissed off and like he was trying to control himself. "You're playing a dangerous game, Ms. Logan." He said "Ms." like he hated it, hated feminists all the way back to Betty Friedan.

"I don't know where he is. If I did I sure as hell wouldn't be here. I'd be maxing out my charge cards at the Beverly Center. Excuse me. Where'd you get the ice cream sandwich?" I turned away and they didn't stop me.

I walked slowly towards the opposite end of the gym. I could see Lupe and Tony working their way towards the edge of the outer circle. The drums came to a sudden halt. The old man who'd led the opening prayer came out into the circle. The dancers looked apprehensively at him. He knelt down amongst them. I moved closer to see what was happening.

He picked up a feather from the floor and examined it. An eagle feather.

He got stiffly to his feet and began to walk around the circle inspecting all the dancers and their clothing. Ferguson and Erhndt pushed through the edge of the circle until they were standing amongst the dancers. Lupe and Tony drifted towards the north end of the gym past the dancers who continued milling around trying to see what the old man was doing. Some of the men glanced at Tony, but quickly turned away as he tried to keep his face turned from them.

Tony and Lupe were still at least fifty feet from the exit. Was the eagle feather a message from Tony? I wondered if I'd misjudged Tony and if he would hurt Lupe if the cops rushed him. What if he took her hostage?

The old man stopped in front of a young guy who'd been dancing near the place Tony had started dancing. The old man checked his ceremonial attire. Finally the old man seemed satisfied the feather had come from that man's clothing and admonished him to be more careful. The old man chanted a cleansing prayer over the spot where the feather had been dropped and over the young man.

The music started again. Tony and Lupe glided out the far door as the dancers crowded the floor. I made my way slowly around the edge of the crowd, keeping Erhndt and Ferguson in sight. The drums shuddered to a stop.

"Folks, we got an unhappy announcement in the announcement part of our program," said the powwow emcee. "One of our young ladies has been killed recently. Shirley Yellowbird. A memorial service will be held tomorrow at noon at Ebell Park."

A silence fell upon the room. Then one woman began the high-pitched trilling of the Lakota women and in a moment the gymnasium echoed with the sound of women wailing.

CHAPTER 15

The parking lot was silent, but for a few couples listening to R&B in darkened coupes. I'd left the gym through a different door than the one Lupe and Tony used and didn't see them, although I checked on the north and south ends of the building. I started to look for Ernie Little Horse's car. It was a Buick and I'd memorized his plate following him down Sunset to Shirley's. There were at least three hundred cars in the lot, but I located his easily enough, in one of the middle rows on the side of the building near Carson Avenue.

I inspected his car with a mini flashlight attached to my key ring. The tires in the rear were low, but overall all four were in pretty good shape. I didn't see any unusual dirt or mud caked in the grooves. Although I could tell where it had been dented in the rear and repaired, the body was polished and well cared for. I turned off my light. There was no flashing red inside so I figured there was no alarm system. I tested all the doors. Locked. I looked around. No one, but the voice of Betty Everett drifting from a radio far away. I took off my shoe and smashed the wind wing, poked out the remaining bits of glass, and opened the passenger door.

The glove compartment was filthy and jumbled with remnants of dirty pink rags and an old play card from Hollywood Park. Ernie Little Horse might be a wizard mechanic, but he was a messy housekeeper. Shoved near the back were two fundamentalist pamphlets with a scourged and anorexic-looking Christ on

184

the front and an address for a church in Reseda on the back.

Shirley had been killed between midnight and two a.m. Why she'd been taken out to the mission I didn't know, but from her apartment to the closest ramp of the Hollywood Boulevard was a slow, cool fifteen-minute drive through the Rampart Division, busiest car theft area in the city. Ernie would have driven slowly and carefully with one taillight out.

There was a wad of pizza coupons and newspapers, including two copies of yesterday's *Times* with an article about Shirley Yellowbird on the first page of the Metro section, on the floor of the passenger side. Shirley could have been knocked unconscious at the top of the stairs, but how had she fallen without any bruising to her face? I shone the flashlight over the backseat. No blood or stains. Certainly he would have put her in the trunk.

A car door slammed nearby and I heard a man and woman get out laughing. I wondered where Tony and Lupe were.

Ernie kept his registration in a brown vinyl envelope attached to the back of the visor on the driver side. Very unwise. Anyone can steal your car that way. I copied Ernie's address. He lived on Beaudry between downtown and Shirley's apartment in Silverlake. Using one of the smelly rags, I wiped off the things I'd touched.

I was about to get out of the car when I noticed a square slip of paper wedged between the driver seat and console. I pulled it out. It was a receipt for food from a place called Guyamas on the corner of Sunset and Broadway, not far from the CCB and not far from the entrances to the Hollywood and 10 freeways out to the mission. I'd parked across the street from it. I'd eaten lunch there a million times. The food was good and cheap. A long block from the southern border of Chinatown, it was one of the few places in that area that stayed open until after two on the weekends. The last time I'd been there a portion of the plate glass window that fronted Sunset had been boarded up. A drunk driver had gone over the curb and taken out a booth near the front door.

The receipt, which was date-and-time stamped, showed that two people had eaten three tacos, a small guacamole, a beef and bean burrito, a beef enchilada (extra sour cream), and two orange sodas at twelve thirty-seven a.m. the morning Shirley was killed.

Women don't usually drink orange sodas. Women drink Diet Cokes. They drink iced tea.

How well did Ernie and Dwayne know each other, I wondered? Perhaps they'd gone together to Shirley's. Dwayne waited in the car while Ernie went to the door. Dwayne stood out of sight at the front door and then stepped into view at the critical instant Ernie wanted Shirley to come outside with him. That was why Angela hadn't heard anything when Shirley left the apartment. Or perhaps once Ernie killed Shirley he panicked and called Dwayne or drove by some bar where Dwayne hung out and picked him up there without telling him why or what he needed him for. This made more sense to me than the conjuring of mystic fabrics that Charley Lomas and Tony Red Wolf were trying to do. Perhaps Ernie and Dwayne met at the restaurant. I imagined them laughing as they studied the menu. Ernie, growing quiet, poking at the salsa with his fork, tossing the fork down, telling Dwayne what he'd done. A big grin spreading across Dwayne's face.

Clutching the receipt, I climbed out of the car feeling nauseous. I headed back towards the door by which I'd seen Tony and Lupe leave the gym. A match flickered nearby, and I heard two men's voices behind one of the cars. I dropped to my knees beside the car closest to me.

"I heard she was butchered like an animal," said one of the men.

The other man mumbled an assent. I crept closer. "They say Tony Red Wolf killed her. You know him?"

"No. Who are his people? Who is his grandfather?"

"They say he's part Choctaw," said the second.

"The old bone pickers."

I saw the first man nod. "Those Choctaws have the strangest damn death rituals of anybody."

"They say he's a skinnywalker."

The first man grunted and puffed on his cigarette.

"They say he can change into a bird. Or a dog. He can walk through walls."

"They got him in a jail downtown," argued the first man. "Gotta feel sorry for any Indian in a white man's jail."

The two men nodded.

"I knew Shirley," the first man said after a moment. "She wasn't as bad as they say. Wild, but not really bad at heart. She used to go to one of my cousins' house sometimes. I met her there. My cousin's wife is church people. She said Shirley had a beautiful voice and knew a lot of songs. Sang "Amazing Grace" in Choctaw. She said Shirley had stopped drinking and was thinking about marrying a Nez Perce guy who came here from Green Bay, but he got killed about a year ago. Wandered out onto the tracks at a train crossing in San Fernando. She started drinking again."

The two men fell into companionable silence. I'd always wondered how people got killed at train crossings. It's not like you can't see a train coming. So Shirley had been with a guy who was drunk or crazy and killed himself dancing with a train. I wondered if that's when she'd turned to crack.

After what seemed like a long time the two men went back towards the gymnasium. I stood up, my knees hurting from kneeling on the ground. As I headed up the row of cars the wind began to blow from the north. A cold, sharp blast. There are only two seasons here. Hot and wet. It was not scheduled to get cold for another two months. I shielded my eyes. The cold licked at my face and stung my eyes. Sand scraped my cheeks and scratched my hands. I was at least five miles from the ocean.

The sand swirled around me so I could barely see the cars in front of me. A sound like thunder giants scraping sandpaper together cracked the sky. I looked up. A thick bank of clouds, normally glossy white from the reflected lights of the city, were black and threatening. It was unusual for the weather to change this quickly. My teeth began to chatter in the cold. I bumped into a car.

A round disc rolled towards me and smashed into my ankle. It was the hub cap from an old American car. I picked it up where it spiraled to a stop. When I turned it over it was full of water, crystal clear, my face reflected and softly illuminated as though in a dressing table mirror in a room lit by candles.

"Whitney." I heard Lupe call my name.

I saw my face dissolve in the water, replaced by the Milky Way and a silver knife with a white handle floating across the stars. It looked like a painting on velvet from TJ. Drops of blood dripped down the handle of the knife. Acid flashback. Except I'd only taken acid once, nearly six years ago.

I dropped the hub cap. It clattered dryly to the ground. Shielding my eyes against the flying sand I saw two figures coming towards me.

"Lupe!" I waved at her with my hand over my head, feeling a bit panicked.

"This is some motherfucking storm," said Tony, closing the distance between us.

"Make it stop," I screamed at him.

"You must have been watching a lot of strange movies," he said. "What do you mean, make it stop?"

"I heard two men say you're a skinnywalker."

"What are you talking about?" Lupe demanded.

"He's the devil."

"Oh, Jesus Christ, Whitney," snapped Lupe. "Get a grip on yourself. We're next to a construction project, in case you haven't noticed. There's enough sand over there on the other side of the fence to remake all the 'Road' movies."

"I'm sure before the night is over people are going to be saying I started the Chicago fire, taught Sirhan Sirhan to shoot, and introduced the Ebola virus to this country." Tony folded his arms across his chest.

"You been acting weird since that old lady gave you that tea this afternoon," Lupe complained.

"What old lady?" Tony asked.

I shook my head. "Clifton's cafeteria. Downtown. We like to go there sometimes. Painted waterfalls on the walls. The lemon meringue pie. We like that. Lots of old ladies work there."

Lupe stepped back. "Yeah. We got the hot turkey sandwiches." She jammed her hands into the back pockets of her jeans and stared at me, then at Tony, with an intentionally blank look on her face. "With extra stuffing and gravy."

"Let's go back towards the buildings. It won't be as windy," said Tony. "Wish we could hear the Forty-niners. They sing them after the powwow. 'I had a girl, her name was . . .' "

I told them I wanted them to go back to my office and to wait for me while I checked in the gym to see that Ferguson and Erhndt were still there. "If they see me, they'll think I'm still waiting for Tony."

"That's sweet," Lupe said. "This is taking on all the dimensions of Romeo and Juliet."

I asked Lupe to ride with Tony so I could take her car to pick up my Chevy.

"Drive my car? You have lost your mind. I don't let anyone drive my car."

189

"You know I'm a good driver. I've got insurance. Do you?"

She didn't answer. I wondered if she was calculating whether it would be worth any money to her if I had an accident. Finally she handed me the keys and told me to be careful when I shifted into third and reverse.

As soon as they were gone I started Lupe's car, got on the 405 north, and headed for Guyamas.

The restaurant was almost half full when I got there, but none of the waitresses I recognized from the day shift were working. Two middle-aged Mexican women in black skirts and white blouses lounged by the cash register; a third, dyed blonde, hovered by the big jukebox that played CDs. She looked annoyed, as though she'd heard enough of Los Panchos for one night. The daytime waitresses spoke English, but I wasn't sure about the night waitresses. There were no Anglos in the place. English seemed a redundancy.

"Hi. *Buenas noches.* Can you tell me which one of you served these people last night?" I showed the two at the register the receipt. The pudgy one took the paper from me and squinted at it like it was something unfamiliar.

"Why do you want to know?" she asked.

"I found this in my boyfriend's car. I want to know if he's seeing someone else."

She handed the receipt to her companion, who looked at it once and handed it back to me. "I don't think he got the money to see no one else."

"American Indian guy. Kinda fat. Long hair. Maybe wearing a t-shirt and cowboy boots."

"Yeah, yeah. Is the same guy. He comes here a lot. Always wants extra sour cream on everything." She smirked at me like I was a chubby chaser. "Leaves thirty-five-cent tip when he comes alone. Eats two baskets of chips. Sometimes three."

I was beginning to feel embarrassed I knew Ernie Little

Horse. "You ever hear anybody call him Ernie?"

She shook her head. "He was with a woman."

"Not a guy?"

The two women looked at each other. "You think is better if he goes with a guy?"

"What did the woman look like?"

"You gonna hurt her?"

I shook my head.

She described Shirley Yellowbird.

"They were having an argument?" I asked.

"Like people been drinking."

"Did the woman look hurt? Like she'd fallen down or been hit?"

They exchanged another look between themselves. "No. But she didn't like what he was saying. She got up and left him. Took his car keys."

"Drove away," added the other with a laugh. "And left him with the check."

"Yeah, he sit here almost another hour eating chips, trying to decide whether to get a bus or cab. Finally took the bus."

I took a foil-wrapped peppermint from a jar next to the register, dropped a quarter on the counter. I raced the Fiat back Sunset to the office. I drove up Shirley's street to the intersection closest to her apartment, turned right and then left. I parked in the dark. There were no streetlights. Not many of the houses had lights on. As I trudged up the hill I saw, between two houses on the opposite side of the street, a sidewalk. It was the stairway. I groped my way to the bottom of it using my flashlight. A pile of dried eucalyptus leaves littered the landing. I kicked them aside.

Blood.

I covered the spot with leaves again.

When I got to the office Tony and Lupe were sitting in the

dark watching the TV on Lupe's desk. I asked to change the channel and put on the news, but Lupe told me they'd already seen it. "The police are still looking for Tony." I wondered if that meant they'd recovered the knife or if it meant they had no other leads.

"Nothing about Dwayne?"

"One of the channels, but not the others," complained Tony. "The blankets, the traditional Indians, want to see me fry. I'm just following my own trail in my own land."

I told Lupe I wanted her to go home.

"What about Shirley's memorial? I want to go."

"The cops'll be there," Tony warned.

"Of course they'll be there. That's on TV every night," she snapped. "They get binoculars. Park far away. Well, I can get some binoculars, too. BFD."

There was a silence and Tony shrugged.

I told Lupe I'd meet her at eleven the next morning. Tony suggested a Bob's Big Boy half a mile from Ebell Park.

After Lupe left we continued to sit in the dark and I heard her clock ticking away. I got up from her desk and sat on Tony's lap. "I appreciate that you've tried to do things my way, but, if we can't find Dwayne tomorrow you have to turn yourself in. I've got the two feather earrings. Dwayne's alibi's not going to hold. I'll make a statement to the police about how I found them."

"How could you be my lawyer then?"

I touched his hair. "Guess I couldn't, if I was a witness."

He shook his head.

"I think I'm falling in love with you."

He dropped his arms from me. "You gotta be kidding."

"I don't think so."

"Why? You've seen what kind of guy I am."

It occurred to me that the reason I let Bill Peters slip away was that he was a nice guy. The reason I never returned the phone calls of any of the sheriffs who'd tried to ask me out, besides the fact they were probably pig Republicans, was that they looked like nice guys. It occurred to me that I didn't like nice guys.

I put Tony's arms back around me.

"Sometimes women went into battle to follow their lovers. In some tribes women were eligible for war honors." He pressed my head to his chest. "The greatest honor is to die in battle."

I tried to kiss him, but he turned his face away. "I can get you another lawyer. The best. Harvey Kaplan."

"Never heard of him." He moved me off his lap and stood up. "You can't go home. Go to a motel. Get some sleep."

"I'll stay in my office. You can sleep here."

Tony didn't answer. He went to the window overlooking Hollywood Boulevard and stood silently a moment, surveying the street before wrestling the window open. A Santa Ana blew in, scattering the neat stacks of papers on Lupe's desk and carrying the incipient promise of fire.

CHAPTER 16

The sun scratched through the window. I had fallen asleep in a chair for nearly two hours. It was a few minutes after six. Tony was already awake, watching TV. A black and white cowboy and Indian movie was on.

"I want to go home for a while," he said.

"The rez?" I was stiff from the chair.

"Hollywood. I need to change clothes for Shirley's memorial. Shower. Shave. I wouldn't want anyone coming to my funeral as funky as I am. I don't even want a funeral. When I die, bury me high. Above the ground."

"Don't go." I reached for him.

He touched my hair. "I been thinking about it all night. I have to do the right thing. Fuck the cops. If they arrest me, they arrest me."

"Tell me what you want. I'll go get it. Bring it back here." I wanted to see the inside of his apartment.

"Gotta go, baby." He told me he'd meet me and Lupe at eleven thirty at the restaurant. "We don't have any words for 'I love you.' We say 'I like your face.' " He kissed me. "I like your face, Whitney." The door closed and the room felt empty.

I glanced down at my own grubby jeans and t-shirt. I washed my face off in the hall bathroom and put on my brown suit I'd left in the office. I looked at the TV again. The cowboys were getting ready to ride on the Indians encamped by a river. A lot of the Indians did look Armenian. The Indians slept contentedly, as though they couldn't foresee the impending attack and their slaughter by the cowboys. I turned it off. I wondered where Dwayne had gone when he left Shirley at her apartment. I had to see Angela again. Like a raid undertaken for personal revenge. There was something she hadn't told me. I was starting to understand dominance over one's rivals was as much about spiritual and emotional reasons as material gain.

The apartment building was dull and flat-looking in the un-tempered gray morning. Angela answered the door looking hungover.

"Ernie didn't kill Shirley," I announced before she could slam the door in my face.

She couldn't decide if this was good news or not. "It was Tony," she shrieked. "I knew it."

"Look, I'm not going to lie to you this time. I'm Tony's lawyer, but if there's real evidence against him, I want to know it." I told her what I'd learned about Ernie at the Mexican restaurant with Shirley.

She let me into the apartment and led me into the kitchen where she was making coffee. She poured me some in a bright orange mug and added sugar without asking if I wanted it. "Dwayne killed Shirley. I think he came back for her after their fight," I said. "Or she went looking for him after she left Ernie."

"I wasn't here when Shirley got home."

I shook my head. "Tony saw you. With a guy. It wasn't Ernie."

"No, it wasn't Ernie." She grinned like she was glad the secret was out. "It was a guy with a real job. A guy who treats me like a lady."

"Cool." I dumped some more sugar into the coffee, but it still tasted like runoff from a dirty roof. "And that's why Ernie was so pissed off when he was trying to break in to see you, wasn't it? That's why Shirley took him to the restaurant, to try to chill him out. I think Shirley got home with Dwayne, something happened between them, and he left. That's why Tony didn't see his car out front. They got here after you'd come home and seen Tony in front of your building. Later, Ernie showed up. Pretty close, isn't it?"

She nodded nervously, putting her coffee down. "Shirley and Dwayne had a fight. They didn't know I was here. Usually I keep my door closed when Shirley has company, but when I came in that night I didn't turn on any of the lights, just went into my room. I must have fallen asleep listening to a CD. I woke up when I heard them in the living room. They were on the couch. I heard Dwayne's boots drop to the floor. After a bit, I heard Shirley say, real angry, 'Again? If your dick don't work, it don't work. And it's not my fault.' She'd told me there was something wrong with his dick. That she had to give him head forever to try to get him hard. It made her feel bad, like there was something wrong with her."

I nodded like this was something I knew from personal experience. "Did he leave?"

"Not right away. She was talking ugly to him." Angela giggled. "She said 'You got a fucking problem, deal with it. Go to a doctor if you think that's what's wrong with it. I'm not holding that thing in my mouth anymore. It feels like a dead mouse.' Then it sounded like they were wrestling. Maybe he was getting dressed to leave and she didn't want him to. I think she must have grabbed his wallet, because she started yelling 'What's this? What is it?' You're not going to let him know I told you this, are you?"

I shook my head. "What was it?"

"Business card. Then Shirley says 'A massage parlor, you go to a massage parlor?' He said 'Yeah, I got a girl there, a good girl. This never happens with her.' Shirley started laughing. It sounded like he hit her or pushed her. Shirley was yelling 'What's her name?' Finally Dwayne said her name was Mary."

I asked if she knew the name of the massage parlor.

She nodded. "After he left Shirley was plenty pissed off. Told me all about it. A-One Oriental Massage on Pico. Near Hauser."

I wondered. Pico near Hauser is predominantly black.

"What happened when Dwayne left?"

"Got worse before it was over. Dwayne telling her how no good she was. Fat, ugly, stupid, you name it. He said, like it was the worst thing he could think of, 'You like to be on top.' "

Ballbuster.

"Shirley was laughing like crazy. She told Dwayne she wasn't so stupid. Said she'd taken a hundred bucks from his wallet a couple of weeks ago and another hundred this week."

"He was dealing?"

"Shirley never said so. But he usually had money."

"She didn't want you to know she used crack."

"She did?" Angela sounded genuinely surprised.

I nodded.

Angela fell silent for a few seconds. I asked her what else had happened before Dwayne left. "She told him that's all he was good for, money, and it was the only reason Mary would go down on him. 'Stupid bitch probably only gets thirty-five bucks.' "

"Did Dwayne say he knew Shirley was stealing from him?"

"Yeah. He said he ought to kick her ass. Then the last thing she said was that she was going to go tell Mary Dwayne had AIDS and that he took it up the ass. That's when he said he'd fuck her up for good."

I pushed the horrible coffee aside. "Shirley was sad when Dwayne split."

Angela looked at me like I was smarter than she'd thought. "She cried."

"That's why she went looking for him later that night," I said, more to myself than to her.

197

"I don't make very good coffee," Angela said, trying to offer me more. "Shirley always made it." She said she didn't feel well enough to go to the memorial service and asked if I was. I told her I was.

I got to Bob's Big Boy half an hour before I was supposed to meet Lupe. I ordered a cup of coffee that was only marginally better than Angela's. I got an address for the massage parlor before Lupe came in, wearing a low-cut black dress with a tiny jacket over it that did little to hide her chest. She carried a black lace mantilla.

"You're not going to wear that, are you?" I pointed at the mantilla. "Rather gothic for an outdoor event. Besides, you agreed that you weren't going. You're going to wait nearby."

"Sorry about that little prevarication, Counselor. Murderers always go to the funeral. I'm not missing this."

"But Tony—"

"Fuck Tony."

I might have blushed.

"You didn't."

I didn't say anything. I finished the coffee. I had enough caffeine in me to take on an army. I could feel my veins pumping against my skin.

"Don't they have rules against that? Having sex with your clients. He's so dirty."

"That's racist."

Lupe grabbed my arm. "Don't ever talk to me like that again."

"Sorry, guess I'm feeling a little on edge." I told her what I'd learned from Angela. "Ever heard of this massage parlor?"

"There's probably a couple thousand of those places in LA."

I wondered why she'd never worked off the streets in a place like that, but didn't ask.

"I know you don't like Tony," I said. "But he didn't kill her . . ."

"I been thinking about it. Last night when I had to ride on the bike with him, I was ticked off, but it was okay. You know I get a feeling about people, fine-tuned in my former line of work, and I didn't get any bad vibe off him. He's a weirdo, drinks too much like some people do . . ." Her voice trailed off and she looked at me critically, but I didn't rise to the bait. "And he's no good for you, but he's no killer."

"Thank you."

"You want to throw your life away on a loser, you want to be disbarred for playing squishy poke poke games, that's your business."

"Nothing's going to happen. Here's what we're going to do—"

"What do you mean 'we,' white girl?"

"Tony's going to be arrested at the service." I wondered if he was really going to come back. It was nearly noon. "I'll testify if I have to, but I think when the cops hear Angela's story they'll arrest Dwayne. Shirley went looking for him after the scene at her place. And I'll bet she found him at the massage parlor. Then there was some kind of fight or problem there. The owner of the massage parlor breathed a sigh of relief when they saw Tony had been arrested, meant cops wouldn't come around asking any questions or threatening to shut them down."

Lupe nodded. "But why did Shirley end up at the mission?"

"I haven't figured that out yet, but I think all the mumbo jumbo spiritual spooky stuff people have been trying to throw at me, because they're Indians, is a load of crap." I didn't say anything about Charley Lomas or the two visions I'd had, but that's what I meant. I started to explain to her what we should do at the memorial service when there was a buzzing in the coffee shop, and then a strange silence.

Tony strode towards us in buckskins, a two-row bone choker, medallions, and a thin strand of Venetian glass beads that bumped against his chest. He had shaved his head so only a scalp lock that he had braided and decorated with feathers and other ornaments flowed down his back.

"Holy cow," Lupe muttered. "Wish I'd brought my camera."

"Didn't think you were going to make it," I said to Tony.

"How about, 'You look great'?"

"Yeah, that too," I mumbled. He did look handsome.

We got in my car. I decided to wait until we were alone to tell him what I'd found out about Dwayne. The memorial service was at a small triangular-shaped park on Plymouth at the edge of Hancock Park. It was two blocks south of the Ebell Theatre, an auditorium and garden built on Wilshire in the early twenties as part of the Spanish Colonial revival. Bungalows had stretched west to Hauser and the beginning of the "Miracle Mile." Not many people remembered that Wilshire Boulevard was named for an oil millionaire who was also a Marxist.

I parked the car. Lupe and I got out, arranging our dresses and checking our hair. Tony sat in the backseat with a glazed look on his face.

"Coming?"

He shook his head. "I need to pray, center myself. I know everybody's going to be looking at me."

"Okay, take care of yourself." I turned away feeling anxious.

"I'll be there in a few minutes."

About eighty people, the majority Indians and nearly all in regular clothes, milled around the west end of the park. I wondered if they were Shirley's friends or just curiosity seekers. I recognized Shirley's mother and brother, who stood by themselves looking uncomfortable. Two long folding tables had been set up. Women laid out containers of food wrapped in tin foil. There were several arrangements of flowers, mostly red and white carnations, which seemed sad and cheap to me, placed near three black folding chairs. Four drummers in a circle played a slow beat. No chairs were set up for the mourners, and they mingled quietly waiting for something to happen. I saw a light green sedan parked on the north side of the park. Lupe nudged me. It was Erhndt and Ferguson in plain clothes.

We joined the mourners. Dwayne stood with some men I hadn't seen before near the front of the crowd. About thirty feet from him, the woman I'd seen him in bed with stood watching him with a frown on her face. She was with a couple of Indian women, but didn't seem to be paying a lot of attention to what they were saying.

"Watch the cops. I'm going to talk to Dwayne." I pointed him out to Lupe.

"Babe-o-rama," Lupe said in surprise.

I started to make my way through the crowd. Dwayne scowled when he saw me coming. "Nice to see you up and about. Thought you might have skipped back to Arizona," I said. I turned to the two men he was talking to, but he didn't introduce me and they stared back at me without saying anything. I turned and nodded at Dwayne's lady friend. The two men glanced back to see who I was looking at. She leaned more attentively towards the women she was standing with. "Didn't realize so many people knew Shirley."

"Excuse me, fellas." Dwayne started to walk away, but I fell into step with him.

"I'm feeling the urge to create a big scene here," I said. "Must be the drums. I'm starting to feel wild and crazy. Guess these people don't know you're banging Tall Bear's widow. Aren't you supposed to be grieving for Shirley?"

"People knew Shirley and I were just friends."

"Then why such a secret about your old lady over there?"

He stopped to shake hands with a guy who said his name.

"Let's go say hi to Mrs. Tall Bear. There's something I have to tell her." I took his arm.

He mumbled some thanks to the guy who'd been offering condolences and moved away quickly. He pulled his arm away from me. "I don't have to talk to you."

"You could talk to the police. Does Mrs. Tall Bear know she was fronting you money for crack?"

"I got witnesses who can say where I was the night Shirley was killed."

"Like Mary?"

He stopped. "I don't know anyone named Mary."

"Everyone knows someone named Mary. Your Mary's a working girl. See that green sedan over there. LAPD detectives." Erhndt and Ferguson were gone from the car. I wondered where Lupe was. "Won't be hard to find them. Dorky-looking white guy and a black dude. It's going to be a little embarrassing for me to tell them you killed Shirley because your dick doesn't work."

"That's a lie!"

Charley Lomas, in a black suit and black penny loafers, stepped to a microphone near the flowers and tapped on it for the crowd's attention. An old-looking necklace with two silver discs hung around his skinny neck. I glanced around for Tony, but he wasn't to be seen.

"Shirley Yellowbird," began Charley Lomas, "was a daughter to me. A sister to us all." There was a moment of silence before a few polite murmurs of assent were heard from the crowd. "Life was hard for her. The bad spirits live here."

Lupe sidled up to me. "You know I can't look at him now without thinking of Wallace Beery. The whole drag bit, but Beery did go on to some macho roles. *Last of the Mohicans*."

Charley Lomas droned on about Shirley for a long time without ever mentioning the crack, the drinking, the bad men. Restlessly I looked the crowd over. Erhndt and Ferguson, who was wearing Armani designer sunglasses, were at the back. Ferguson caught my glance and nodded. I turned away. Where was Tony? I decided I didn't want to tell the police about Dwayne until I could get Tony safely away from the service. "Wakanda, take your daughter. We could not help her here. The old men are all dead. And now she has gone where people go at last."

When Charley Lomas began to pray I heaved a sigh of relief. The drummers beat the drums. The ceremony came to a halt as suddenly as it had begun. The smell of coffee filled the air and the crowd began to move towards the food. A young man offered Charley Lomas a plate of food, but he shook his head and began to walk with a sad, lonely look on his face towards the far end of the park where there was a cluster of eucalyptus trees.

"I think the food's going to last a while," I told Lupe as we watched Dwayne get into the line. The Tall Bear woman drinking a cup of coffee looked edgy. Tony still hadn't joined the memorial service.

"Yeah, let's get some."

"We're going to the massage parlor. Talk to Mary."

Lupe rolled her eyes. "What! Now I'm supposed to interpret?"

A-1 Oriental Health and Massage Center ("Open 24 hours. We take Visa, MasterCard and Diners Club") was a stucco bungalow with its windows coated gray and covered with bars. It was about two and a half miles from the park and two blocks from Roscoe's Chicken and Waffles, which Lupe pointed out, complaining she was hungry. I told her to look in the glove compartment for a chocolate bar. Habit I learned from my father. He got in a car and never stopped. Lupe pulled out an old Hershey bar, no almonds, and looked disappointed, but she ate it anyway. "What's wrong with you? You can afford the European kind. I like the kind with cappuccino filling. Or pistachio."

There were no cars in the small parking lot. "Probably a back lot, too," Lupe said licking her fingers unhappily. She followed

me to the black metal screen door that had enough bars on it
for the main gate of a state prison. I rang the bell. A buzzer
sounded. I pushed the door open. Inside the room was lit with
red lights and perfumed with sandalwood incense. A black
woman and a Vietnamese woman sat at an empty desk looking
as though they were about to nod off.

"I want to see Mary."

The black woman scowled at me through her fog, but the
Vietnamese woman sat up attentively. "You two want to see one
girl? We got two girls. Is better."

"I just want to talk to Mary. I'll pay for her time."

"Cops?" The Vietnamese woman stubbed out her cigarette,
which had burned down to the filter.

"No, I'm trying to solve a problem before I have to call them.
It's about a guy who was here last night—"

"Five minutes. Forty bucks. Cash," Lupe interrupted. "She'll
pay you."

The Vietnamese woman put out her hand. "Mary, the black
chick? Or the Virgin Mary?"

"The Virgin Mary?"

"Yeah," said the black woman. "She's a white girl, blonde.
Looks sorta like you."

"Which was the good-looking Indian guy here to see last
night?" Lupe asked.

"Around one in the morning," I added.

"I know, I know," said the Vietnamese woman. "He's been
here before. The Virgin Mary."

"Let me see her." I dropped the money on the table. The
Vietnamese woman scooped it up and dropped it in a metal
box.

"She's not here," the black woman drawled.

"We'll wait." I was in a hurry to get back to the memorial
service, but I wasn't going to let them fuck with me. I sat down

in a red plastic chair that sagged in the middle. The incense was starting to make my head pound and I felt more anxious and crabby by the second.

"Won't be back 'til ten tonight."

"Where's she live?"

They both shook their heads. "Don't even go there, girl," the black woman snapped. "She left here last night right at midnight. When the Indian got here about an hour later, he was mad. And drunk."

"Did he call to book her?" Lupe took one of the business cards from the desk.

They shook their heads again. "I think he thinks she likes him." The Vietnamese woman giggled in agreement, adding, "He brought her a rose one time."

"Sucker," Lupe whispered.

"He left madder than when he got here. Drove off drunk, tires making a lot of noise." The Vietnamese woman clasped her hands together briskly on the desk as though signaling she was through with us. Dwayne had met up with Shirley then. Flipped on her without intending to kill her. He mutilated her to cover up what he'd done.

"Something else happened last night," I insisted.

"Mmmm huh," the black woman said. "But that's a different story. That's a hundred-dollar story."

"Okay, that's it," I shouted. "I'm calling the cops. I got a car phone. I'll sit outside 'til they get here."

"Maybe it's more like a fifty-dollar story," Lupe said soothingly.

The black woman nodded her head, tapping her long, curved, sparkly baby blue nails dreamily on the desk.

"Fuck no," I glared at Lupe. "A woman came here looking for the Indian. An Indian woman. Drunk, too. Later, you saw her on the news. Murdered."

The two women exchanged a surprised look.

"You ought to give her the forty bucks back," said Lupe.

"Forget it. It's yours." I peeled myself off the sticky chair and went out leaving the door open. "I like to see my sisters sticking together."

"Give me your beeper," I told Lupe when I got near the park. "A is one, B is two . . ."

I heard an owl hoot.

"That's Tony!" I shoved the beeper in my purse as I slowed to a stop. "Find the Virgin Mary. I need to hear from you as soon as possible. Take a cab back to the office." I took out a folded hundred-dollar bill I kept hidden in my wallet for emergencies and handed it to her.

Lupe shook her head as she climbed out of the Chevy.

I found Tony three houses down the block at the end of an empty driveway, sitting on the stair of a side door that was nearly obscured with bougainvillea.

CHAPTER 17

The mourners began to straggle from Ebell Park. I motioned Tony to get in the car. Holding a flicker feather roach that had come loose from his braided scalp lock, he got up slowly. He looked tired, although his eyes glittered when he saw me.

"Where have you been?" I demanded.

"I tried to go to the service, but I couldn't get myself to cross the street. Then I saw you leave. I didn't think you'd come back. Glad you recognized the owl hoot. Lots of people think owls are bad luck. That they mean death."

"You know I wouldn't leave you." I wondered if this fear of abandonment went back to the time he was kidnapped from his parents and taken to the Indian boarding school. I reached to touch his hair, but he shook his head.

"It's wrong to touch a scalp lock. If you were another warrior, I'd have to kill you for it," he grinned. "Some people say scalp taking evolved from headhunting, but it just represents a warrior's spirit. The Sioux used to do scalp raids against an enemy to replace the lost spirit of a member who'd recently been killed. I shaved my head in honor of the dead woman."

I backed the car slowly down the driveway.

"Where's Lupe?"

"She went home," I lied. I didn't want him to know I was still checking his story. Love had not come easily to me in my life. I parked so we could see the departing mourners. Ferguson and Erhndt were standing near the folding tables and holding paper plates of food, trying to blend in more. "Go talk to Charley Lomas," I pleaded. "Put your mind at rest. Ask him who killed Shirley. He's at the service."

Tony shook his head. "I'm not purified. I don't feel right in my skin. That's why I couldn't go over there."

"You don't have to be afraid anymore. I can prove it was Dwayne." I explained it all to him. Dwayne's impotence. The argument. The massage parlor.

"The Virgin Mary. Don't that beat all," Tony laughed. "Talking shit about me. When it was his problem."

We saw Dwayne cross the street alone. I started the Chevy. "I have enough evidence to make a citizen's arrest."

"Whoa, girl. You can't do that. You think this is the Wild West?"

"What are you going to do? Hide in the car again?" I was torn and running out of choices. Tony was still a suspect and I was still an officer of the court. I didn't want to have to take him to the police. That was something he had to initiate. He'd be in custody a long time before a trial could begin, unless the police turned their attention to Dwayne.

Tony looked away from me.

"Sorry, I just don't want you to get arrested. You're not safe 'til Dwayne's out of the way. Behind bars."

Dwayne got into his car. I eased the Chevy away from the curb and followed him to Olympic, then to La Brea. He didn't seem to know I was there. Thinking he was going east on the Santa Monica freeway back to Vernon, I jumped over a lane so I'd be able to cut him off when he wanted to make a left turn.

Instead he turned west.

I slid over two lanes, turning in front of two cars that had to slam on their brakes. Dwayne looked in his rearview mirror when he heard the commotion. He turned and glared over his shoulder at me. He sped up the ramp without stopping for the metered light. A two-hundred-dollar fine. I tore after him without stopping, either.

"He's going to drop dead when I tell him I know Shirley showed up looking for a fight at the massage parlor while he was there. Busted!"

Tony put his hand on my thigh.

Dwayne swerved to the fast lane. I stuck to him. "Where's he going?"

"Not Hollywood, that's for sure. This was the original Route 66. Bet Dwayne thinks it's 666. Probably going to some devil worship place."

"There are devil worship places on the Westside?"

"Particularly there. Kinky white folks."

We passed Fairfax, then Robertson, where I'd gone to a Sikh chiropractor when I hurt my knee falling off a bench at Gold's while doing a step-up lunge with sixty pounds on my shoulders. Dwayne was doing eighty as he headed towards National and I was less than fifty feet behind him. "You think I'm kinky?"

"Do you want to be?"

"A bit."

"Can't be a bit thing. You either are or aren't."

Turning the wheel suddenly, Dwayne rabbited across two lines of traffic towards the slow lane.

"Shit." Tony pulled his hand from my thigh.

"Don't do that. I like it." I put his hand back where it had been and turned the Chevy almost ninety degrees so we flew across honking traffic until we were behind Dwayne again.

He pulled towards the slow lane to get off the freeway.

I gunned it, following him towards the lane. I almost cut off a black Ford with tinted windows, but it hit the gas and sped forward, passing Dwayne, then dropping into his lane barely a car length in front of him. I was parallel to Dwayne, who looked scared. Jerkily, he swerved to the right as he hit the brakes. He went up onto a long, narrow concrete barrier that was about seven inches high. His car soared into the air as I flew past him. The last thing I saw, in the rearview mirror, was Dwayne's car as though suspended, arching in a sickening half circle to the right as it hit the zenith of its flight before starting to fall.

Charley Lomas said Dwayne would be killed in his car. Charley Lomas said things and they came to pass. Everything he had told me was true. About my father. The vision he'd given me of the stairs. The woman in Cambodia.

I tried to remember how to pray, but I could only negotiate. I told God I'd do anything he wanted. I'd quit drinking, I'd go back to Maryland. I stopped. I couldn't promise that.

We heard a crash behind us and the sound of a car rolling. Then an explosion.

Tony had killed Shirley Yellowbird.

"Don't say his name," Tony said in a flat voice. "We don't say the names of the dead."

I nodded.

"Where's that goddamn bottle?" Tony said. "We can't get pulled over with an open bottle in the car. Did you put it in your bag?" He reached for my purse. I didn't want him to know about my gun.

"No. It's here, under the seat." Hastily I pulled the bottle partially out and showed him. I didn't know where to go. I was afraid of Tony. I hadn't seen the license plate on the Ford and I hadn't seen its occupants. I wasn't sure what model of car or year it was. Could I get Angela or the women at the massage parlor to talk to the police if Dwayne was dead? Could I prove Tony was innocent if I knew he wasn't?

"Let's go to Malibu," Tony said, settling back against the seat.

"You think this is a good time for the beach?"

"The mountains."

"A picnic? You want to pick up something to eat?" If we could stop I could use a phone. I would get my head out of my ass. I would call the police. It would be Tony Red Wolf's word against mine.

He shook his head. "We can't eat now. Time for a ceremony. We have to get there before dark. Purification. Then I'll turn myself in."

"Promise?" Perhaps I was wrong about Tony.

He nodded and squeezed my leg.

The freeway ended at Pacific Coast Highway and I kept going. Although it was past four, it was still sunny and glorious. The sun crackled on the waves in Santa Monica and many happy people rode bicycles or skated in parking lots. Some played volleyball on the sand. I couldn't remember when I'd last done anything fun. I put a Cleanhead Vinson tape in the player. Cleanhead Vinson pleaded for the love of a good woman. I wanted to believe Tony was innocent.

Had I really killed Dwayne as Charley Lomas predicted? I ran the accident through my mind in slow motion from all possible angles.

I had.

We passed chaparral-covered hills out to Topanga Canyon. "Here?" The canyon was full of old hippies who called themselves names like Gentle Moonbeam and Sky Warrior. Tony pointed north with his lips.

We passed the Getty Museum, which houses classical art in a building modeled after an ancient Roman villa that was buried in an eruption of Mount Vesuvius. The beginning of the Malibu beachfront housing strip, of gray Cape Cod shacks in need of paint, but with Jaguars and red Ferraris parked next to their doors. An inviting-looking bar called Tonga Lei I'd always meant to visit. I felt more afraid the farther we went. We passed the Malibu pier, where a dozen or more rubber-clad surfers waited beyond the waves for the evening glass off. We passed the Malibu shopping center, which sold clothes made of hemp as well as organic papayas and eighty-dollar Italian aromatherapy candles. A castle with towers high on a mountain guarded the inland approaches to Malibu. I could wait until he got out of the car and then drive off. Tony had killed Shirley Yellowbird in a rage. I would do anything I had to, to keep him calm. PCH crested into a hill at the top of which was Pepperdine University on one side and on the other a Little League park, which had at its entrance a tepee made of exposed poles and a bunch of feathers flapping in the breeze on top. "Is that it?" I asked, to break the growing silence.

"Before the white man came the largest number of Indians lived here, California, along the coastal strip." He glanced towards the ocean. "We're going up near Trancas."

Finally Tony told me to turn into one of the canyons. He started to look calmer and more interested in the landscape. I pretended to relax. "This is good," he said, more to himself than to me. "Eucalyptus. Oak. We might see a hawk. That would be a good sign." He told me to keep driving towards the top of the mountain. The Chevy was having some trouble with the grade and it felt too big on the curves. I began to feel I was driving in a dream and the road stretched endlessly in front of me.

I thought of the gun. Of pushing it in Tony's face. "Can I have a drink?"

"If you have to, but it's not good for the ceremony." He turned from the trees and looked at me disapprovingly.

"Guess it can wait."

He grunted and nodded his head. The Santa Monica Mountains are full of rabbits, skunks, deer, rodents, rattlesnakes, dozens of species of birds. Brazen coyotes that carry off pet cats and small dogs. I kept driving until I reached Mulholland, at the top of the mountain. Stretched out below in the twilight to the east was the vast and densely populated San Fernando Valley, where lights were beginning to glow.

"All this used to be Chumash land. Before the white man and his stinking missions." He pointed back towards the ocean. "And that," he turned and pointed out into the valley, "was Fernandeno land. No one remembers the names of the original tribes. I don't. Who were they? The Quechan and Maricopa? And no one remembers where they came from." He saw a dirt road and told me to turn off and park past a gatehouse.

He got out of the car and surveyed his surroundings.

I started to take my purse with the gun in it.

"Let's go." Tony began to walk down the dirt road. "You don't need anything. You're free. Nothing here, only the footprints of coyotes."

"Makeup. Can't live without it." I shoved the bottle into my purse on top of the gun. "Isn't this private property?"

The road descended quickly towards a small wood and stone structure. "Is someone living here now?" Tony continued walking as though he hadn't heard me. Once past the building he left the road and headed into the dark brush. "Are there snakes up here?" I tripped in my heels, turning my ankle slightly, as I followed him into the brush and trees. I was pretty certain I didn't like camping and hoped the ceremony wouldn't take long. Or did he plan on killing me here?

I looked for the main house that should have been below the two buildings I'd already seen. There was a large space that had been leveled in preparation of construction, but it had been reclaimed by the fast-growing brush and some scrub oak.

"Where's the house?"

"Never built."

Had the owners run out of money? Or had they, like many in Los Angeles, moved restlessly on to fulfill some other dream?

"Place was called 'Eagle Feather.' "

I stopped. "I don't like this. Can't we go somewhere else?"

"Don't worry. We're alone. Nobody's going to bother us. Back in the twenties some of the big-name architects got into a kind of 'Native American Revival' period and were decorating everything with our art. 'Pre-Columbian' they called it."

He took my hand and he felt warm and solid. I was appalled at how nervous and edgy I felt. What he said made sense. I'd seen an apartment house built like a pueblo in Hermosa Beach when I'd gone there once to go body surfing. I squeezed Tony's hand and he squeezed back.

" 'Pre-Columbian' doesn't sound very politically correct."

"Christopher Columbus was a goddamned liar," Tony growled. "Like he brought civilization to a new world. My people, the Choctaws, had a civilization. City councils, poetry." He stopped and let go of my hand. He tied a red bandana on a tree. "Here we do the purification."

"Is this safe? I think it's illegal to have open fires here . . ."

He pulled a small medicine bundle made of tattered animal skin from the waist of his buckskins. It contained beads, stones, and dried herbs. A stone pipe was set aside. He took out a wand of sage braided with sweetgrass and bound with red twine. Matches appeared, and then he placed a tiny cream-colored leather pouch on the ground. He gathered leaves and branches together. He dropped a match on the pile of leaves and it burst into flame. Then he lit the sage and sweetgrass and washed his body with smoke. Tony called me forward into the circle and bathed me with the smoke. He scooped up some dirt and spit in it until he formed a paste. He smeared the dirt all over his face. He scooped up more dirt and made paste again which he painted across my nose and forehead.

Raising his hands above his head, Tony closed his eyes and began to chant. It seemed to echo in the surrounding woods. I wondered what he was saying, but kept quiet. Eventually the chanting stopped and the echoes faded away. Tony squatted to the earth, motioning me to do the same. He undid the leather pouch and dumped some animal teeth on the ground. Wolves' teeth?

He picked them up, rolled them in his hand, and threw them on the ground like dice. Tony studied the teeth for several moments without speaking. "Things are fine. The moon rises above the trees . . ."

And the sun sets in the west. My legs were starting to get crampy. I wondered what the Virgin Mary would be like. I'd threaten her with the police about her drug problem if she didn't want to cooperate. But how reliable would the jury consider the testimony of a crack addict? I was sure Harvey would help me after Tony was in jail. I pictured myself in a black suit entering the courtroom amidst the buzzing speculation of reporters. A surge of love for Tony ran through me. I glanced up from the teeth and looked at him in the light of the fire, his scalp lock flowing across his shoulders and onto his chest, his beautiful face hidden in the dark.

". . . the Navajo's death was an accident. No one could have predicted it."

I imagined Charley Lomas at his table, a magnifying mirror in front of him, applying a cheap pair of black false eyelashes to his wrinkled eyelid, and I felt unbearably lonely.

"You, Whitney, will learn to stand alone and face your fears. I will help you." He withdrew a silver knife with an ivory handle from his waist and laid it amongst the teeth.

The knife that had floated upon the stars in my vision.

"I will be found innocent with your help." He studied the teeth again before collecting them and putting them back into the pouch. "Did I ever tell you there was a chief called 'Lawyer'?" He stood and embraced me.

"Where'd you get the knife?" I pulled away from him.

"It was the Navajo's."

I looked into his black-painted face, but couldn't see anything except Charley Lomas's eyes and I knew everything Tony Red Wolf had told me was a lie.

"I took it from him during the fight yesterday."

There had been an instant as they rolled on the floor of the Tall Bear woman's living-room floor when Tony had been on top and I couldn't see what was happening. Tony put his arms around me again. I couldn't stop trembling. He kissed me and my lips opened.

Then we were on the ground in the light of the fire. Tony pulled my skirt up. The buckskins fell to his knees as he got on top of me. He was in me before I could speak and we rocked on the earth. I felt a confusion of burning wetness. Tony called my name and clutched me tighter. Then he lay quietly on me.

The beeper in my purse went off.

"What's that?" Tony pushed himself up.

"Nothing," I lied. "But I have to go pee." I peeled myself away from him, pulled down my skirt, and found my purse. "Got to check my makeup."

Tony grinned. "Don't get lost. It's dark out there." He rubbed my calf as I went by. "There might be snakes. Or ghosts."

I stumbled down the hill about a hundred yards to a clump of trees where I pawed through my purse for the beeper and flashlight. I took a drink. A garbled series of numbers shone on the beeper and I counted off the alphabet, scribbling on a note-pad. As soon as I cleared the first numbers, a second sequence appeared, then a third and fourth. "Saw Mary. D one am. Mtl. Free luv."

Mary had been with Dwayne. There was no doubt Tony had killed Shirley. If Mary and Dwayne had been in a motel, there had to be a record of it.

"Whitney!" Tony's voice sounded as though he was coming down the hill to find me.

"I'm on my way," I called back. I ripped up the notes and dug a shallow hole that I dropped them in and covered it with dirt and leaves. Then I stuffed the gun into my waistband.

Tony was sitting near the fire, bare-chested. I stopped in the darkness beyond the glow of the flames. "Charley Lomas told me you lied about Cambodia."

"You're making that up. He's my spiritual elder."

"I went to see him at his hotel."

"He said I wasn't in Cambodia?"

"He said you tortured and killed a peasant woman. You told me you tried to stop the other men from hurting her."

"He's lying. He's jealous. I have spiritual powers he doesn't."

"You tried to hit on him when he was dressed as a woman."

"Never."

"Put your hand up his dress and feel his dick?"

"I like women."

"You hate women. You killed Shirley."

"Don't say her name."

I felt come running down my leg. "Dwayne was in a motel with another girl. Ernie was at a Mexican restaurant when Shirley was killed."

"She has no name!"

"Like the Indians in the mission cemetery? That's why you killed her there. To make her a nobody."

Tony jumped up and gave a scalp yell. A necklace sparkled against his chest. The silver discs Charley Lomas wore at Shirley's memorial.

"You killed Charley Lomas, too." I pulled out the gun.

He reached towards me.

"You left the eagle feather because you wanted it to look like your god wanted Shirley dead. Don't come any closer. I'll shoot

217

you if I have to."

"Aren't you a brave girl? With your thunderbird?" Tony laughed. He stepped towards me.

I shot at him. The bullet went through his left shoulder.

Tony laughed again. There was no hole where I'd hit him and no blood. I pulled the trigger again. I saw the bullet hit him in the throat. No hole. No blood. He was a skinnywalker.

"Want to try for two points?" Tony leapt closer, opening his mouth.

I fired wildly. Tony caught the bullet in his teeth and spit it on the ground.

I darted forward with a branch that I lit from the fire. The stinky smell of crushed sumac exploded in the air. I hurled it at him.

He caught the burning branch in his hands and threw it up to the sky where it disappeared. A rain of eagle feathers fell upon me, sticking to my hair and face. I wiped the feathers from my mouth.

"You killed Shirley because she made you feel like you weren't a human being. You wanted to take all that was human from her."

"I fooled you. You thought I was a man." Tony dropped to his knees. He changed into a red wolf with flashing red eyes.

"My love was weak. And selfish. If you'd been a human being you would have known that." I fired again, but the wolf threw back its head and howled. It leapt at me. I jumped towards it, kicking out as hard as I could with my left leg, but I passed through the wolf's body as though it was a hologram. An icy blast of air knocked me down. I landed on my side, my shoulder and elbow scraping the ground near the fire and the ivory-handled knife. I grabbed the knife. When I looked up the wolf was gone and Tony was walking away.

Drums beat. I saw a group of Indians dancing among the

trees. The Ghost Dance. Tony approached the group to join them, but they turned away from him. He followed them at a respectful distance deeper into the woods. I kicked off my shoes and ran after him. He didn't seem to hear me come up behind him as he tried again to join the dancers.

"Grandfather, I have wanted to see you!" Tony shouted in a cry of mourning.

I thrust the knife as hard as I could up into his ribs. He glanced back at me almost gratefully for giving him a warrior's death. Then he turned into a king snake and vanished into the dust. The dancers danced for another minute before fading into silent darkness. I picked up the knife and plunged it into the ground to clean it.

Still clutching the knife, I stripped off my suit and tossed it along with my panties, my torn stockings, and my bra into the fire, where they blazed and crackled. I cut a small wedge out of my left thigh and threw it into the blaze and I thanked the Great Spirit. I sat next to the fire until it went out. I never realized so many stars were visible above Los Angeles. I imagined my parents in their separate bedrooms in the house that was too big for them. I saw Lupe laughing with Joey and her mother at a dining table covered with food. With the knife I scattered the remains of the fire.

I stepped out of the bushes onto the dirt road that glowed dully in the moonlight. I threw the knife away into the undergrowth without looking. I would call Lupe and tell her I was okay. I would get tested for all the STDs. I would have to wait six months to take an AIDS test. I pulled on a sweat suit and some tennis shoes from the gym bag in my trunk. I took a drink before starting the car. I headed east on the empty road towards my apartment in Sherman Oaks. The Santa Anas had stopped. To my right the moon played on the Pacific. To my left the lights of the valley stretching into Hollywood and on into downtown shimmered like stars in a bowl, their cold light pulsing in frozen gasps.

THE LOBBY OF THE
ALEXANDRIA HOTEL

Photo credit: Security Pacific Collection / Los Angeles Public Library

HAUNTED:
AN AFTERWORD

BY LUCAS CROWN

Ghosttown haunts me.

It haunts me as story, as artifact, as history, as obligation, as evidence.

As story, *Ghosttown* ends with a frozen gasp. Were we witness to magic? Hallucination? Madness? A dream? Did Southern Comfort and loneliness finally push Whitney Logan over the brink? Was the author yearning to take the notion of a mystery into another dimension?

As artifact, the manuscript has haunted me for nearly a decade, since it was rejected by the publisher of her two previous, critically acclaimed Whitney Logan mysteries—a publisher that would neither publish it, nor relinquish its contractual hold on Whitney and Lupe as characters, which would have allowed the author to find another publisher. The manuscript remained tucked away in a cardboard box, its two heroines held captive.

Ghosttown haunts me as history, both personal and public. I knew Mercedes Lambert, whose real name was Douglas Anne Munson, for nearly twenty years. I knew her as she wrote and published all of her books, and I witnessed much of the sadness and hardship she faced in life, some of which she expelled into fiction. Writing became her counterbalance, a way to keep level and steady. I knew her as she struggled to revise and then reinvent *Ghosttown* in hopes of publication. She tried out new names for Whitney and Lupe, new personalities. She wanted to salvage the story and the glimpse it provided of an almost-invisible subculture lost in a teeming and trembling city.

Ghosttown extends itself to a more public history by encapsulating a time before blogs, Blackberries, and the cacophony of ring tones that now fill our public spaces, when the Lakers still played at the Forum, and most people still walked into bookstores to buy their books, and did so without wondering who might be tracking their purchases. It seems like a time far more distant than it really was. In the decade since Douglas/ Mercedes wrote *Ghosttown,* Los Angeles has continued to shape and reshape itself. Subcultures have shifted, fault lines have shuddered, the sprawl continues to spread. Notorious Winston Alley, which the LAPD frequently and ineffectually targeted with raids, only to find the bustling marketplace for bootleg videos, stolen electronic equipment, and crack cocaine resume business the next day, was finally cleaned up by a female cop who quit the force and joined a community group. The Alexandria Hotel, sadly, still remains a ghost of its former glory.

Ghosttown haunts me as obligation. For the decade it went unpublished, three of those years, following Douglas's death in 2003, the manuscript was in my hands. In the last few years of her life, when she knew she was dying and claimed to no longer care, I promised to find a publisher and allow Whitney and Lupe to live again, as she had intended. Even after Five Star Mystery accepted the manuscript for publication, I still felt compelled to do everything within my power to make it a success.

Finally, as evidence, I knew *Ghosttown,* along with the journals and letters and emails that Douglas left behind in a half-dozen dusty boxes, might hold clues to perhaps her greatest mystery: why Douglas Anne Munson, in 1998, broke with her career, her city, her friends, and finally her writing—to start a new life, a different life, in the Czech Republic.

★ ★ ★ ★ ★

I met Douglas in John Rechy's writing workshop at UCLA in the early 1980s. She was writing her first novel at the time, which was then called "Glass Candles." She was an attorney who worked in LA's dependency court, where matters of child custody were decided when abuse or neglect had been alleged. It was nothing less than a personal hell for someone who herself carried the scars of childhood trauma, something she had never been able to talk about, except in flip references that might spring from an otherwise mundane conversation, or buried like clues in the seeming minutia of a letter or email. Popular culture shapes its myths to turn victims into avengers. One can only imagine how the self must be divided when the abused must defend the abusers. She was able to advocate for the victims at times as well—but it was never anything less than horror that filled her days . . . and infused her writing.

Douglas, who earned a degree in Latin American studies at the University of New Mexico, had been in Quito, Ecuador, organizing local hot dog vendors into a union when she decided to enter law school at UCLA. After passing the bar, she worked as an attorney for an insurance company, tried making it in private practice, then ended up in dependency court. Douglas started writing as a way to cope with the agonies of her day job. When she was diagnosed with cancer in the mid-1980s, it changed her life completely. She stopped drinking, stopped engaging in dangerous relationships, and started taking care of herself. She beat the cancer into remission. In 1990, "Glass Candles" was published as *El Niño*, then issued two years later as a mass-market paperback titled *Hostile Witness*.

El Niño is nothing less than a raw scream from a savage place, and nothing less than a work of art.

In 1991, Whitney Logan, attorney-at-law, made her debut in *Dogtown*, wearing her Charles Jourdan heels and dodging her eccentric landlord. Before the end of the first chapter, Lupe Ramos makes a grand entrance, worthy of any of the great Hollywood legends she revered, standing in the shade of a pepper tree wearing a black leather miniskirt and a screaming pink stretch top, disrupting the flow of traffic along Hollywood Boulevard. Whitney knew the law and how to formulate a plan; Lupe knew the streets and how to revise a plan when things went wrong. Perfect sidekicks, in 1996 they would team up again with the publication of *Soultown*.

By 1990, LA County Juvenile Dependency Court was receiving up to 1,500 new cases every month. There was less staff, fewer resources, more demands on the attorneys. Douglas, who had been there for a decade, continued to be shocked by the ever-increasing agonies inflicted upon the young and helpless. Like Sandy Walker in *El Niño* and Whitney Logan in *Dogtown*, Douglas had become an attorney to serve the people, to protect the rights of the accused. But the fault line dividing the fair trial deserved by all, and the deeds perpetrated upon the victims, was becoming an ever-greater divide. Douglas was losing ground.

She suffered migraines, bouts of depression. She worried about money. She dreaded her job. Fears grew out of proportion. One afternoon she invited me to dinner at her place in Marina del Rey. She spent the day cooking coq au vin. When I arrived, she was in a state of alarm. She had been awoken in the middle of the night by a shrill and intermittent screech coming from the back of one of her kitchen cabinets. She was certain that something was in there, dying some horrible death—an insect, a small animal. She asked me to help. On the top shelf, pushed to the back, I discovered a smoke detector left by workmen months before while painting her ceiling. The sound was not the death scream of some suffering creature, but an alert that the alarm batteries were weak. Douglas couldn't bring herself to open the cabinet and find the source of the noise, but she had spent the entire afternoon methodically combining a complex array of ingredients to make one of the best meals I've ever eaten.

In 1994, her mother died, leaving her without any remaining family. An only child, she had never married, had no children of her own, claimed no surviving aunts, uncles, or cousins. The men in her life came and went. Her lifelong fear of always being alone increased as she got older and believed—incorrectly—she was becoming less attractive, less capable, less competent. She wrote in the pages of a journal of finding her mother, dead for days, in a sparsely furnished room . . . and feared the same fate for herself. She wrote in those same pages of wandering the slips of Marina del Rey, searching for someone willing to take her out beyond the three-mile limit to scatter her mother's ashes into the ocean.

By late 1995, she had reached a point of complete burnout with her work in the court system. She described her drive every morning from her place at the beach to the court in Monterey Park. There's a tangle of freeway interchanges and off-ramps near downtown LA where traffic slows to a crawl regardless of the time of day. She called this the "chokepoint." She had come to dread her work so much that every morning she would start to cry uncontrollably when she reached the chokepoint.

Like Whitney Logan, Douglas resisted mysticism but yearned to believe in something beyond the facts. The previous year, she had a series of astrological charts drawn. One time when I visited her at the marina, she spread the charts out on the floor of her apartment like a series road maps. I glazed over as I looked at the widening rings with transits marked by numbers and indecipherable symbols. She summarized: next year her life would change completely and the next seven years would be filled with adventure. Whether she believed in celestial stagecraft, or accepted the results as prescriptive, her life did change completely the following year, and as far as the next seven years, they would be her last.

In 1996, Douglas resigned her job with the court system, gave up the apartment she loved at the marina, stored her stuff in the garages and attics of friends throughout LA, and went to San Francisco to work towards a certificate that would allow her to teach English as a second language abroad. She was making the final revisions to her new Whitney Logan mystery, *Ghosttown,* in anticipation of sending it to her agent. She had also braced herself for what she half-jokingly referred to her colleagues as a trajectory of "downward mobility" and told them of notes she had begun to keep of the best public bathrooms to use were she to become homeless.

The following February, Douglas wrote me from San Francisco. She had received a letter from her agent saying she didn't like the book. There were a number of problems, but mainly her agent didn't get the ending and felt Whitney was too tough. Douglas responded with a willingness to work on the book, make revisions, but indicated, "The ongoing struggle is for Whitney to become streetwise. She can't remain naïve forever. She has to extend herself."

For a year, Douglas struggled with revisions. After earning her teaching certificate in San Francisco, she went to Bainbridge Island in Washington State to stay with former friends from the court system. In Washington, she grew weary of the constant rain. She ferried to Seattle every day to earn five dollars an hour selling concert tickets for a national ticket broker.

In June of 1997, Douglas sent a revised draft to her agent, which her agent forwarded to her publisher. Our letters by this time had become emails that she sent and received from the local library. Douglas sounded optimistic. She talked about considering the next Whitney Logan mystery and planned to start researching the skinhead subculture.

In July, Viking rejected *Ghosttown*. "Let me dump my bad news now," she began in an email, "so we can then commingle our anxiety and depression. Viking rejected my book. They didn't like the story, they didn't like the writing, it had been too long between books, the other 2 books hadn't made any money and I, they said, refused to cooperate with promoting the last book. I am in a grief cycle. Think I'm still in shock with some overtones of denial (like they might call me and say it was a mistake)." She learned this in a fax from her agent that morning, who went on to inform her the book couldn't be sold to anyone else since Viking owned the characters.

Douglas spent the rest of the summer struggling with the book, worrying about money, waiting for job offers from overseas. Her migraines worsened. She grew increasingly isolated on that island and uncomfortable with the living arrangements. After a radiologist spotted something irregular on a chest x-ray during a routine medical exam, she was certain she was dying. Douglas never completely believed the cancer from the 1980s was gone.

Her struggles to reshape and reinvent *Ghosttown* survive on a dozen three-and-a-half-inch disks. Some files contain pages comprised of single-line notes, shaped like poetry but as uninspired as a grocery list. Several almost-finished chapters read with a tentativeness not found in her other work. She was lost, fumbling, trying to satisfy the directives of others. Apathy saturates what must have been her very last attempts: unfinished sentences, incomplete thoughts, typos and punctuation left uncorrected. I can imagine her in the constant rain on that island, consumed by migraines and the fear of cancer returning, ferrying back and forth to a job taking ticket orders, all the while tearing apart piece by piece in her mind the characters she had created and the book she had written.

We have never known Whitney Logan in any of the three books to be anything less than a reliable narrator. She could be duplicitous and dodgy in circumstances when warranted: when others claimed to be who they were not, or their deceit needed to be met with equal subterfuge. But always, with us, her voice was true. If anything, she wanted to tell us more—but couldn't.

Whitney could be hard-boiled to meet the occasion. She was changing from the very start, shedding her skin. She was growing, toughening. How could she possibly, after the experience of *Dogtown* and the events of *Soultown*, remain the same naïve attorney, whose best advice at the start of her journey had been to keep up her subscription to *Town & Country*? Harvey Kaplan may have been her mentor, before his fall from grace, but Lupe was her guide through the dark places where they ventured, and no one emerges from those shadow worlds the same. A lesser writer—a less honest writer—might have left her characters stunted. Not Douglas. One of the reasons we were not allowed *Ghosttown* until now is because of the creative conflict over whether Whitney should grow as a character or remain the same. It was a dynamic that seemed to work—naïve white girl and street-wise Chicana, moving from adventure to adventure. It was a good starting point, but Douglas was too talented a writer not to keep true to her characters. If *Ghosttown* had followed on the heels of *Soultown*—if Mercedes Lambert had not, out of frustration and disappointment, abandoned it all—one can only imagine—and mourn the impossibility—of what new towns would she have given us?

Another reason we have waited so long for *Ghosttown* is the book's ending. Mercedes was deliberate in challenging the boundaries of the genre. If it can be said that solving the smaller mysteries allow us some solace in our futile struggle with the greater mysteries, then *Ghosttown* transgresses convention with a vengeance. On the final pages, when Whitney Logan thrusts a knife into flesh and then plunges it into the ground, Mercedes Lambert simultaneously sunders the comfortable certainties we have come to expect, exposing the limits of our knowledge and intimating further mystery beyond the thin membrane of our skin and the mutable boundaries of our cells.

We are left to wonder where another Whitney Logan mystery might have taken us after that inexplicable night in the Santa Monica Mountains.

The version of *Ghosttown* you hold in your hands is one that Douglas intended, without compromise or concession.

In August of 1997, like a fugitive, Douglas slipped quietly back into Los Angeles one last time.

She asked that I not tell anyone she was in town. She stayed briefly with a friend, then rented a room for several months in one of the worst areas of Venice. She was halfhearted about starting again, trying to resume her life. We spent one long, hot day looking for places she might live. A studio over a bar with a pair of handcuffs left cinched to a radiator from the previous tenant. Transient hotels off Hollywood Boulevard with caged-in front desks. Desultory apartments south of Wilshire Boulevard that reeked of accumulated sorrows. Places where events from her own books were likely to end badly. Years later, she would email me a recollection of that day: "Remember when you drove me around looking for a place to rent and we went to a building behind the Ambassador? We walked into a courtyard which had some tall jacaranda type trees and the ground was littered with dirty diapers people had thrown out their windows. Those dirty white plastic diapers like doves turned out of paradise. I think we were too numb to comment on it."

She didn't ask to look again. She hadn't mentioned her health scare, and changed the subject when I mentioned it. She vanished for nearly a month. Much later I would learn that an ex-client, whom Douglas had helped out of addiction and homelessness, had seen her living on the streets of Santa Monica, filthy and disoriented. Douglas described that time of homelessness to me in an email much later: "At the first shelter I was at in LA there would be strange food donations—like people bringing leftover wedding food at 11 at night and then groups of gangsters, guys into complex Kennedy conspiracy theories, Jesus freaks, all of us falling ravenously on brie and brioche, shrimp quesadillas . . ." In another email from Prague: "Yesterday on the bus I had a very vivid flash of a silver and onyx bracelet, Mexican, from the 30s I bought in LA and brought my left arm in front of my face and really saw it there for an instant. I was surprised to feel a sharp pain of longing. I rarely ever think of what I used to own (except for my Montblanc pen which was stolen in homeless shelter) and if I do think of them it's without attachment. The pen, well, the loss of it really cemented my loss of identity as a writer."

Before she left LA for good she called and asked me to visit. She had rented a room at the Alexandria, the ghost hotel and welfare flop in *Ghosttown*. The Alexandria is one of those places that will eventually be lost forever, like so many other LA landmarks, to the indifference of a city too steeped in youth to have a concept, much less an appreciation, of history. In 1906, when the doors first opened, the hotel was called a "gem set in tile, steel, and marble." Meeting place and residence of Hollywood stars and presidents alike, it began to fade as early as the twenties, when other grand hotels opened and began the trend from downtown to the west. Briefly closed by the Depression, the hotel reopened four years later as a shadow of its former self. The grand ballroom once frequented by royalty became a training ring for prizefighters. In the 1970s, the

Alexandria received a two-million-dollar facelift. When I arrived in Los Angeles in 1975, I emerged from the Greyhound bus station with no idea where to stay, and wandered fortuitously into the grand lobby of the Alexandria, then in the full flush of its comeback. I'd arrived from Massachusetts to attend college, and was a week early. I needed a place to stay until the dorms opened. I wandered the renovated corridors starstruck by rooms and suites named for the famous who once occupied them. The comeback was short-lived. The hotel's decline was rapid. By 1988, Mayor Tom Bradley called the Alexandria the "worst drug trafficking spot in the city."

When I visited Douglas there in 1997, I parked in the underground garage and noticed a sign above the elevator that must have been hung during the heady optimism of the 1970s: "The Alexandria. A Return to Elegance." In the lobby, a security guard in a stained shirt looked up at me with indifference. Only a few of the remaining electric candles throughout the hallways still worked. It was nearly impossible to see the room numbers in the darkness. An eerie green bulb dangled from a broken ceiling fixture, making shapes and shadows indistinguishable. I finally found Douglas's room. She had a cast on her leg from a fall while getting onto a bus. We went to Colima, which she called "Guyanos" in *Ghosttown*, the place where Ernie Little Horse and Shirley Yellowbird sat in a booth and argued the night Shirley ended up decapitated in a trashcan. We ate chips and guacamole. We watched the traffic along Sunset Boulevard. We made awkward conversation. I drove her back to the Alexandria.

Although we would remain in contact—sometimes daily—for the next four years, I had no way of knowing this would be the last time I would see Douglas alive, framed there by the entrance to the Alexandria. She may have known at this point she'd never be back. I don't know. But it was the only time in all those years we had any physical contact. She left a kiss on my cheek before turning and disappearing into the darkness of the ghost hotel.

When I heard from Douglas again, several months later, she was in the Czech Republic, in Prague. By then, email had become prevalent, and she had a Yahoo account that let her send and receive email from anywhere. She complained about the food, but seemed content, even at times happy. She moved from Prague to the smaller town of Hradec Králové. We exchanged long emails, sometimes several a day. The topics were rarely profound. We talked about movies. She told me about watching *Titanic* in Czech, of the Czech fascination with old American country music performers like Bob Wills and Kitty Wells. During the week she taught English to missionaries, mink farmers, and soldiers. On the weekends she would visit spas or travel. I received travelogues of visits to Germany, Paris, Krakow. She visited the chateau at Duchov, where Casanova wrote his memoirs and made his final home. We talked about books we were reading. Music. Politics. We complained about the lines we had to stand in at grocery stores, or bad service we'd received at restaurants. Once, we devoted a dozen emails to the topic of poaching the perfect egg.

We were linked by separation. Distance drew us closer. In relinquishing our corporeal selves, we had found an intimacy that would not have endured proximity. In one email, while pondering her future in the Czech Republic, Douglas observed, "It would be nice to talk to you face to face about this—maybe not face to face as it is hard for me to talk about some of what's at hand or beneath all of this, but to sit next to each other, stare at a tree and talk."

Email and the Internet was that tree we could stare at and talk without facing one another. I woke each day eager to find a new email waiting. Fueled by caffeine, I would reply, tapping out thousands of words, my fingers barely able to keep pace with my thoughts. Away from the computer, there were times I would face my wife across the kitchen table, or friends in a restaurant, and find myself inarticulate, at a loss for conversation, fumbling with small talk.

Douglas had broken with the city she loved, with her career, with all of her friends. I had the sense she had broken with writing, as well. When *El Niño* had been published, she'd told the *Los Angeles Times,* "Dad always told me that I couldn't write, that I shouldn't write. He told me it's a tough gig; he didn't think I could cut it." Her father was a newspaperman who eventually wrote industrial films. Long after she proved him spectacularly wrong, she added this in the middle of an otherwise chatty email: "Did I ever tell you that when I was a junior in high school my mother asked me one afternoon why I wasn't filling out college applications and I told her I didn't want to go to college. I wanted to go on the road like Kerouac, work Mcjobs and be a writer. She took a coffee pot off the stove and threw it at my head. Isn't it strange that at this age I am doing that (except not writing???)."

The "except not writing" was touchy ground between us. Since the miserable experience of *Ghosttown,* she was silent on the topic. I did not know if the "not writing" was intentional, something intricately connected to her downward mobility, a part of leaving everything behind, the last of what made her her that she had jettisoned—after career, city, friends.

The cliché of reinvention, worn thin by overuse, did not seem accurate in describing Douglas's trajectory from southern California to San Francisco to the Puget Sound and finally the Czech Republic. Bleaching her blonde hair, then dying it red might be reinvention. Trading in the old Mercedes that had belonged to her mother for a red '64 Chevy Malibu might be reinvention. This felt more like Douglas was un-inventing herself, in the same way that you cast aside things you have clung to for so many years, things that had once been valuable and sacred. You purge yourself of them. You put them in boxes and leave them at the back door of thrift shops in the middle of the night. In a way, that's what she did with all the boxes she left scattered in garages and attics throughout Los Angeles. Maybe she inverted the Kerouac thing by doing the writing first then going on the road. She had once confided that all she had to keep her coping with life was her writing. Now—had she abandoned that, too?

I asked if she might consider resuming work on "Erotomania," a partially completed manuscript that I felt contained some of her best writing. She didn't acknowledge the question. I persisted. I asked her bluntly: had she given up writing? She explained that someone had told her she was a great writer but a lousy person. That didn't ring true. I could imagine it being said, in a moment of meanness, by one of the men she had been involved with—one of the men who used her—but I couldn't imagine her accepting it as a verdict. It sounded like one of the flip lines that she would often toss out dismissively to be done with a subject. Then she added, in an email that followed: ". . . being homeless changed something in me forever. All my self confidence and courage are gone and it feels like it will never come back. I guess it could be said that I am a broken woman. It changes everything to be unsafe, to have people in the street spit on you, to become afraid to go into supermarkets. If I don't write am I less valuable as a person? I imagine you would like me to be happy or serene and that you see writing as part of me fulfilling myself. My task is to try to re-form my broken self and put some type of skin around it. I can't say now what that will involve. It's not a 100% picnic living in a small town in the Czech Republic and I wouldn't be doing this if I had been able to think of something better to support myself.

It's like trying to set one's own arm or having to do a tracheotomy on yourself."

For the next month, I received no emails. She made her point. I knew not to mention writing again.

The year 2000 was half over. "Getting old sucks," she wrote me. "It's a long stretch of road with bad motels, indifferent diners, and gas stations with dirty toilets before you reach, uhm, Florida."

"This is a bad letter," I woke to read on March 1, 2001. "Things have changed and I can't stay here. I am going to live in CT . . . Please, I ask you to help me. I don't want to drop a bundle of hysteria in your lap. This is the worst situation I have ever been in." She needed a ticket to New York. She knew people who had relocated from California to Connecticut, and planned to stay with them. I wired her the airfare. Her last email from the Czech Republic summed up her feelings in three words: "Scared. Excited. Sad."

Less than a week after arriving, she learned she could not stay where she had planned. "Now I am putting my things together," she described. "I will leave my things here except for a little day pack and what money I have. Am going to wash my hair, look for some paperback books to take with me, and ask them drive to me to an emergency shelter when they return."

She had come back to America to find herself homeless again. As she moved between shelters, and underwent various medical tests, she continued to correspond from library computers or Internet cafés. When the test results were conclusive, she told me what I suspected. The cancer that had been successfully treated in the 1980s had returned with a vengeance.

· She was given six months to live.

During this last season of her life, packages from her began to arrive by mail at my house every few weeks, supplementing our continuing email correspondence. Books that had meant so much she carried them halfway around the world and back. The Montblanc pen she bought to replace the one stolen in LA. Ten single-spaced pages of a journal she had kept when her mother died and she scattered the ashes at sea, which she had promised to send me before getting sick and then changed her mind. I started to look forward to the arrival of the mail, checking immediately to see if there were any packages addressed in her familiar handwriting. It was bringing the tangible back into my life. I realized how insubstantial we had become. Ghosts in the ether. Disembodied, translucent, protoplasmic. Now, touching what she touched, I yearned for the tactile, and realized how much time had really passed since her lips brushed my cheek that drizzly night on the corner of Fifth and Spring Street, and how little time remained.

Douglas began addressing the business of her dying. She pre-paid for her cremation. She arranged to execute a will. She emailed me a request. She wanted her ashes to be scattered off the waters of Marina del Rey. She wanted this done from a sailboat. Besides the captain and possibly a first mate, she wanted no one else to be present, not even my wife, who was my fiancé at the time. No prayers. No words. Just the flutter of the topsail and the slap of water against the side of the boat.

After we had exhaustively covered all the aspects of her death, she closed the subject by writing, "Now let's get back to talking about the trivia of our neurotic lives."

She dug in. The allotted six months passed, then a year. She described a chauffeured trip she was able to make to Manhattan by a local car service, stopping at all the great stores, lunching on oysters. She complained about the constant medical appointments, "the indignity of having to spend one's last days reading old issues of *People* magazine." In December of 2003, I received an email that said simply, "Going to Prague. Back in a week. Will write then." I didn't know what to make of this. The suddenness. A long and arduous trip in the middle of winter to eastern Europe. Was her heath improving? Did this signal some kind of finality? A week later, she sent a hurried note: "At home. Tired. Have cold, flu or pneumonia." The next day she seemed better: "Sunday snowed all day. Today sunny, cold, snow on ground. Don't feel like getting up. Watching CNN & TCM. Nice with sun coming in. Waiting for laundry to be delivered. Hopefully someone will go to market for me today. The last meal I had in CR was beef goulash with dumplings and it was so delicious I can't stop thinking of it. Didn't have any food in house when got home but lentil soup, cheese-it crackers and peanut butter. Ugh. Hope it doesn't take long to get back on track/schedule eg apt cleaning, pilates appointment etc. love, d."

A week passed. That wasn't unusual. Our correspondence might lapse for a few weeks, only to resume in a flurry of notes as we both spent afternoons or evenings staring at our computer screens. I had changed addresses that autumn but Douglas hadn't updated the information with her caregivers. When the hospice nurse was finally able to reach me, Douglas had been rushed to the ER unable to breathe, and had fallen into a coma. She was not expected to last the night. She held on two more nights before dying the morning of December 22, 2003.

Several weeks later I was sitting at the kitchen table when I saw the postal carrier come through the front gate with his usual clutch of bills, junk mail, and advertisements in one hand, and a package in the other. For one brief, forgetful moment, I thought it might be another package from Douglas. Something else that she was divesting herself of, another artifact I might hold in my hands and feel some residual connection. When the doorbell rang and I saw the unusual seal on the box, I realized what it contained. This was the last package I would ever receive from Douglas. She had come home to California.

The box weighed less than eight pounds. It cost $23.30 to mail from Westport, Connecticut, to Claremont, California. When I unsealed the tape and pulled open the flaps, I found the inside filled with that pink foam popcorn used to pack appliances, electronics, or other fragile objects that might be damaged in transit. There was something simultaneously horrible and hilarious, incongruous and appropriate, about these pieces of foam surrounding the thick plastic bag that held Douglas's ashes. The weight, the cost, the pink foam popcorn—these are details that Douglas would have appreciated, would have—in different circumstances—delighted in, made the topic of several emails. It was the kind of mundane detail, freighted with greater weight and meaning, that might have ended up in one of her books.

Douglas was specific and firm about the conditions of the scattering, but had not stipulated about a separate memorial service. After an obituary appeared in the *Los Angeles Times*, and was picked up nationally by the AP, I received calls every day for weeks from old friends, coworkers who remembered her from thirty years before, former students from the brief time she taught writing at UCLA, close friends from the courts who were bewildered by her disappearance and brimming with questions. She had compartmentalized her different worlds. I knew her in relation to her writing, from the group of talented and successful authors who emerged over the years from John Rechy's writing workshops. She navigated many worlds. Even the forms of her name changed with context and time. Some knew her as Doug, others Dougie, others as Douglas, still others as Douglas Anne. There were subtle variations and permutations of character to accompany the names. Doug, who had worked briefly for a large insurance company after passing the bar, smoked an occasional cigar. As Mercedes Lambert, she not only invented a name but a brief biography for the jacket flap: "lives in Montebello with two children." Her friends and hospice workers in Connecticut during her last years knew her simply as Anne. They were surprised to learn after her death that she had published three books. Douglas was not alone in transmuting herself. She is the basis of numerous characters that populate Kate Braverman's fiction, and in particular is the inspiration for Carlotta in *Squandering the Blue*.

I was certain Douglas would have been as dismissive about a tribute as she had been about her books in those last months, and so I had deliberately avoided the topic. Memorial services are for the living, those left behind, a chance to come together and grieve.

We found a hotel on Venice Beach—blocks from where Douglas lived and wrote all of her books—willing to allow us the use of their sitting room. The Cadillac Hotel stands across from an art gallery where Kerouac read in the sixties. A chunk of the Berlin Wall resides in its lounge, crammed against a brightly lit Coke machine. When you step outside, you are instantly swept up in the tumult of the speedway, a concrete strip that separates the beach from the shops, hotels, and homes that face the ocean. On almost any warm day of the year, the walkway is filled with people strolling, Rollerbladers, bicyclists, street performers, musicians. It's loud, raucous, full of life. It's a place where elements of all the "towns" of Douglas's books would most likely intersect.

The room was crammed beyond capacity. People spoke about knowing Douglas. Some read from her books. A former judge praised her work in the courts. After the tribute, alone or in small groups, her friends asked the same questions.

Why had she left?

Why hadn't she said goodbye?

Could they have done more?

Douglas had ended one life and started another. How intentional? At what point deliberate? When irrevocable? They say people disappear every day. Leave home one morning with a sack lunch for a job at a bottling plant in Islip, and a month later return from stocking the shelves of a grocery store to an apartment in Scottsdale. With Douglas, I had seen it happen in degrees, her breaking. (Even giving it a name, framing it by a single word, seems counterfeit, suggesting singularity for something complex and manifold). For those who looked to me at the memorial service for an explanation, this breaking-leaving-disappearing-fleeing-exile had been abrupt. No letters, no cards, no emails. No one knew she had even left the country. All I could do was shrug my shoulders.

The saddest fact I know about Douglas is that while she was far too intelligent not to have known how many people loved and cared about her, that wounded part of her, which always expected abandonment and loneliness, dismissed all evidence to the contrary. When she still lived in LA, we had worked on a screenplay version of *Dogtown* together. I had to leave the effort because of other demands. She wouldn't return my calls for months. Then a postcard turned up in my mailbox. "I am basically over being pissed off that you abandoned me on this hideous project. . . . I'm willing to work on friendship recovery if you are and if you promise you will never leave me again in said fucked up way. I have enough residue of childhood trauma." Her leaving, her flight, her exile—was it preemptive? By leaving us all, had she shielded herself from the expectation of our leaving her?

A month after the memorial, the rains that had been constant that winter relented briefly. I drove down to the marina with Douglas's ashes on the seat beside me. Maybe I was too early. Maybe the skies were still too gray or the wind too high. The marina was deserted. Access to the slips was prevented by locked gates. I can only imagine what a suspicious character I must have seemed, carrying a bag under my arm and rattling metal gates. I finally stopped at a rental office for one of the anchorages and explained my plight to a receptionist. She looked at the package I was carrying with distress, but agreed to take my phone number and see if she might find someone interested in earning a few hundred dollars to take me out to sea. By the time I made the long drive home, my cell phone rang. Captain Paul Muggleston had a forty-two-foot ketch. He told me he once participated in a funeral at sea as part of a flotilla of eight boats that included the firing of a cannon. I told him I had something more subtle in mind. We worked out the details, and set a date for the following week. Later that evening, I consulted *Merriam-Webster* for the meaning of "ketch." "A fore-and-aft rigged vessel," I read, "similar to a yawl but with a larger mizzen and with the mizzenmast stepped farther forward."

I had no clue—but thought Douglas would be pleased.

On my second trip to the marina with Douglas's ashes, I planned a more circuitous route. I left before dawn and arrived at the corner of Hollywood Boulevard and Western in the weak light of sunrise. This was where Whitey Logan's office was located, where Lupe Ramos stood under the pepper tree. I drove west to where Tony Red Wolf had an apartment, then zigzagged back towards downtown LA, passing MacArthur Park and the bars along its eastern fringe where Whitney and Tony drank beer at the Bucket after finding Shirley Yellowbird's body. I drove past the Criminal Courts Building, where Division 40 doled out cases to keep Whitney barely able to pay the rent, then joined the commuter gridlock through the waking streets of Koreatown and along Pico Boulevard towards the ocean.

When I reached the marina, the weather was starting to change. Clouds were massing against the inland mountains.

Captain Paul and his first mate worked quickly to steer us beyond the breakwater with the engine throttling. Once on the open sea, engine extinguished, the main sail carried us swiftly along. Overhead, the underbellies of jumbo jets swooped above us on their ascent from the LA International Airport. The farther out we sailed, the quieter and more peaceful the world became. When we reached the three-mile point, I made my way along the side of the boat and undid the seal of the plastic bag, allowing the grit of Douglas's ashes to pour slowly into the Pacific and vanish in our wake.

We had beaten the storm, and we sailed slowly back towards the marina. Captain Paul made coffee and prepared lunch below deck. We sat silently, the wind blowing our hair. I sipped coffee and ate a ham sandwich with a fine dusting of ash coating my hands.

I drove the most direct route back to Claremont. When I reached the chokepoint and passed the exit for LA's dependency court, the rain began to fall in sheets.

In the years that I worked on getting *Ghosttown* published, I remained haunted. I had not yet brought myself to sort through the boxes Douglas had left behind. Some had been left with me when she went to San Francisco. Others she had stored in the attics and garages of friends. Four sealed boxes had been forwarded from Bainbridge Island and two thick envelopes arrived from Connecticut. They collected around me in the library of our home. They were always going to be next weekend's project. I spent a lot of time in that room. Reading other books. Working at the computer. Sitting.

Avoiding.

I had been talking with UCLA for over a year. They were interested in archiving her papers in their Special Collection that included the works of Raymond Chandler. I needed to provide them with an approximate idea of what remained. I delayed. I made excuses.

I knew roughly what the boxes contained from rummaging through them to find the various drafts of *Ghosttown*. I felt a gravitational pull keeping me in their proximity, and an equal force pushing me away.

One weekend, when my wife was away visiting her family, I woke at four in the morning from a dream about Douglas. My heart was racing. In my sleep, I had pulled the sheets from their corners, tossed pillows to the floor. I went straight into the library and started picking through the material.

I skimmed the pages of journals she had kept for almost fifteen years, the unfinished manuscripts in three-ring binders. I glanced over notes for future books, newspaper and magazine clippings that suggested story ideas, pages of poetry. I flipped through dozens of photographs of Douglas through the years. A baby pushing herself up on a mattress. A teenager in cap and gown graduating from high school. A young woman in the jungles of Ecuador.

I found, but did not read, a seven-page psychological consultation, and a vocational aptitude test. I located grade-school report cards, her diplomas, her California bar certificate.

When I opened her passport, I found one of her blonde hairs caught in the fold. I brought the document she had carried through so many countries close to my face and could smell her on its pages. After all these years, a part of her still clung tenaciously to this world. A hair, her fragrance. I stared at the passport photo. She stared back, beyond the camera, into an uncertain, worried future. I stuffed the passport back into the box, along with the other documents I had let scatter around me. I had to flee the house. I drove to an all-night donut shack along Route 66 and sat on a cold bench sipping coffee until the sun was up.

I had only skimmed the surface. I knew I had to go through every page, each photograph, all the documents. When my wife returned that Sunday night, she sensed my distance—a greater distance. My preoccupation had been obvious for some time. All the hours I spent alone in our library. My increasing distraction. These are usually the telltale signs of a dalliance, an affair. In this case, I was keeping company with a ghost.

When *Ghosttown* was accepted for publication by Five Star Press, I could no longer avoid this postmortem. I wanted to offer some kind of coda for the book, for my friend. I could not do this without immersing myself into what Douglas left behind, the evidence of her innermost thoughts. I needed to sum things up as best I could. I needed—at long last—to grieve. I realized, with the arrival of the book contract, that I had not allowed myself that process. I had kept busy, first with the arrangements for her memorial service and the scattering at sea, then with the relentless letters and phone calls and emails to publishers. This is what I do for a living. I manage projects. I had used the skills of my profession to construct a firewall to protect me from the pain. Now I needed to grieve, all-at-once, in isolation, away from home.

I knew exactly where to go.

The Alexandria Hotel is a haunted place.

The woman dressed in black from head to toe who appears at the far end of the hall in chapter 13 of *Ghosttown* is rumored to be a resident of the hotel who died while in mourning for some loved one. "Stricken with grief," describes Laurie Jacobson and Marc Wanamaker in their book *Hollywood Haunted*, "she barely noticed her own passing and continued to grieve for more than seventy years."

It was the practical Whitney Logan who saw her—"I couldn't see through her, but she wasn't solid, either"—and then watched her disappear through a wall. Whitney's toughening brought with it a wider range of possibility; the typically more intuitive Lupe Ramos—steeped in Hollywood lore, and infused with the mysteries of the Catholic Church—showed the more practical side, flatly insisting there were no such things as ghosts.

For me, the Alexandria will always be haunted. Haunted by the first days I spent in a city I came to fiercely love and occasionally hate. Haunted by the stunning transformative chapter of *Ghosttown* where Charlie Lomas serves tea to Whitney Logan. Haunted most of all by Douglas Anne Munson, whom I last saw alive vanishing into its blighted lobby. This is where I would go to excavate her life, to attempt to comprehend the mysteries that consumed her, and to expel the grief that I had held suspended for far too long.

As I stood in the lobby of the Alexandria, which is now predominately a welfare-voucher hotel, I was wearing an old t-shirt, had a week's worth of stubble, and was weighed down by an oversized duffle crammed full of binders, notebooks, photo albums, and printed emails. I was told, curtly, that there were no rooms available. There might not be for months.

I was sitting dejectedly on one of the lobby's sofas, when a man in his mid-thirties approached me. He had heard my conversation with the desk clerk. He was paid up for a month at the hotel but needed to get to Fresno. A buddy of his had ten days of work to offer, off the books. He didn't want to lose his room. "Ain't got much up there," he nodded towards the once-grand ceiling and the twelve stories that rose above it, " 'cept a radio and some books. Figure whatever you were gonna pay for a week would help me get to Fresno and get a room until I start drawing on my pay." I wondered if he was on the grift, if I was being hustled. I looked down at what was once called "the million-dollar carpet" because of the movie deals that transpired in the lobby, long before the drug deals took their place. I had been too long in suburbs. I'd lost whatever savvy I might have had in those younger days when I rode busses, slept in cheap rooms, read books in libraries, and killed time in coffee shops and barrooms. What choice did I have? I would be subletting at the ghost hotel. I accepted his offer.

He showed me the room and told me after a week to leave the key on the bedside table. When he returned, he'd tell the front desk he locked himself out. I handed him two hundred dollars. He gathered his clothes and swung them in a pack over his shoulder. "Oh, hey—" He turned back before closing the door. "Feel free to read any of the books. TV reception sucks."

I stayed five days. I reread our correspondence. I found a letter from the editor of *Dogtown* pleading with Douglas to consider writing another Whitney Logan mystery. I reread a long and chilling letter written to her from a convicted serial killer on San Quentin's death row, prompted by a story on her in a legal publication and their shared first name. I paged through lavishly bound journals and sketchbooks and imagined her buying each one, invigorated with the prospect of filling its pages, and then losing that enthusiasm after only a few entries. I traced months and years of her life through a narrative of calendar appointments and things-to-do jotted in numerous Day Runners.

I lived mostly on snack food and bottled water. I left the hotel only once. I roamed the corridors frequently, when the room became too oppressive, or when the enduring charm of the place itself—undiminished by neglect—drew me through its corridors. I avoided the lobby, fearing someone might ask questions and discover I was not a registered guest. I didn't even know the name of the man who had rented me his room. I had completely cut myself off from everything familiar: computers, my PDA, daily routines. I'd even left my cell phone at home. All that I had from the world I knew were the keys to my car, which was parked a block away, and to my house, thirty miles east of downtown.

I grew disoriented. I felt furtive. I realized how deeply embedded one becomes in regularity. I noticed myself frequently reaching into my pocket to touch my key ring, or brushing my hand against it, seeking reassurance that a familiar world awaited my return. How strong Douglas must have been—how brave! Chucking it all, her whole world. What talisman did she have—if any—to allay what must have been at times crushing anxiety and despair? Had our emails provided some scrap of continuity? A virtual bridge?

In my exploration—my investigation—I arranged materials on every available surface. I covered the bed with photos. I arranged and rearranged them. Chronologically at first, then in like sets: Douglas alone, Douglas with others, Douglas smiling, Douglas sad.

I paged through large books that she had filled with images torn from magazines: models from advertisements, landscapes. I tried to understand the relationship between the images and her, between the images themselves. Were they telling a story?

I snuck up on the journals, and when I finally started on them, I let them subsume me. She had kept journals from the 1980s until she died. The earliest ones were nearly ruined. She had printed them out on the backside of drafts from *El Niño*. Time and the elements had worked them over. Brittle, their edges brown and curling, some pages had to be carefully peeled from the next. Words from her novel and words from her journal bled into each other from their opposite sides, rendering her life and her fiction into an indistinguishable blot. The lines of other pages had completely vanished, leaving gaps in an almost daily narrative, like the fade of memories.

Douglas told me she had kept some of the journals in a storage space in the parking garage beneath her building. She was mortified one day to find a homeless man had gotten into the boxes and was reading her journals. For months she was certain she saw him in various parts of the city, watching her.

Reading these most intimate passages, I felt like a voyeur. I wondered if I were much different than the homeless man who had stolen a glimpse of someone else's life. Maybe worse: he had been a stranger—I knew Douglas. But she had left them. She had not, in all of her clear and careful instructions, asked that they be destroyed.

I had come to find evidence. Expecting—perhaps fearing—that there might be something Douglas had not told me, had not told anyone. Something that she might have been able to articulate only on these private pages. Something that demanded expression if only after her departure.

I found no revelations, no epiphanies. The pain I expected to find—that had kept me away so long—filled the pages. This was another voice, another sensibility. There were so many. The Douglas I knew in person as a friend. The Douglas I knew as a storyteller from her books. The Douglas I knew as a correspondent. And the Douglas who kept journals—sometimes obsessively. I saw no discord in the occasional contradiction, when the words of a journal entry might be at odds with the words of an email I had received on the same subject, or when two contrary emotions might be expressed. Each was true. Expecting the unified, we find the quantum. Some of us align ourselves with ourselves more effectively than others. Douglas contained the complexities and incongruities that made her both the talented writer and the troubled woman. Honesty is refusing to abrogate our many contradictions.

She was never not honest.

She did, I discovered, continue to write, forced herself to write. Her last journal entries are often little more than a date and a single event that transpired. Bought groceries. Read Flaubert's letters. Ate strawberries.

In the end, what broke me completely, were the lists. A half dozen of them. None longer than a page.

The sheer bulk of her journals, their cataloging of sadness I so dreaded, left me numb. The lists ambushed me. They were dispatches of hope from a place of siege and despond. Simple. Plain. Direct. Evidence of an optimism that persevered beyond abuse, abandonment, disappointment, heartbreak, rejection, homelessness, and cancer. Fewer than thirty-five words in all. A list of things she liked. A list of tasks she should do every day to be happy. A list of the things she thought were beautiful. It was evidence of indomitability, of the valiant stand that some of us are never too lost, too frail, or too fearful to make against all that opposes us.

I had told her this once—now I felt it all over again: she was my hero.

I opened one of several blank tablets I had brought and began to scribble.

Around noon on my fifth day at the Alexandria, I gathered all I had come with, placed the room key on the battered table, and left my paperback copy of *Dogtown* for the room's rightful tenant. I walked one last time down the stretch of corridor to the elevators, imagining Charlie Lomas in one of the rooms making tea on a hot plate. I stepped from the lobby's dimness onto the bright sidewalk of Fifth Street feeling unburdened. I was ready to let go of it now, all the stuff in the duffle bag that swung from my shoulder as I hurried towards my waiting car. I was ready to surrender it to the archivists who would know how to preserve it for those who might one day want to know more.

I wrote most of these words from a fetid room in the Alexandria Hotel. Later, I typed them into a computer, tidied some of the syntax, reordered some of my thoughts; I preserved the feelings and the emotions as I had frantically jotted them in that room, even where they seemed mawkish upon rereading. I resisted revision.

Douglas had been involved in several cases where exorcisms had been performed upon children believed by their parents to be possessed by demons. They were squalid affairs, as she described them, performed in ugly apartment buildings in places like Pacoima. None of the elaborate rituals with evocations in Latin as depicted in the movies.

I felt like I had exorcised something in that room: the grief that had possessed me, that I could not expel at home. Grief is a bitch. It can gather in density and grow inconsolable. It makes one wish for magic, yearn for the impossible. It makes one want to reshape history, alter reality. I had wanted to protect that beautiful child in those photographs from the hurt that was awaiting her. I had wanted to obliterate the cancer that neither surgery nor chemotherapy could abate. I had wanted to be in the room in Connecticut to hold her hand as she died and let her know she had not been abandoned.

I had not seen the ghost that is supposed to haunt the hallways of the Alexandria Hotel, who is said to have died of a grief so complete and inconsolable that she failed to notice her own passing. But I could understand how such a story could affix itself to such a place.

I will always feel haunted. My ghost is metaphorical. My haunting analogous.

Good mysteries continue to haunt. They disallow us too much complacency with their reminder of the ineffable and inexplicable. We do our best in assembling the evidence, connecting the events, establishing the timeline, determining the motivation, deciphering the meaning. We strive to make our case ironclad. Bulletproof. Whitney Logan, Sandy Walker, and Douglas Anne Munson, like all those who have come before, and all those who will follow, grapple with injustice and struggle to right the wrongs, hoping to restore, as much as possible, some sense of order and righteousness.

I arrived home satisfied by a few certainties: I was enormously lucky to have known Douglas Anne Munson. She was my friend. She was supremely talented and relentlessly haunted. The pages of her books—often brilliant, occasionally flawed—reflect the wonder and pain of her life, and leave us all with a frozen gasp. Although we never said goodbye, we managed to say in cyberspace what the damage of our pasts might never have allowed face to face: that we loved each other.

Here is your book at last, Douglas, just as you intended. I hope you are pleased. I hope this rights at least one wrong. I miss you.

Farewell, my lovely.

ACKNOWLEDGMENTS

There were many generous individuals who helped to make the long overdue publication of this book possible. I thank them all. Below are a few who deserve special acknowledgment.

Melodie Johnson Howe, who provided invaluable suggestions and who pointed me in the direction of Five Star Mystery.

Bill Fitzhugh, who answered my endless stream of emails with helpful advice and encouragement.

John Helfers at Tekno Books, who accepted the manuscript for publication and guided me through the process, and Tiffany Schofield at Five Star™, an imprint of Thomson Gale, who took it the final distance.

Michael Connelly, who responded to a letter from a complete stranger asking for help and generously took time from his hectic schedule to contribute an appreciation of Mercedes for no other reason than he thought it was the right thing to do.

Amy Crown, my wife, who provided support and encouragement, shared my ups and downs on the long journey to getting this book published, and never minded—too much—the time I spent preoccupied by a ghost.

And to John Rechy, teacher and friend, for his unwavering encouragement through the years and his enduring lesson of perseverance.

—Lucas Crown

ABOUT THE AUTHOR

Writing under the name **Mercedes Lambert,** Douglas Anne Munson was an author, attorney, and teacher. Born in Crossville, Tennessee, in 1948, she lived most of her life in Los Angeles before moving to the Czech Republic in the late 1990s. She died in Connecticut in December 2003. More can be found about the author at www.mercedeslambert.com.